About the Author

Mrs. Diane Martin was born in Chicago, Illinois and currently lives in the Chicago-land area. She earned her Master of Arts and Bachelor of Arts degree from Chicago State University.

My writing legacy would be my true depiction of life; exploring the entire colorful spectrum of people, both good and bad, capturing it in words and exposing it to all cultures in a respectful manner - In a way that would stand the test of time. - Diane Martin

Peaches

Diane Martin

http://dianemartin.weebly.com

First Edition

Cover Design by Denise Billups of Borel Graphics Email: denise.billups@gmail.com

Book Layout and Design by Diane Martin

Edited by Dr. William Martin & Diane Martin

United States ISBN Agency:

ISBN - 10: 0-9975761-0-3

ISBN - 13: 978-0-9975761-0-8

Disclaimer: This is a book of fiction and is not based on actual events. Any similarities to current events, characters, names and locations are purely coincidental and based solely on the imagination of the author.

Dedicated to
the
Middle Child

Butterfly, butterfly,

Fly away home,

Your house is on fire,

Your parents will burn.

Except for the little one whose
name is Grace,

Who's stowed away in her hiding

place.

Prologue

This ain't no Cinderella Story...I've gone through things that would give the average person nightmares. I had sex before I even knew what a penis was and my family's response to that traumatic experience was to pretend that nothing happened. *How do you do that? I guess it's easier when you're not the victim.* Now, that I really think about it, and thinking about it has been something that I've tried not to do since it happened, I think our need to brush it under the rug, was as painful as the abuse itself. Maybe my parents felt like I was too young to understand, and believe me, I didn't understand. But once an adult forces themselves on you, I think that adults have to realize that you just can't go back to a place of innocence. You can't go back to "normal." "Normal" is gone – never to be seen again. The forfeiture of my youth should have prompted them to help me regain it, or some form of it, but because of their refusal to talk to me about it, I always felt like a broken little girl stuck in an adult's body. And I knew that I needed to figure out a way to find closure – to close that chapter of my life because I didn't want this to be my story. I didn't want the rape and abuse to define me. I spent all of my life hiding my pain and hiding my scars, but suffering the constant torture from my sisters never allowed me to heal. Every time, a wound would try to heal, something stupid would happen and I was left "raw" all over again.

But like every story, this too had to end. Contrary to popular belief, there is no "happily ever after." You live and you die. What you do in the meantime defines you. Until the end, you just want to be happy. Is that too much to ask?

Chapter 1

Peaches...That's what they called me. They alternated between that, my real name, or whatever else they could come up with based on how they were feeling that day. No one ever called me by my real name until I got older. Until then, I was Peaches, the baby girl. I was always told that being the youngest child was a blessing. But sadly, being the "last" of four girls was more of a curse than a blessing. I would have gladly given up my spot in that line if I thought that it would have made my life any easier.

Early on, I felt like I got "tails" in this coin toss called, "life." I always felt like I was being punished for something that I've done in another life. Like maybe, I was an asshole in a past life and I was brought back into this world to atone for my sins. I could never have predicted that life would be so hard for me as a child. I mean, I knew that there were kids who unfortunately and sadly, have really fucked-up lives. It's tragic, but no child is capable of predicting that. Kids just want to be kids. We want to be loved and cared for and it's not a lot to ask for, but there are people who, for some bizarre reason feel otherwise.

And it wasn't like my parents were bad parents, on the contrary, they were fantastic based on my definition of the word "fantastic." They weren't bad people and they loved me to death. And we had it pretty good. We lived in a nice home. It wasn't the "best" home, but it was "home." My parents were always kind to me. They worked hard, they took care of their family, and they believed in God, so much so that they made sure that we attended church twice a year – Easter and Christmas.

They always quoted Scripture. All three of them. The one that says, "If someone puts their hands on you then you have every right to knock the shit out of them," the one that talks about, "How tomorrow is not promised, so you better have fun while you can," and the last scripture that gives parents' permission to beat the hell out of their kids because God said so." That last one is my dad's favorite one.

As a child, my parents didn't really need to discipline me that much. All they had to do was give me the "look" and I straightened up. I never wanted to be on the other end of my Daddy's belt and he used it often. He felt punishment should fit the crime and he had no problem making sure that folks got what he felt they deserved. But I'm sure that the other folks in the house felt differently about his "brand of justice." I, for one, thought that he was fair, but I wasn't the one getting hit every time that I did something stupid or bad. I made sure that I stayed out of the way.

Yes, I was the baby and being last made me cognizant of what that meant. It meant always having the focus on you even if you don't want it. It also meant that there is always going to be someone to resent you for it even though you had nothing to do with it.

But enough about me…back to the reason why we're here…the person who said, that "'Girls are made of sugar, spice, and everything nice'" never met my sisters. They were made out of salt, venom, spiders, worms, horror movies, and pure unadulterated evil.

Might as well start this off by being absolutely honest. I hate 'em. Hate 'em, hate 'em, hate 'em….Did I say that I hate em'? If not, let me say it again. I hate 'em. Now, it wasn't hate in the beginning. When you're little and don't know any better, you assume that people will just love you. It never crosses your little mind to think that the people charged with loving you would do everything but love you. And the weirdest thing is, I actually thought that what they did to me was love because again, I didn't know any better. When you don't have any point of reference, then what you see and experience becomes your point of reference. I mean, if your sisters lock you in a dog cage every day until you're six, you assume that all six year olds sleep in dog cages until you find out that that was some bullshit that they thought would be funny; without thinking about how it would affect you in the long run.

And they loved it...

While other kids were out jumping rope, going to the park, hanging with friends, "The Evil Three" were looking for ways to make my life a living hell.

Regan, the oldest, was a bitch. I know that that sounds harsh, but there is no other way to describe her. I could try to say something nice, but if it walks like a bitch, talks like a bitch, then, what more can I say?

I honestly believe that when she was born, the doctor tried to slap her on the ass, but she probably looked up at him and scared him so bad that he just put her down and walked away. It is through her, that I learned what darkness is and learned to fear it. She was cold and unfeeling. My baby dolls were more "human" than she was. I'm sure that being the oldest came with a lot of responsibility and that the expectations for the first born were great, but being the oldest made her angry, evil, and it was sad, because she was actually truly beautiful. Now, I know that there is no correlation between beauty and a person's capacity to make another person's life miserable, a living hell, but her beauty made it easier for her to be cruel to people. I used to look at my sister and wonder how someone could be both beautiful and ugly at the same time. I'm sure that it wasn't an easy task, but one that she'd perfected.

She had the most beautiful long jet black hair and she made sure that you saw it because she was forever throwing it in your face, literally. I mean that she actually threw it in your face. She was forever swinging it. You couldn't talk to her without getting an eye or mouthful of her hair. She also blossomed early, so at age nine, she had breasts that were more than a mouthful and an ass big enough to sit a complete table-setting for one on it. And the boys loved her for it. She got a kick out of letting them touch her. She would give them just enough to make them "hard" then she would leave them standing there looking stupid with an erection that they couldn't do anything with, but wish or rub away.

When she was younger, she played with boys like I played with dolls. They used to chase her like she had the latest video game stuck up her butt. It was so easy for her to use them too because she convinced each one of them that they had a chance to be the one to take her virginity. Little did they know that that honor was already given to her fingers and anything else she could stick between her legs. From as far as I could remember, she was doing that – rubbing her vagina on things like a dog that dragged its ass across the floor because it itched. Maybe that's why she did it, but there was not a pillow in the house that didn't smell like musty vagina. Perhaps someone should have told her about soap or told her that little girls are not supposed to get freaky with the furniture – a practice usually performed by animals, but until she reached the big times, the furniture would just have to do. She had this thing. She used to walk around the house sticking her fingers in our faces and saying, "Smell my fingers." Who did she think wanted to smell her booty-fingers? Who does that nasty shit? She did.

At some point, boys had become boring to her. I guess it was right around the time when she realized that they couldn't do anything for her, but make her panties wet. No, she wanted more than that, so she directed her energies toward the "more-seasoned" of the male species. She used her sexuality to get men to give her what she wanted and if they didn't, she took it from them.

When she was fourteen, she dated a man so old that I think he was the waiter at the Last Supper. She was always stroking those three strands of hair on the top of his head like that would make the rest of his hair grow back. It didn't and when she rubbed his head, he purred – making his dentures whistle. When I heard it, I knew what was going to happen next.

One day, when my parents weren't home, I saw them playing with each other. At least I think that's what they were doing. It sort of reminded me of what I saw some dogs doing at a park one day. My mama called it "A Party for Two," but that didn't look like any party that I wanted to be invited to.

When I opened the door, I wanted to turn and run out of the room, but there was something so odd about it that I couldn't look away. I looked, squinted my eyes, and tilted my head in every direction just trying to take it all in. She was pulling on his penis like she was trying to start a lawnmower. He was moaning and groaning so loud that I thought that he was going to "stroke-out."

"Hurry up and cum you old bastard!!!!" she yelled, pulling on him with one hand and wiping sweat from her forehead with the other;

while he huffed and puffed like the "Big Bad Wolf."

She seemed exhausted like she'd been pulling on him for a while and then suddenly, as if someone had smacked him in the back of his head, his false teeth shot out of his mouth and flew clear across the room.

"Weeeeeeeeeeeeeeeeee!!!!" he shouted as he clinched the sheets. His toes curled as he convulsed. His eyes rolled up into the back of his head. He twitched, and then his body went limp. When it was all over, she stared over at me, smiled, and wiped her hands on a towel that was sitting next to her. He was in a "coma" and wasn't waking up anytime soon.

This was her opportunity. While he slept, she went through his pockets and wallet and took every dime that he had. She counted the money as I watched. She was so proud of herself. "Shhhhhhhhhh," she said, before telling me to get the fuck out and I was happy to leave because I knew that mess was going to give me nightmares or be the cause for future therapy sessions.

Then there was Raven, Regan's identical twin. Raven was Regan multiplied by 100. She was hard-core. I bet that when she was born and the doctor slapped her, she probably turned and slapped his ass back. She was a bitch too, but she was more calculating in her "bitchness." She was a thinker – a planner. She didn't just go about torturing folks haphazardly. No, she was too smart for that. She was serious about what she did and who she did it to. Everything had to be perfect – from the day, the time of the day, to what she was wearing when she was hurting her victims.

She was scary. She was the type of scary that you didn't know that you were supposed to be afraid of until it was too late. Not like "a tarantula falling in your lap" type of scary; even though that's pretty damn scary. No, she was more like a tarantula, dressed-up in a sexy stripper's costume, while carrying a loaded .22, type of scary.

Oddly enough, everyone liked her. Everyone else but me that is. She was very popular in school. She had her own little clique of girls who were bullies just like her. Interesting enough, high schools have a full supply of them; angry little girls who like taking their anger out on others.

She was a great dresser and all of the girls emulated her. If she wore plaid on Monday, by Tuesday, every girl in the school was wearing plaid. She was cute and had a walk that was almost hypnotizing – intoxicating and she knew it. It gave her great joy knowing that she had that kind of power over people, and power was what she wanted.

Her pleasure came in the torture of ANYTHING that had breath. I mean ANYTHING. She had this way about herself. She was a magnet. She drew people and animals into her circle, making them love her, want to be with her, and then punishing them for their choice.

Now, her "thing" wasn't just using or hurting men. Matter of fact, I'm not really sure if she even liked men. If she did, that part of her was kept a secret and I don't think she liked women either. The more that I think about it, I don't think she had an affinity for anyone or anything. You see, that would require something that she wasn't capable of – liking anyone or anything other than herself.

You couldn't have anything around her. She would destroy it just because she could. Because of her, I had a lot of blind bald-headed baby dolls. When she was bored or when she wasn't bored, she used to rip the heads off of my dolls, shave their heads, poke out their eyes and then hand them back to me. That's horrible, but it could have been worse. She could have buried them in the backyard with all of her dolls that she no longer had any use for – buried – never to be seen or played with again.

I was around four and I vaguely remember that my mother bought me a goldfish. After watching that movie about a whale, I just knew that I had to have one. Of course, I couldn't have a whale, so a goldfish was the next best thing.

I begged and pleaded until my mom and dad gave in. The night before we went to pick one up, I spent the whole night thinking of what to call him. After several hours, I decided on the name, "Blinky" because goldfish have the biggest eyes.

I remember the trip to the store to pick one out. I was so excited. I skipped and hopped all the way to the door of the store. When we entered there were wall to wall animals, puppies, birds, turtles, bunny rabbits, mice, and gerbils. I was like a kid in a candy store.

When we found the tank full of goldfish, I thought that I'd died and gone to Goldfish Heaven. There were about a hundred in the tank, but there was one that stood out. He was both silver and gold and had the prettiest eyes. I pressed against the glass so hard that I thought that I was going to break the tank. "That one!" I shouted. "That one!" When the salesperson put him in the plastic bag and handed him to me, I held him up to see him in the light. "Mommy, look at his eyes. Don't he have pretty eyes?"

My Daddy answered, "Yes, Baby Girl, he does have pretty eyes."

Raven looked at me and frowned. "How do you know that it's a boy?"

I held the bag up and looked closely at the fish not really sure what I should be looking for. "Daddy, is he a boy?" I asked.

He smiled and said, "It's whatever you want it to be." He glared over at Raven.

"Then it's a boy," I said, smiling. Looking at the fish, I saw two eyes, blurry, staring back at me through the plastic bag. I lowered the bag to see who the eyes belonged to.

Raven stared at me, smiled, and said, "You better hide him from me."

I held the bag close to my chest and said, "No, don't."

She smiled and looked at Regan who smiled out of the corner of her mouth. "You better hope that she gets to him first."

I could only imagine what they were going to do to him. Afraid, I ran to my mother's side and said, "Mommy, I don't think I want him."

She kneeled down and said, "Sweetie, what's wrong?"

Looking over my shoulder at my sisters and trying to figure out a way to save the fish's life, I said, "He's stupid and ugly. I don't want him."

My father looked at me and said, "Baby Girl, don't be silly. He's not ugly." He took the bag from me, held it up, and grimaced. "Well, he's no Denzel, that's for sure, but of course…he's a fish."

I pulled on his pants, pleadingly, "Daddy, please…"

Regan walked away and began to flirt with the store employee, but Raven's eyes were fixed on me and the fish. She licked her lips like a cat watching a mouse before it pounced on it.

I continued to plead with my parents when my mother finally said, "Stop it…now, we came to buy a fish and now, we got a fish." She began to walk to the front of the store. I kept looking over my shoulder at my sister. She continued to smile and she did that all the way home.

I tried not to think about the things that they said. I got so caught-up in loving it, that it never dawned on me that someone was on the other side of the house making other plans for it.

For the next couple of days, everything was fine. I fed him, talked to him, sang to him, and just loved him. Then it happened. One day, after coming home from the babysitter, I ran to my room to say "Hi" to Blinky, but he wasn't in his bowl. I called out to him expecting that the fish would run into my room and jump into my arms, but that didn't happen. I looked for him under my bed, everywhere, but there was no Blinky. Then I heard Raven call my name. As I walked towards the door, I could smell something cooking. I was so glad because I was so hungry. I ran down the hall still calling his name, but there was no response. When I walked into the kitchen, I asked everyone had they seen Blinky, but they all said, "No." My dad looked around the table and said, "I don't know where that fish is, but he better appear before the night is up…do you hear me?" My sisters, responded with a resounding, "Yes" that was met with giggles.

That night when we went to bed, I cried myself to sleep. I cried all night long. I looked down to find that my pillow was soaked with tears. The next morning, Regan called me for breakfast. I stretched and sleepily slipped my feet into my house-slippers and immediately felt something wet and "slimy". I rubbed the sleep from my eyes and slid my foot out of the shoe. As my toes started to reveal themselves, I saw two black things sticking to them. I leaned over to inspect the stuff that was sticking to my foot and then I saw them. Blinky's eyes. I shook my foot violently, trying to remove them from my feet. I jumped up and was headed out of the room when Raven stopped me in my tracks. She laughed and said, "I saved you the best part…didn't you say that you like his eyes?" I was about to scream when she said, "You better not…you don't want to end-up like your friend." I muffled my cries. Regan walked passed and said, "The rest of him wasn't bad either," and she began to lick her fingers while she sucked her teeth. She rubbed her stomach like she'd just finished eating a hearty meal. They both laughed and walked away. I walked back into my bedroom and just stared at the empty fishbowl. When my Daddy found out, he punished them all – made them save their allowance to buy me a new one, but I didn't want any more fish after that.

My other sister, the quiet one was named, Ivy. According to my parents, she was not a cute baby. Ivy was the inspiration behind the joke about the baby that was so ugly that the doctor slapped the Mama instead of the baby. They used to joke that when she was born, the doctor wasn't sure if my Mama was delivering a baby or if she'd just "shitted" on herself, but to me, she was beautiful too, but in her own special way.

If you weren't there to see her born, you wouldn't even know that she ever existed. When she walked in the room, she blended in like wallpaper while the others stood out like a puss-filled pimple on the tip of a teenager's nose. Even now as I look back over the years, I can't really say much about her. Other than her being evil too, she had a weird fascination with picking her nose and eating everything that came out of it. She was not the prettiest one or the smartest one. She was just Ivy and Ivy really didn't want any trouble. Although, she was always involved in it, she kept her degree of involvement to a minimum. She knew better than to get in their way, or get hurt for doing so. When they called her name, she ran like her life depended on it. She moved like someone had set fire to her house-shoes. Her share in the mess was more of a matter of survival. She was just buying her time until she was old enough to move out.

And then there was me…

Chapter 2

My real name is Grace. It means "Blessing or Favor." My mother said that I was her little miracle baby. She became pregnant with me at the age of 40 after being told that she couldn't have any more children. That placed me eight years younger than Ivy. My older sisters were born a year apart making them very close, so they weren't happy when I came along. I was the outsider. The disrupter of their perfect little lives. Even though my mom and dad were happy and couldn't wait for my arrival, my sisters were already plotting my demise.

They were so lucky that I didn't die. My mother told me that I was born three months premature because she slipped and fell down a flight of stairs. She said that she didn't understand how it happened but remembers tumbling and landing on her stomach. She remembers looking up and seeing the girls standing at the top of the stairs, but when she looked again, they were gone. She cried out for them, but they didn't come to her aid. Instead, she lied there in a pool of blood until my Daddy arrived home from work. They thought that they almost lost me, but due to God's "Grace" and mercy, their little 'peach' pulled through.

I was the typical baby. I cried. I slept. I ate and I pooped. That's all I did and my parents loved it. I couldn't do anything without them tripping over each other to see it. They took pictures of me sleeping, eating, yawning, stretching, spitting-up, and doing absolutely nothing. As a baby, I'm sure that it didn't bother me to have a light constantly flashing in my face, but when I became a toddler it really got old fast. By the time that I was a teenager, I felt like I was surrounded by a bunch of stalkers. Even though my parents showered us all with love, there was something about my mother's "near-death" experience, as she often called it, when she was carrying me that made them feel like I deserved just a little extra attention.

They thought that I was the cutest thing on the planet. By the time the "baby" comes along, all questions have been answered, all mistakes fixed, and there were no dreaded "hand-me-downs." They used to talk about hand-me-downs" like someone was passing down a virus – no one wanted it. I wore a new outfit every day and had a new pair of shoes every month. My mother stayed in my hair – which consisted of bangs, ponytails, and barrettes to match every outfit. When my mother used to sit me on the floor between her legs to do my hair, I could see my sisters staring at me. I would wave at them at first, maybe even smile, because, I guess, I loved them and wanted them to love me, but the looks on their faces told me that that could and would never happen.

At the time, I wasn't capable of understanding what they were feeling or why they were feeling it. I wish I could have convinced them that I wasn't their enemy. As a baby, you just don't understand such things. You just want everyone to be happy and to love and be loved.

My mother told me of instances when I was an infant, where she couldn't explain it, but she would always have to cut my fingernails, because as soon as she would leave the room, she would always return to me crying with bleeding-welts drawn across my face. She also told me that I pulled my hair a lot too because I often had bald-spots in my head.

One thing that she could never figure out was why I would never let my sisters hold me. Every time that she tried to hand me to one of them, I would scream to the top of my lungs. It was so bad, that she had to carry me everywhere because she was so worried that something was wrong with me. She noticed that after a while of never leaving my side, I stopped scratching myself and pulling my hair and attributed my odd behavior to me missing her. Yes, I missed her. I needed to be with her, but not for the reasons that she suspected.

I learned how to walk at an early age. I was barely eight months old when I took my first step and I was getting into everything because that's what babies do. If my little hands could reach it, I was getting into it. I was very curious and loved exploring my new world, but not everyone in the house was happy about that.

As I look at a scar that still lingers on the back of my hand, I cringe as I remember the memory tied to it. It was during one of my exploring days, that I was burned badly by a hot iron. My mother could never figure out how an iron that was normally kept on the kitchen counter was now, plugged-up and sitting in the middle of the kitchen floor.

When I burned myself, my mother asked my sisters how the iron got on the floor. Initially, they claimed that they didn't know what she was talking about. Then, they blamed it on the two invisible children in the house named, "I don't know and It Wasn't me." It's funny because a lot of stuff gets blame on those two. But after a lot of pressure, my oldest sister told my mother that she should be glad that it wasn't worst and that she should be careful about leaving me alone.

This answer made my mother extremely angry. She did not enjoy being disrespected or being told what to do. Especially, by a child that she insists is the reason why she can't wear a bathing suit anymore. My mother did not react immediately. She took a moment to process Regan's words and then without warning, Regan was tasting her wedding ring. Regan grabbed her mouth. "Why did you do that?"

My mother leaned in and said, "Because I can…and don't forget it." She smiled, raised her eyebrow, and continued, "Does it hurt?"

Fighting back tears, Regan mumbled, "Yes…" as she wiped blood from her mouth.

Picking me up into her arms, she said, "Then my job is done…the next time that you fix your mouth to tell me what to do, I want you to remember that pain. You should be glad that you still have teeth…my mistake…maybe next time."

Regan began to breathe heavily – inhaling and exhaling through her mouth. My mother laughed. "Unless you're trying to put out a fire, you better go and sit down somewhere."

Regan slowed her breathing and quickly remembered that she was standing in front of the only woman who wasn't afraid of our Daddy.

She picked me up again and said, "I thought so. Now, put some ice on that lip and go lay down somewhere." Regan wiped her mouth as she watched me disappear down the hall.

My mother felt so guilty behind the incident, but her guilt only made things worse. The more love that I received, the more that she tried to make it up to me, was countered by their vengeance.

In my short lifetime, I could never remember my mom and dad putting their hands on my sisters except to punish them. They weren't the type of people who woke-up, looked at their watches and said, "Guess what time it is? It's time to beat our kids?" and they didn't look at their calendars and say, "Guess what day it is? It's National Beat the Shit Out of Your Kids Day." While they may have felt like such a day should exist, that's not who they were. No, they didn't beat their kids because they could, but when they had to, they got it done. Otherwise, they were such loving people. They loved us the same, but it felt like my older sisters believed that since they were born first that should have afforded them some type of special treatment. I guess every kid probably feels that way, but they felt almost entitled.

The interesting thing is, is that I knew early on that something wasn't right. The way that my mom and dad treated me made me feel good and the way that my sisters treated me, was horrible. Their kind of love hurt.

I learned early on to fear them, so I began to avoid them as much as possible. When my mother left the room, I would walk so close behind her that I walked on the back of her shoes. I'm surprised that she had any skin left on the back of her heels. I wouldn't let her leave my side. Even when she used the bathroom, I was right there. I used to sit on the floor right in front of her and wait until she was done. I didn't care if she was doing #1 or #2. I just knew that I didn't want to be left alone with the 3 that were waiting for me on the other side of the door.

My fear completely extinguished my parent's sex life. As soon as they put me to bed, before Luther could finish his first chord, I would climb out of my crib, walk to their room, and crawl into their bed. My Daddy used to get so angry, but as a baby, I didn't think nor did I care about that. I needed protection and plus, they didn't need any more kids anyway.

Early on, I had dreams of them standing over me – watching me as I slept. All three of them were standing in the darkness, watching me as if they were waiting for me to take my last breath. In my dream, I reached out to them and one of them leaned over and bit the tips of my fingers. I screamed and that's when my mom and dad would run into the room to save me. While I thought that this was a dream, on many occasions, I would awake from my dream to swollen red fingers.

I showed my mother my fingers and said, "Bite…bite…" as a way of trying to tell her that I thought that her daughters hurt me, but she didn't understand what I was trying to say, so she stared at them and nibbled at the tips. I would snatch my hands away and think to myself, *It already hurts. I didn't give you my hand so that you could cause me more pain.*
"Did mommy hurt you?" she would ask.
YES Damnit!!! I thought, before she kissed them to make them feel better.

Things like that happened so often, that it felt normal – my nightmares being a part of my reality. The pain, the dread, and the fear, was a constant reminder to never get comfortable, because evil lurked in the bedrooms down the hall and it wears a skirt, ponytails, and lip gloss.

Chapter 3

When I was five, my mother went back to work – often times leaving me with my sisters. It wasn't an easy decision for her, but when you had four kids and you wanted to give them a good life, you did what you had to do. She took a job as a typist at a company nearby, so that she was able to pop in on us, but after a while, she became comfortable with leaving me in their care – so comfortable, that she didn't bother checking on us anymore. They were so excited when it happened. They waited for that moment like kids waiting for Santa to bring them gifts on Christmas day.

It was amazing what they were capable of hiding from her. You should have seen them in action. It was fascinating to watch. It was like watching serial killers in training. They would get up in the middle of the night, when they thought that everyone was asleep, holding their little meetings in their rooms to discuss all of the dirty stuff that they had planned for the day. I would climb out of my bed and crack my door, to find them creeping back and forth from room to room. One time, I tried to listen in but was greeted with a pillow to the face. After that, I never did it again.

They were really good at being deceitful. They smiled in mom's and dad's faces, promised that they would be good, and as soon as the door closed, the torture began. Now, don't get me wrong, they didn't focus all of their attention on me. Sometimes they had other things and people to do. On those days, I was just something that got in their way like a pair of shoes sitting in the middle of the floor. They'd just push me to the side so that they could get down to business, but when it was my turn, nothing else in the world mattered.

When they were forced to babysit me, they would sit me in front of the TV, stick a bowl of food in my face, and dare me to move. When I got up because I needed something, they would tie me to a chair using a pair of my mother's pantyhose. After a while, every day, I went straight to the chair. They called it playing "Cowboy & Indians," but often times, I was an Indian and there were no Cowboys.

I remember one night, I fell asleep in the chair. I woke up to a "crook" in my neck. I couldn't reach up to rub my neck because my arms were tied down, so I tried to readjust myself in the chair. Still half-asleep, I looked over at the television but it was being blocked by two black things moving around in front of it. I looked closer and found that they were shadows of who, I didn't know. One shadow was on its hands and knees, while one shadow was behind it, pushing itself into it. I couldn't really tell what was going on, because the room was so dark. I tried to lean-in close to see what was going on and accidentally moved the chair. The shadow that was on its hands and knees heard me and said, "Go back to sleep." Afraid, I closed my eyes and did what I was told.

The following day, Regan tied me up immediately after Daycare. I wasn't allowed to go to the washroom after snack time at school so I was really looking forward to going once I got home, but she wouldn't let me. We were barely in the house before there was a knock on her bedroom window. She looked at me and said, "I better not even hear you breathe…you hear me, you runt?" I nodded, "Yes" and climbed into the chair. Hours had passed. I started to "dance" in the chair, but was afraid to say anything. I couldn't hold it anymore. Suddenly, I surrendered to the urge and allowed my bladder to relieve itself – all over the floor. I was so happy. I began to relax when I finally thought about the mess that I'd made of myself. I was completely soaked when I heard a door open. I was sure that I was about to get in trouble, so I tried to pretend that nothing happened, but it was kind of hard to ignore the puddle of yellow water pooling underneath my chair. Ivy walked into the room. She looked at me and then turned and walked out of the room. Soon she came back with a change of clothes. "Shhhhhhh," she hissed. Then she removed the stockings and pulled the wet clothing off of me. She used my wet clothing to clean the floor, dressed me and stuck me back into the chair. She threw the clothing in the garbage and no one checked-up on me again until moments before my parents were to return home. They were able to do this for a while until…

The situation came to a head one night after my mother came home from work early. She was tired and looking forward to seeing her girls, but found one of them tied to a chair and the other three were nowhere to be seen. She untied me. "Who did this to you?" she asked, kneeling down to pick me up. I screamed in pain. She called out to them, "Regan, Raven, and Ivy…where are you?" Their doors swung open.

When Raven and Ivy entered the room, they looked and then tried turning around. "Hold up!!!!" my mother said, "And where is your sister?" Suddenly, Regan entered the room, fixing her nightgown and yawning, "What's going on, Mother? You're home early. You look beautiful today. Is that a new dress?"

She put me down and began to undress me. When she saw the rash on my private area, she began to cry. She glanced up at my sisters. She didn't say anything. She just pointed towards the hallway. Shortly after, my Daddy walked in. He saw me standing in the middle of the floor. "What is going on, Baby Girl? Why are you naked?"

I pointed between my legs and then looked down the hallway. My Daddy saw the red inflamed skin and began to take off his belt. Without asking any questions, he began to swing his arm and with each blow, my sisters screamed.

I ran to see what was happening. My mother was screaming, "You better hit them before I kill them!" I began to cry. My father continued to swing. My sisters tried to run, but my mother held them in place so that my father could hit them. They pled for him to stop, but he didn't.

I ran to him, grabbing for the belt. "No, Daddy....noooooo." My mother grabbed me and said, "Peaches, come here...get out of the way before you get hurt." When she said that, Raven and Regan stopped crying. My father swung some more, but there were no more screams, cries, or tears from them. They held hands and took the blows as if they were being hit with a feather. Ivy continued to plead with him.

This went on for a few minutes before he got tired. When he was satisfied with what he thought was punishment for their treatment of me, he yelled, "Clean-up this damn room and take your asses to bed." Ivy was the only one who responded, "Yes, Daddy."

This incident, like many others, was always followed-up with a practice that my Daddy often called, "A Laying of Hands." I often found it weird that this practice of "laying hands" never required the use of his hands – well, except to hold something. For a long time, I thought that hands was another name for belt until I got older and realized that it wasn't.

The next day, my mother decided to stay home from work to care for me. She started a bath for me to soak in. I could hear the water running so I rummaged through my drawers for a nightgown, a t-shirt, and some panties. The phone rang and my mother called out for Raven to watch the water to make sure that it didn't overflow. I was lying in my bed when I saw Raven limp by. She was still sore and angry from the whupping that she received the night before. She walked pass, but then walked back and looked into my room. She didn't say anything. She just stared, turned, and walked down the hall. Next, she came back and said, "Come on....mommy told me to put you in the tub."

When she reached out her hand, I hesitated.

"Come on...I'm not going to hurt you...I promise."

I didn't take her hand. I crawled out of the bed and followed her down the hall. When we arrived at the door, I stopped. I saw the water in the tub. She walked in and said, "Come on...I don't have all day."

I stared at her.

"Come on, you little brat and get your butt in the tub." She began to pull on me.

I screamed, "Noooooooo....stop it!"

My mother must have heard us because she came running down the hall. "What are you doing? I only told you to watch the water."

Raven responded, "I did."

My mother walked passed her towards the tub. She stuck her hand in the water and then drew it back quickly. "Oh my goodness…this water is so hot. It's a good thing that you didn't get into it…it could have burned your skin."

I glanced up at Raven who was staring at my mother's back as she leaned over the tub. She walked towards her with her hands stretched out in front of her. My mother was still looking at the water when I called out to her, "Mommy" and she turned around. She stared at Raven. "Why are you still standing there? Go do your homework or something." Raven looked at her, looked at me, and then whispered, "Next time."

Later that evening, while my mom was making dinner, I was playing with my dolls when I heard someone say, "Peeeeeaaaaches." I continued to play with my dolls when I heard it again. "Peeeeeeeaaaaaacccccchhhhes." I stood to find out where the voice was coming from. I looked out into the hall where I saw a finger motioning for me to come towards it. Slowly, I began to walk down the hall. I passed the kitchen where my mom and dad was until I arrived to find my sisters waiting for me.

"Do you wanna play house, Peaches?"

I stood at the door and saw them peeking out at me.

"Come on," Regan motioned. "It'll be fun."

I didn't move. Regan punched Ivy in the arm and said, "Tell her that it'll be fun."

Ivy hesitated, but then said, "Come on, Peaches..." She glanced at Regan and Raven and continued, "It'll be fun."

Slowly, I walked into the room. They took the doll from my hand and began to play with it. For a moment, it felt okay to be around them. They were smiling, so I began to smile and when they laughed, I laughed. It felt great.

Raven took some gum from her pocket. "You want some gum, Peaches?"

Happily, I nodded, "Yes." *What kid doesn't like gum?*

She removed the gum from the silver piece of paper and handed it to me. I smiled and took it from her and began to chew. She handed Regan and Ivy some gum and they began to chew. We were all having fun and chewing gum.

They asked me if I wanted them to comb my doll's hair. I immediately said, "Yes," because my doll's hair looked a "hot mess." Until that moment, I'd been styling my doll's hair. After I

45

styled her hair, she was left looking like Buck Wheat with a big pink ribbon in her head. When they were done, she looked like a completely different doll. That made me extremely happy. Then they asked me if I wanted my hair to look like my doll's hair. Again, I immediately said, "Yes." Suddenly, they took my hair down. They began to comb it while laughing the whole time. I was having so much fun that I didn't realize what they were doing to me.

My mother called for us to come to dinner. We stopped playing and proceeded towards the kitchen. When we walked in, my mother looked at me. Startled by what she saw, she dropped the plate that she was holding. "Peaches!!!!!!...What have you done?"

I was still chewing the gum when she ran towards me. "Oh my Gawd, Baby Girl...what have you done?"

My Daddy walked over and looked at me. "Baby Girl," he said, shaking his head. "Tsk, tsk, tsk...what a mess." He grabbed the broom and dust pan and swept-up the broken plate. "Awwwwww damn...come on here," she said, dragging me down the hall. She put me over the sink and as she did that, I caught a glimpse of myself in the mirror. I looked funny, so I began to chuckle, but my mother didn't find it funny. She grabbed a bottle of shampoo and generously poured it over my head. She pulled, tugged, and then rinsed, but it was still a mess. She looked at me and frowned. "Daddy, please bring me some ice." I sat there, still holding onto and playing with my doll – fascinated by how pretty she was. My father entered the bathroom. He handed my mother the ice tray, shook his head, and exited the room. My mother applied the ice until it began to melt. The cold water oozed down the side of my face. She let out a big sigh and yelled, "Daddy, please bring me the scissors."

I continued to play with my doll. My dad entered the room holding the scissors. "Here," he said, before shaking his head and leaving the room again. Suddenly, I could hear, *snip, snip, snip,* and then I saw some black stuff fall pass my face and onto the floor. She kept snipping and more black stuff fell on the floor. I looked down and then back up. I stood up on the toilet and glanced into the mirror. My eyes widened, my mouth fell open, and the gum fell out. I caught it before it hit the floor and put it back into my mouth. Chewing, I grabbed my head. It was gone. It was all gone.

My mother grabbed my arm and dragged me back down the hall. "What did you do?" she asked my sisters. Regan answered, "Why are you always blaming us for what she does?"

Raven chimed in. "Yeah, don't you see her...she got a mouth full of gum."

My mom looked down at me and I was still chewing the gum that they'd given me earlier. "Did you do this to yourself?" she asked, frowning.

I opened my mouth to say something, but something caught my attention out of the corner of my eye. It was Regan. She balled her fist up and pretended to punch herself in the right eye, left eye, her nose, and her mouth. I knew what that meant. That meant that I better keep my mouth shut or I was going to be the lucky receiver of a punch in the eyes, nose, and mouth, so I looked at my mom and nodded, "Yes."

Regan and Raven seemed satisfied with my answer. They smiled.

She sighed. "Well, at least you know what will happen the next time that you stick gum in your hair."

We all sat down for dinner and no one said another word while my dad chewed his food and shook his head.

Chapter 4

My home was like living in a house of mirrors. Can you imagine being tortured by people who look just like you? Every day, it felt like I was kicking my own ass. It is so hard to understand how siblings could be so mean to each other. I often thought that being cruel to them was like being cruel to myself and you would think that they would feel the same way, but they didn't. We were sisters, but they treated me like I was more of a consequence of my parent's behavior and love for each other than an extension of themselves.

Because my older sisters were born so close together people called them "The Triplets," but when I came along, we became "The Triplets" plus One and it was something about that "plus One" that singled me out. When people said that, Regan would "check" them right away. "Plus one, nothing...that little runt...she's nobody...she ain't a 'one' of nothing...not that half-pint." I'd just stare at her and smile. Oblivious to the fact that she'd just excluded me and insulted me. I just thought that she'd given me another nickname.

The twins couldn't or wouldn't be ignored. They thought that being twins would automatically make them stars of the family and while it did in the beginning, when Ivy came along, their light started to dim, and when I arrived that totally put their light out. They weren't getting the attention that they were accustomed to. They'd been replaced – kicked to the curb by the new kid and they weren't having it.

Now, I was the "one" and I didn't like it. Even when we were all together, people would want to see and get to know the "little one." They would "coo", and hug, and kiss me and I hated that and I don't think that my sisters realized that. There was nothing great about having a bunch of strange folks always up in your face. I'm sure that when they were little, people did the exact same thing to them, but maybe they felt like they were supposed to get that type of attention all of the time – all of their lives. Personally, I didn't see the excitement in it, but clearly it was something that they wanted and needed.

They felt like they'd been replaced instead of realizing that their roles as big sisters was special in its own right. I wasn't trying to take their place. No one could do that and I'm sure that no child is born with the intention of stealing the spotlight from their older or younger siblings. They are just born. That's it. But for some odd reason, my sisters acted like I had a say in it. Just like their births, this was all of God's doing, but they wouldn't dare punish Him. No, they wouldn't do that because a bolt of lighting up the ass wouldn't feel good, so messing with me would be their payback. Their way of balancing things out.

They pushed me away. They didn't want to be seen with me and when they were over their friend's houses, they would make me stay outside – no matter the weather, I was left outside. One time, they brought me home soaking wet. My sisters always had a plausible explanation for it. "She wanted to play outside…so we let her play outside." Of course, this was far from the truth, but the truth would be more than my mother could accept, so they told her what was necessary to keep them out of trouble.

Every time this would happen, my mother would warm me and tell me that playing in the cold would make me sick. As my mother said these things, my sisters would wait to hear my response, but there would be none. I just looked at her, looked at them, and kept my mouth shut. While looking at her, I thought to myself, *"You need to tell this to your other daughters, who you left to care for me, instead of talking to the kid wearing wet clothes and freezing to death."* Of course, I never said this out loud because I knew better, but I wanted to.

We weren't able to keep this a secret for long though. One day, they took me with them over one of their friend's house. Again, they stuck me outside on the front porch alone. Luckily, it was nice outside. While sitting there, a baby wearing nothing but a diaper walked passed. I looked at him and said, "Hi baby." He looked at me. I waved. Curious, he walked towards me. He crawled up the steps and sat next to me. I smiled at him and said, "Would you like to play with me?" He smiled back, but he didn't say anything. I handed him a doll and he looked at it and smiled. "Her name is Gracie," I said. He smiled again. When he moved, I noticed that he didn't smell right, but it didn't matter because I was so happy to have someone to play with that I didn't care. We continued to play when suddenly, he crawled back down the stairs still holding my doll. "Baby, give that back to me," I said, but he continued down the stairs. I didn't know what to do. I looked at him and then at the door of the house to see if my sisters were looking at me, but they weren't there. I turned back to look at him and he was headed down the sidewalk with my doll. I walked down the stairs to follow him.

He walked towards a house whose door was sitting wide open. I called out to him. "Baby, give me back my doll." Now, the little boy was out of sight. I hesitated before entering, but I had to get my doll back. Suddenly, I heard a baby crying. I walked in.

The house was filthy and wreaked of soiled diapers. In the first room, I saw two boys who were wrestling with each other. One was a really big boy and the other was a little boy – not much older than me. The big boy was pulling on the little boy's private parts and the little boy was doing the same to him. They both laughed as they pulled on each other. I thought that this was odd, but I wasn't there for that. I was on a mission. I interrupted them. "That baby has my doll..." They stopped, looked at me, then turned, and went back to playing with each other. I shrugged and continued through the house.

I entered another bedroom where a baby was lying on a bed, screaming at the top of his lungs. I walked up to him. "Baby, what's wrong?" The baby screamed louder. He smelled worse than the other baby. Closer, I was able to see why he was crying. He was covered in poop and bugs were eating him. He had sores all over his body. I tried to get the bugs off of him, but the more that I tried to get them away the more that he screamed. I didn't know what else to do for him, so I said, "Okay, baby, I have to get my doll. I'll be back." The baby continued to scream as I left him lying there, alone.

I called out to the baby who had my doll. "Baby, I need my doll. I'm going to get in trouble," but there was no answer. I continued through the house. Finally, I landed in the kitchen where a big woman was sitting at the table polishing her fingernails. "Excuse me lady...your baby got my doll." She looked at me and pointed towards a sink full of dirty dishes with flies buzzing all around them and underneath sat the baby who was playing with my doll. I walked over and took the doll away from him. "You can't play with my dolls anymore. You're not a nice baby." He smiled and looked at me. I walked back passed the woman sitting at the table. She stared at me as I left the room. I walked back passed the screaming baby, the room where the boys were playing with each other, and then walked out of the house. I went back to sit on the porch like nothing happened.

During dinner, we were all talking about our day. I was sitting quietly, thinking about the screaming baby, when my mother asked me what was wrong. Her question shook me and I erupted like a bottle of soda pop. "Mommy, I saw a baby, today…he had poo-poo all over him and bugs were all over him. He was crying, Mommy…crying so hard." My mother looked at me in complete horror. My father's mouth fell wide open as a fork hung from his bottom lip. The looks on Regan, Raven, and Ivy's faces was a combination of a "deer caught in the headlights" mixed with a little "I'm going to kill you for telling on us later." When my mother was able to speak again, she said, "When did you see this baby, Baby Girl?"

I looked at my sisters and then back at my parents and just shrugged my shoulders.

She looked at me again. "Peaches…you shouldn't tell horrible stories about others if they are not true."

Regan looked at me and said, "Yeah, Peaches…you shouldn't make up stories about people."

Finally, the fork fell from my father's bottom lip snapping him out of his daze. "Baby Girl, are you lying to your Daddy?"

Raven chimed in. "Stop lying little girl."

My Mama and Daddy glared in her direction. She dropped her head and pretended to eat.

I became frustrated and in one breath, I said, "No, I'm not lying. I saw it. A baby took my doll when you made me sit by myself on the porch and I followed him in the house and I saw a big boy playing with a little boy's wee-wee and the baby was crying and there was a lady in there and…"

My father starting choking. My mother slapped him in the back of the head. He stopped choking and gave her a dirty look. Then they turned and looked at my sisters. My father stood and started removing his belt. "Get up," he instructed.

As they were walking towards the door, my mother grabbed Regan's arm and said, "Not you…not yet."

I went back to eating.

Later that evening, after everyone settled down, I went to my room to play with my dolls. My mother looked into my bedroom.

"What cha' doing, Baby Girl? You're supposed to be sleeping," she said, walking in.

I looked at her and said, "Awwwww mommy...can I play...just a little longer?" I asked.

She walked towards me. "Come on," she instructed. "You and your babies have to go to bed."

I crawled to the top of my bed and climbed under my blankets. I placed my dolls next to me. My mother tucked me under the covers.

"Mommy?"

"Yes?" she asked.

"Do you believe in monsters...?"

She laughed for a second and then said, "Why do you ask?"

I grabbed one of the dolls and held her tight. "'Cause...I wanna know."

She paused for a minute and said, "Well...I don't believe in monsters per se...you're probably thinking about the ghouls and goblins that you read about in your story books. I don't believe in them but I do believe in good and evil. I do believe that there are some truly bad and scary people in the world. Why do you ask, Sweetie?"

"'Cause…" I began to answer when I heard my door opening. I looked over her shoulder to find two eyes peering at me through the door. My mother looked back and said, "Take your butts to bed!!!" She turned back to me and said, "You don't have to worry 'bout no monsters…not as long as I am here." She leaned towards me and kissed me on the cheek.

I turned my back to her and said, "Leave the light on anyway, Mommy…just in case."

The next morning, my mother called the police and reported the situation. I can only assume that the police did something about it because we weren't allowed to leave the house or see the sun for several days.

It was a Saturday morning when my Daddy decided to add a little "exercise" to their punishment to teach them a valuable lesson. We were all sleeping when each one of our doors were thrown open. You can hear him screaming over the sound of thunder coming from outside. "Get up and put your clothes on!!!!!"

I looked around trying to figure out what was going on. I thought that we were having a fire drill. I jumped up and ran around my bedroom collecting everything of importance – my dolls and their clothes; just in case it was cold out. Then as I rubbed the crust out of my eyes, my Daddy entered my room and said, "Baby Girl, get up…let's go."

"Okay, Daddy…coming," I confirmed.

Groggily, I heard them all complain, but that noise fell on deaf ears. "Get some damn clothes on and get your asses outside!!!"

The whole time that we were dressing, we all mumbled. We dragged ourselves outside. It was raining so hard. My Daddy was pacing back and forth, wearing a yellow raincoat, some galoshes, and one of my mother's rain scarfs. "Okay ladies…"

"Okay, what?" Regan mumbled, rubbing her eyes.

My mother slapped her in the back of her head. "Ouch," she yelled.

My father continued. "So…you thought that it was cute to sit your little sister outside while you sat inside…with your friends…away from the elements…"

Raven interrupted him. "Didn't we get punished for this already?" As soon as she said it, she ducked to avoid any incoming blows from my mother, but my mother just smiled.

He paused and looked at her and said, "Yeah, I did, but I think beating y'all isn't working. I'm starting to believe that y'all are getting immune to it, so today, I've decided to switch it up a bit…give you a taste of your own medicine."

They all turned and looked at me and then back at him.

"Guess what you're going to do?" he asked.

They didn't say anything. "Nothing? No one wants to take a guess?"

They remained silent.

"You ladies are going to cut the grass…," he said.

Ivy frowned. "The grass…really? But it's raining."

"Yes, it is…I'm glad that you noticed that…means that those expensive-ass glasses on your face are doing their job."

They were all frowning now.

"Yes, ladies…you are going to cut the grass…in the rain."

Raven interrupted. "Won't that hurt the grass?"

He stopped pacing and said, "Wow…how vegetarian of you…if only you acted like a humanitarian, you would have thought twice about leaving your sister on the porch while you do what you do. Somebody else could have taken her…"

"Somebody should have taken the little brat," Raven mumbled under her breath, but my mother still heard her. She knew that she was going to get hit. She tried ducking, but she was too slow. *Pop!* Right in the back of her head. "OUCH!" she yelled as my mother smiled, waiting for the next person to say something.

My Daddy continued, "…and you wouldn't even have known it. So you need to know what it feels like, but you're lucky…I'm going to be right here making sure that you don't come to harm."

Ivy said, "Let me go and get my coat…"

"Nawwwwwww…I want you to feel every freakin' raindrop…now, get your butts out here." They stepped away from the warm porch. As the rain hit their bodies, they began to shake. They stared back at me as I remained protected from the rain.

He started the lawnmower and watched as each one of them took their turn at mowing the lawn. At first, I watched, but then my mother took me inside, fed me, and got me ready for a bath.

I could hear the roaring of the lawnmower from outside of the bathroom window. I began to sing as I dunked each of my dolls into my makeshift swimming pool. Suddenly, the roaring stopped, then I looked up to find that one of the window panes was being opened from the outside. Before I could say or do anything, an avalanche of grass clippings was being poured on top of me. When the lawnmower bag was empty, I could hear them laughing. When I opened my eyes, the tub was full of grass, leaves, paper, spiders, millipedes and other debris. I started to scream. I stood trying to shake the stuff off of me. "MAMMA!!!!!!" I screamed.

She ran into the bathroom. "What the hell?"

"MAMMA!!!!!" I screamed again, swatting the bugs and grass out of my hair.

She looked towards the window to find Regan, Raven, and Ivy staring at her.

She immediately began to wash the grass off of me. She dried me off, helped me get dressed and sent me to my room. She stomped out of the house and then seconds later, you could hear her screaming. Then there was some knocking and banging and more screaming proceeded. Then my father began to scream. There was some more banging and then there was silence.

At the dinner table, there was only the three of us. My father told my sisters "that if they were hungry, they could eat that shit that is in the bathtub."

Later that night, while everyone was still asleep, I went to use the bathroom. I was swinging my legs and having a good time when the bathroom door opened slowly, I looked over and found Regan staring at me. She walked over to the sink and slowly removed the hot bulbs from the vanity. Quietly, I watched her exit the bathroom, but before she left she said, "Try wiping your snitching ass in the dark." And I tried. I grabbed a wad of toilet paper and wiped myself until my skin started to burn. When I was done, I slowly peeked out of the door to make sure that she wasn't waiting for me in the hall – waiting to throw those bulbs at my head. When I realized that it was safe to go, I ran across the hall, locked my door and jumped into my bed. A moment later, I heard a door open, I pulled my blankets over my head trying to protect myself for whatever they had in store for me. Suddenly, I heard someone say, "Who took the damn bulbs out of the bathroom?!!! Why would you take the bulbs? Who in this house is taking a piss in the dark? Who? DAMN KIDS!!!!!"

Chapter 5

After all of the strange things that were happening to me, my mother and father set their schedules so that someone was always at home. My mother worked days and my father took a job that allowed him to work nights. Everything was "abnormal" for a long time, and I was glad. I liked abnormal because abnormal didn't hurt and I could sleep at night. Every day, my sisters went to school and came home. When they got home, they each went into their rooms and did whatever girls like them do. And that was wonderful for as long as it lasted.

I was now old enough to go to school too. I'd started Kindergarten, but I wasn't too happy with that idea at first. On the first day of school, I walked into the classroom and saw all of the different faces and wanted to turn and run back to the car. I grabbed my mother's leg and held tightly because I didn't want her to leave me.
"What's wrong, Sweetie?"
I grabbed harder. "Mommy, I want to go with you."
She tried to free herself from me. Pulling at my arm, she said, "Stop it...now, let mommy go."

I saw all of the faces watching me, but all I could see were new people who wanted to hurt me. The more she pulled, the more that I held on. The teacher who was watching the exchange, walked up behind me and said, "It's going to be okay...I promise."

She reached out for me, but I turned to my mother and screamed, "Nooooooo!!! I don't want to!"

Finally, my mother had enough. She kneeled down and said, "You better stop this. Now, do you really want to go home?"

I thought about that for a second and said, "No." I released her and turned to look at my new world.

It was bright, colorful, and loud – so very loud. There were kids all over the place. The teacher told them, "Gather around everyone...we have a new friend...everyone say 'Hi' to Grace." They all swarmed around me screaming, "Hi Grace!!!" With open arms, they reached for me. I tried pushing them off of me, but the more that I pushed, the more they kept coming. "Hi Grace...Hi Grace," they all yelled as each one of them took a turn hugging me and while I struggled at first, by the last "hug", it felt okay, but I knew that stuff like that didn't last for long.

Being around other kids was weird. They were happy, they shared their toys, and they wanted to play with me. They really wanted to play with me and not hurt me. It allowed me to drop my guard for a while until they gave me a reason to put it back up. I laughed…a lot. It was so much fun that when my Mama came to pick me up, I didn't want to go home. I begged and pleaded for her to leave me there, but she told me that I couldn't stay. I couldn't understand why, but she insisted that we leave. I refused so much so, that she had to pick me up and carry me out of the building. As I struggled to get out of her arms, I waved "goodbye" until the teacher was completely out of sight.

When we got home, I remained in my car seat. She reached out to me. "Come on, Sweetie." I turned and looked out of the window at the house.

"Come on," she insisted. "Mama's had a long day."

I did not move. I continued to look out of the window. She tried reaching out to me, but I pulled away from her.

Frustrated, she said, "Well, okay…I'm going in now…"

I looked at her and waved "goodbye."

She started to walk away. "Okaaaaaaayyyyy… Mama's going in now… she's going to leave you."

I didn't budge. Now, we were staring at each other – having a War of the Wills – who would blink first and it wasn't going to be me. I continued to look at her. She walked away as I sat there and watched her. When she approached the front door, I saw the curtains move. I stared back at her. She waved. "Mommy's going in the house and she's going to eat all of your chocolate chip cookies."

I said, "Okay," and waved back. *Goodbye.* I looked at her and then back at the eyes peering through the curtains. She waved again and I sat there.

Frustrated, she stomped back towards the car and began to pull on me. I started kicking and screaming. I grabbed onto the seatbelt and held on for dear-life. "Girl, I don't have time for this shit…now, bring your little ass on."

"Noooooooooo!!!!" I screamed. She tickled me under my arms and I let go of the belt. "No, no, no, no…" I struggled to get out of her arms.

She put me down and said, "Look…what is the damn problem?"

I quieted, looked at her, and then back at the window.

She looked towards the window. "What's wrong? That's your sisters…they miss you…and can't wait to see you."

After hearing this, I ran back to the car. She ran behind me, caught me by the arm, and said, "Look…enough of this shit. Now, I don't know what's going on with you, but this has to stop. I'm tired. I still have to cook dinner and I don't have time to play with you."

I cried as she dragged me to the door.

When I walked in, there was no one there. The coast was clear. I snatched my hand from my mother's and ran down the hall to my bedroom. Shortly after, I heard my door open. It was Ivy. She walked in slowly and whispered, "Hey Peaches…how was your first day of school?"

Suspicious, I looked at her and said, "Nice…it was nice."

She grabbed one of my dolls and began to stroke her hair. "What did you do, today?" she asked.

I took my doll from her and said, "We played… we had cheese and crackers…ummmmmm, we had recess….we played on the swings…"

She interrupted me and said, "That sounds like a good day."

I smiled and said, "Uh-huh…"

She smiled back and said, "I wish I could have been there with you." She looked down and then looked away. Then she said, "Do you want to play with me?"

I hesitated at first, but then said, "Okay…" I grabbed a couple of my dolls and we began to play. She was acting like her doll was a Fairy Godmother and my doll was a beautiful lost little girl. We were both laughing when we heard a squeaking sound that was coming from across the room. We both looked towards the sound. Regan stared into the room. She gazed at Ivy. "Let's go," she demanded.

I looked at Ivy because I knew that she wasn't talking to me. Ivy dropped the dolls and walked towards the door. In the doorway, she glanced back and smiled before walking down the hall. Regan frowned at me before closing the door.

After dinner, I was put to bed. I was sleeping when I heard a sound down the hall. I tried to go back to sleep when I heard it again. I got up and walked towards the door. At first, I placed my ear to the door to see if I could hear anything, but I couldn't. I slowly opened it. The whole house was dark except for a sliver of light coming from

Regan's room. I walked back to my bed and grabbed my doll before venturing into the darkness. As I walked towards Regan's room, I could hear voices. I put my ear on the door. I couldn't hear what was being said so I opened the door.

When I looked in, I saw Regan's bed, but she wasn't in it. Instead, there was a boy on her bed. My eyes drifted to the floor where Regan was on her knees with her face in the boy's lap. His eyes were closed. Slowly, he opened them and saw me standing in the door. He tapped her on the top of her head and said, "Pssst, we got company." She jumped up and ran towards me. She grabbed me by the collar of my nightgown and said, "You better not say anything or I'm going to kick your little butt." She snatched my doll from my hands and said, "Do you see this?" She held up my doll by her head and twisted it until it came off and handed the two pieces back to me.

"Leave her alone and get back on this dick...I have to get home before my parent's realize that I'm not there," the boy said, rubbing himself.

She leaned into my face and said, "Now, get your butt back in the bed." She pushed me out into the hallway and I hit my head on the wall making a loud sound.

Suddenly, the light came on in my parent's bedroom. The door flew open. My father came running out of the room wearing nothing, but a pair of black dress socks. "Daddy!!!" My mother yelled.

He looked down, realizing that his "manhood" was showing. He turned and ran back into the room. Seconds later, he returned back into the hallway dressed and carrying a gun. "Who's there? Who's there?"

Shortly, my mother was right behind him. "What's going on?" she asked, tying the belt on her robe.

I was crying and rubbing my head when he approached me. "Why are you out of your bed?"

I glanced towards Regan's bedroom door. My father turned and looked inside. Suddenly, he ran in. "What the fuck...?"

We heard some shouting, scuffling, and then *BANG!!!!*

"Daddy, nooooooooo!!!!" Regan shouted. *BANG!!! BANG!!!!*

"Daddy, nooooooooo!!!" She shouted, again.

We heard the boy struggling to get out of the window.

Suddenly, my father ran out of the room. "That slippery son-of-a-bitch...," he said, running down the hall to the front room. We heard the door open and then there were two more BANGS!!!!!

He walked back in, stomping towards us. "That motherfucker was in my house…getting his dick sucked? What in the hell? Ain't but one motherfucker getting his dicked suck in this house and that's the motherfucker waving the gun. DO YOU HEAR ME??!!!!!!!"

Raven walked out of her room. When she saw what was going on, she turned and closed her door. Ivy walked out and saw me on the floor. When she saw what was happening, she turned and went back into her room. My father went into his bedroom and then walked out with a belt in his hand. He mumbled as he walked passed. "You have gon' crazy…you have lost your damn mind…in my house? Oh no you won't." He walked passed me so fast that I felt a chill from the breeze that his body generated. He walked into Regan's room and slammed the door. My mother scooped me up and took me into my room. She looked at my head and said, "You're going to be okay, Peaches." She kissed it and said, "Mommy's going to check on you in the morning. Now, go to sleep." She walked out of the room and closed the door. I heard her walk down the hall and open another door. "Save some of that ass for me, Daddy."

When I woke up, the next day, I ran to the door. I could still hear Regan screaming. Suddenly, they both walked out of her room – exhausted. "That child has lost her damn mind...fucking in my house..." Daddy mumbled as they walked pass me and went into their bedroom. I walked down the hall and into Regan's room. She was on the bed, curled-up into a ball. I walked over to the side of the bed to look at her. She had her face covered with her arms. I reached out and touched her hand. She snatched away from me. She glared at me and said, "I hate you...you fucking bitch...I hate you." I mumbled, "Okay," and turned and walked out of the room.

During breakfast, my Daddy read all of us the *Riot Act* – his rules of the house – his house. As we stared at our empty bowls, he walked behind us, circling the table as he recited each rule. "Look at those empty bowls...they will be empty until I put something in it." He turned to my mother and said, "Put some cereal in Peaches' bowl."

My Mama did as he instructed. My sisters were seething.

He continued. "You see that? You don't even get to eat unless I feed you. You know why? Because that's my damn cereal, those are my bowls, that's my spoon, and that's my damn milk...in my

74

damn house. All of that shit is mine. MINE!!!! Now, clearly I've done or said something that makes you folks think that some things are just automatic....you can do whatever the hell you want to do and still get to eat my cereal out of my bowls...with my damn milk...in my house. Y'all are crazy. Stuff is just automatic for y'all...like food, lights, heat...all of that shit...But I'm the one who works for that and all I ask you to do is go to school, get good grades and follow my rules. FOLLOW THE DAMN RULES!!! How hard is that?" He stopped, slammed his hands on the table, and looked at all of us. "Now, clearly you've forgotten what those rules are. So let me remind you. NUMBER ONE, this is my house. YOU..." He stopped and pointed at us. "You motherfuckers are just VISITORS... a bunch of folks just passing through...in my house. YOUR NAMES AIN'T ON SHIT....THIS HOUSE, THE FOOD, YOUR SHOES, NOT EVEN THOSE DAMN DRAWERS THAT IS ON YOUR ASSES...YOU DON'T OWN SHIT ...VISITORS...remember that. NUMBER TWO, YOU DO WHAT THE HELL I SAY, WHEN I SAY IT! You don't like it, GET THE FUCK OUT! NUMBER THREE, THIS AIN'T NO DAMN MOTEL. THE ONLY PEOPLE GETTING THEIR FREAK ON IN MY HOUSE ARE THE TWO PEOPLE WHO CAN

AFFORD TO GET THEIR FREAK ON...IN MY HOUSE. NUMBER FOUR, WHENEVER YOU'RE IN DOUBT, REFER BACK TO NUMBER TWO! AND NUMBER FIVE, I AIN'T SCARED TO GO TO JAIL! BRING ANOTHER MOTHERFUCKER UP IN HERE AND I'm BUSTING a CAP IN HIS ASS! Do you understand?" he asked.

"Yes," they mumbled.

"I CAN'T HEAR YOU!"

"YES!!!" they yelled. Regan, Raven, and Ivy were glaring at me, so I said, "YES!"

My Daddy walked over to me, kissed me on the forehead and said, "Not you, Baby Girl...I'm talking to them."

The way that he said the word "them" made me uncomfortable, because again, we were being divided, but I kept my mouth closed by filling it with cereal.

He continued. "Keep on...you gon' catch some shit...messing with one of those triflin' boys." Regan frowned.

Finally, my mother poured my sisters some cereal. We were eating when the silence was broken. "Ma...Dad...I can't go to school like this," Regan said, pointing to the bruises on her arms and legs. Everyone stopped chewing, but me. My father looked up and said, "Oh...you're going. I want you to show

76

everybody and I dare them to say something. When they do, and they come up in my face screaming Child Abuse, I'm going to tell them what you did to earn those stripes and dare them to do something about it. Now, if you don't want folks to know that you're training to be somebody's whore, you're going to do what you have to do to get through the day and bring your ass home....*Humph*...That's the problem with you kids...you are so worried about what other people think of you, but don't give a damn about how your parents feel about you. How do you think I felt when I saw that mess in your room?" Regan was about to answer, but knew better.

He continued. "Huh? Do you care about that? No, you don't and since you don't care about how I feel, I don't care about how you feel. If you don't want your ass whupped don't give me a reason to whup it. It's that damn simple. Do you understand?"

"Yes," she mumbled.

He sighed. "You better be glad that you're still alive. If I'd pulled that mess in my Mama's house, she would have killed me, buried me, dug me up, and then killed me again. You got it good...believe me. The fact that you're still above ground proves that. *Hmph*...worried about what you look like. PLEASE...you better hurry up and get out of here before I let loose on your butt again...got a lot of damn nerve...in my house," he said, shaking his head in disbelief.

Chapter 6

I could feel the rays of the sun burning through my eyelids. I opened them, but the rays were so bright that I covered my head to protect me from them. I was nestled under my blankets, but through them I could see various shades of darkness. I hesitated but something told me to remove the blankets. I peeked through the covers to find a set of knees. As my eyes slowly moved upwards to reveal what was connected to them, I saw her – waiting. She leaned in. "Happy Birthday, Baby Girl," she whispered. I threw the covers back over my head, hoping that she would go away.

Suddenly, my blanket was snatched from my bed. I jumped up and drew my knees to my chest. When I surveyed the room, I found that I was surrounded. They were all holding something. One had a belt, one had a brush, and the other one had an extension cord. Raven was swinging the extension cord back and forth. "It's your birthday…and we want to give you something special."

My eyes moved back and forth trying to keep them all in sight.

"Yeah, something truly special. Have you ever heard of Birthday licks?" Regan asked.

I didn't say anything. I just watched them.

Regan continued, "Birthday licks are for special little girls…it's what people give you when they love you."

Curious, I asked, "Soooooooo, when Daddy hits you, it's because it's your birthday?"

Regan frowned and said sarcastically, "Yeah, it's because it's my birthday and it's because I'm soooooooooo freakin' special."

I smiled and said, "Boy, you must have a lot of birthdays…"

Raven and Ivy laughed. She glared at them and they immediately stopped.

She frowned again. "So now you're big enough to get what we've been getting….because…" She turned away for a second and continued, "Because we love you."

Ivy didn't say anything. She stared outside at the sun still hitting the brush against the palm of her hand. Regan held the belt high above her head and said, "It's going to hurt a lot at first, but after a while, you won't feel a thing."

Raven held the extension cord high above her head. Ivy continued to look outside.

Then at the same time, their hands came down hard. When the belt and cord hit my skin, it felt like I was being cut with a razor. I screamed. Next their hands went up and before coming down again, I screamed again. This time, I began to cry. "Noooooooooo...stop it!"

Regan glared at Ivy. "You better hit her or I'm going to hit you."

Snapping out of her daze, Ivy turned and looked at Regan. "I'm not going to hit her." She dropped the brush on the bed and began to walk out of the room. Regan grabbed her by the arm and said, "Okay..." and pushed her on the bed on top of me. Their hands went up again and this time when they came down, I didn't feel anything. I heard it, but didn't feel anything. This time, Ivy screamed. Their hands went up and Ivy screamed again and this happened over and over until we heard a sound coming from the front room.

"Girls," my mom cried out. "We're home...and where is our little birthday girl?" Regan and Raven stopped and looked at us. "You better not say nothing...do you hear me?" Through tears, I agreed and nodded my head. They ran out of the room. I crawled over to Ivy who was crawled-up in a ball. I threw my arms around her. She whimpered and cringed to my touch. Through tears, she mumbled, "Happy Birthday, Peaches."

I had a big birthday party. Some of my friends from school were there. I watched as everyone laughed and had fun. They played games and ran around without a care in the world, but I couldn't have fun. I was still thinking about what'd happened earlier that day. I would have enjoyed myself if my skin wasn't still stinging from the Birthday licks.

Suddenly, my mother walked out of the house holding a cake and everyone began to sing, "Happy Birthday to you." Soon everyone gathered at the table. My dad called out to me, "Come on, Baby Girl...come and make a wish and blow out your candles."
Slowly, I walked over. I climbed onto the chair and stared out at all of the faces surrounding me. I could see Raven and Regan staring at me. They were having the time of their lives. I looked at Ivy who was sitting by herself.

My father lit the candles and smiled at me. "Make a wish, Baby Girl." I looked at him and at all of the faces surrounding the table and then I looked at the candle. *I wish that they would go away.* I thought to myself and then blew out the candles.

It was time to open the gifts. I opened them one by one and slowly, I began to feel a little better. I got two new dolls. I got a car for my dolls to ride around in. I got some necklaces, some coloring books and crayons, and some clothes. I got a lot of really nice things. I was starting to feel really happy when Raven approached me.

"Open this one…it's from me, Regan, and Ivy." She was holding it for a minute as I stared at the thing in her hand. The whole room stopped to see what it was that she was handing to me.

"Go head and open it, Baby Girl," my father said, standing over me. My hand was shaking as I reached out for it. Raven smiled as she watched me. I slowly took the item which felt very heavy. I removed the ribbon and wrapping paper. It was a tin, a very pretty tin that was covered in pink roses. I smiled but then I remembered who gave it to me and slowly began to open it. Inside of the tin was very dark. My mom and dad stood quietly, carefully watching me. There was an odd silence hoovering over the yard.

At first, my mom, my dad and I leaned in to see what it was. Next, the people sitting close to me leaned in to see what it was. We were all staring at its contents when all of a sudden, we saw something black peeking its head through the lid. It screeched and jumped into my face. My father fell backwards onto the ground and my mother followed behind him. The other people ran and screamed – running in every direction. People kicked over the table and chairs. Cake and fruit punch was everywhere. People knocked each other over as they tried to figure out what it was that jumped out of the tin.

Then we saw it. It was big, black, and had a long tail. It screeched as it tried to get away from us and we screeched as we tried to get away from it. When my dad figured out what it was, he ran into the house and reappeared with a rolling pin. My father ran around the backyard until he had it cornered. Most of us gathered on the other side of the yard – cowering in fear. With one swift blow, my father swung and hit it. It screeched again and my father swung again. The crowd watched in horror as blood splattered across the white picket fence.

There was silence except for the noise coming from the other side of the yard. We all paused to look in its direction. Crying from laughter was Raven and Regan. They were laughing so hard that they didn't realize that we were all staring at them. On the other hand, Ivy was as white as a sheep. Unexpectedly, she bent over and threw-up all over the lawn.

My father walked up and stood over them. When they realized that no one else was laughing, they stopped and looked up. My father held the blood-covered rolling pin over his head. He was about to swing it when my mother ran up behind him and caught his arm. They both stopped and noticed the faces of the people in the yard staring at them. My father put the rolling pin back down as my mother fixed her dress.

One of the mothers of one of the kids said, "I think we should leave."

My father agreed. "Yeah….that sounds like a good idea," he said, looking back at Regan and Raven.

Everyone began to gather their kids and then exited the yard. My mother gazed at Regan and Raven and ordered, "Clean-up this mess." My mother took my hand and dragged me into the house.

An hour had passed before the girls had finally come into the house. During this whole time my father had been pacing the floor while my mother screamed at someone on the other end of the phone. When they walked in, I just knew that he was going to give them some of those "birthday licks", but he didn't. He glanced at them and calmly said, "Girls, come and have a seat. I want to talk to you."

They all sat down. He pulled up a chair in front of them. He sat there for a while, smiling at them. Nervously, they glared back and forth at each other. He leaned over, placing his elbows on his knees, and then placed his head into his hands. Ivy opened her mouth to say something, but my mother gave her a look that said, "Now, is not the time."

Minutes had passed before he looked up. Then he sighed and asked, "Why?"
They all glanced at each other like they were trying to figure out who was going to be brave enough to answer the question. He waited for them to answer.
Finally, Regan answered. "It was just a joke, Daddy. We just wanted to have a little fun." They nodded their heads in agreement – like this was the perfect answer.
My father smiled. "Ohhhhhhhhhh, that's what it was...a joke?"
Raven laughed and said, "Yeah...a joke...that's all it was."
Ivy was just staring when Raven nudged her in the ribs.
"Ain't that right, Ivy? It was a joke, right?"
Ivy glared at me, my mother and father, and then at my sisters and said, "Yeah...," she sighed and continued, "A joke."
My father nodded and said, "Awwwwww....it had to be. I mean, why would you be foolish enough to ruin your little sister's birthday...I

mean...that's cruel and who could be that cruel?"

They looked and nodded in agreement. Then there was silence. My father scanned the room and then out of the blue, he started to laugh. We all looked on. He started to laugh harder. My sisters looked at each other and started to laugh with him. Suddenly, the room was full of laughter. My father glanced over at my mother and nodded his head. She laughed and walked out of the house. My father and sisters continued to laugh.

"Did you see the way that those kids scattered all over the place?" My father asked.

"Yep...that was too funny...they looked like roaches when you turn the light on," Regan joined in.

"They were tripping all over each other," Raven said, laughing and holding her stomach.

Regan tapped her on the shoulder and said, "Did you see when Ol' boy slipped and fell into the cake?"

Raven gazed at her, still laughing, "Girl, I almost pee'd on myself when they knocked that old lady down...I'm going to be laughing at that all night."

Ivy didn't say anything. She just studied them. My father chimed in. "Yeah, your mother spent our vacation money trying to make that party special for your sister." Suddenly, they choked on their laughter and the room became quiet again. Then my mother walked into the house with piles of what resembled cake that had been dumped in the garbage. It had blades of grass and other debris sticking out of it. She walked into the kitchen and grabbed three plates and three forks and sat them in front of them. My father leaned towards them and smiled. "This cake cost us a lot of money. No one had a chance to eat the cake and you know how I HATE to waste money...don't you?"

They stared at each other. "Yes," they said, together.

He smiled. "Well...eat up."

Their mouths flew open in shock. Regan protested. "I'm not eating that mess. It just came out of the garbage." She turned-up her mouth and folded her arms.

"It wasn't garbage until you decided that a rat for a birthday gift was a good idea. Now, you can eat this or..." he stuck out his hand. My mother walked out of the room and subsequently returned with the rat spread out on a piece of cardboard.

"You can eat this," he said, as my mother placed the rat in front of them. They stared at each other in horror.

Again, Ivy turned white as a ghost. She tried to throw-up, but because she'd thrown up the first time that she saw him, there was nothing left, so she just made a gagging sound.

"Awwwwwwww, hell NO!" Regan yelled.

"What did you say?" my father asked.

Raven spoke. "Daddy, you can't be serious."

"Serious as a fucking Heart Attack," he responded.

"Man, I'll take a butt-whupping, but I ain't eating no garbage or no rat," Regan said, defiantly.

My father smiled and said, "Oh, you're going to eat one of them and if I have to wait any longer, you're going to have to eat both of them." Suddenly, you could hear something making a "clinking" sound. We all stopped to look at where the sound was coming from and it was Ivy who had obviously made her choice. She picked the grass out of the cake and ate it in one bite, licked the fork and said, "Can I go to my room?" My father glared at her and said, "Yep."

She stood and left the room. We all watched as she walked down the hallway. Turning his attention back to Raven and Regan, he said, "Next."

They both took a deep breath and filled their plates with the cake. He watched them as they forced the cake down. When they were done, he said, "Now, get out of my face."

We all went to bed early. It'd been a long day and I was really glad that it was all over.

The next morning, I was awakened again by the bright rays of the sun. As I lay there, I thought about the events of the day before. I turned over on my back and stared at the ceiling. As I thought about the mean things that my sisters had done to me, my eyes began to fill with tears. My thoughts were interrupted by the silence – it was too quiet. I knew that if I didn't hear my mom and dad that meant that I was left at home with the babysitters from hell. I immediately became afraid. I knew that they would blame me and find a way to get back at me for yesterday.

Slowly, I turned to my left to look at the door and when I did, I saw two eyes looking back at me. I screamed and jumped up. Lying on the pillow next to me, was the dead rat that my Daddy had killed the day before. As I scrambled to get out of bed, my bedroom door opened. Raven looked in. "Happy Birthday, you little Bitch," she said, before closing the door.

The closet

Chapter 7

*F*or the next couple of years, it would be pretty much the same old crap - a daily dose of dumbshit was how I defined and lived my life. Cookies that were made out of feces for a Christmas gift, shaving off my eyebrows while I slept, putting hot sauce in my cereal, cutting-up my doll's clothes, stealing money from my parents and then blaming it on me, and making me clean the bathroom floor with my toothbrush and afterwards making me brush my teeth with it, etc., You know? Dumbshit. It was always something, but when my mother started a new job caring for the elderly at night, the real torture was about to begin.

It had been a while since Regan had been caught with a boy. I don't think that she stopped seeing them after that. I think that she'd just found other ways to be "fast." When the "gate-keepers" went back to work, stuff went back to normal and fast. Boys…men…were coming in and out of my sister's bedroom like she was passing out free tickets to a basketball game. Every time that you looked up, it was somebody new.

Having me at home was again crimping her style – making it difficult to do what she had to do. So I'd graduated from the "chair" to the closet and I would have to stay there until they were done doing the "do."

This went on every day for a while. We went to school and when we got home, she forced my other sisters in their rooms, took a shower and when she was done, she would grab me, warn me not to make a sound, and throw me into the small dark place.

On purpose, just to be extra cruel, she never closed the door completely. She wanted to make sure that I saw everything that happened in her bed. She enjoyed laughing and pointing so that the people she was having sex with would see me and do the same. They'd look at me, but no one thought that it was odd that a little girl was sitting in the closet watching them have sex or at least no one cared. Some of them even found it amusing as they stared at me while her head bounced up and down between their legs.

And I watched…I watched each one of them have sex with her…sometimes one, sometimes two, and sometimes, three at a time. She took great pleasure in being used. She took the money that they gave her, folded it and slipped it into her bra, and called the next one in like those people who called numbers at the store's deli department. *NEXT!*

This went on for months, but over time, the different faces stopped, leaving only one man who came by almost every day. He was old – old like my Daddy, and he was nice too. He used to hand me candy through the crack in the door when my sister left the room. He always said things to make me laugh, but as soon as Regan came back, he'd run and jump back on the bed. He was funny and I'd become comfortable around him because I really liked him.

One night, after they finished doing what they were doing, when he knew that the coast was clear, he crawled over to the door, and asked me if I would like some candy.

I said, "Yes."

He handed me some and we ate it together. We were laughing and having so much fun when he said, "Would you like to try something cool?"

I shrugged my shoulders.

He touched my arm. "It'll be okay…I promise."

The last time that someone said that to me, everything was okay. I ended-up having a really good time – surrounded by really nice people, so I said, "Okay."

He stuck a piece of candy in his mouth and said, "Now, you have to use your mouth to get it."

I frowned and said, "No."

He rubbed my arm and said, "It'll be okay…see look…put the candy in your mouth…"

I hesitated for a second, but complied. "Okay."

Then he took my doll from my hands and said, "Now, we're going to let…" He gazed at the doll for a second and said, "What's your baby's name?"

I closed my mouth and swallowed the candy and said, "It's Gracie…almost like my name but better."

He chuckled. "Okay…I'm going to give you another piece of candy…this time don't swallow it."

We both laughed and I said, "Okay." I put the candy in my mouth.

Then he placed the doll's mouth against mine. "You see…that wasn't bad. Now, was it?"

I giggled and said, "No."

He said, "Now, I'm going to do it to you."

"Ummmmmm, okay."

He leaned over and stuck his tongue in my mouth to retrieve the candy. I jumped back. "Ewwwwwww, that's nasty."

He said, "That's because we have to practice…okay?"

"Ummmmmmmm…okay?" I said, feeling uncomfortable, but trusted that he knew what he was talking about.

He leaned in to do it again when we heard the flip-flop of Regan's house-shoes coming down the hall. He glanced at the door and then back at me. "Now, you can't tell your sister or she's going to get mad at you and you don't want that, do you?"

I shook my head back and forth. "Noooooooooo."

"Good, then it's our little secret," he said, crawling back to the bed.

She walked in, still drying her moist skin. She sat at the end of the bed and braided her hair. Afterwards, she crawled on top of him. I cracked the door and watched as Regan took candy from his mouth.

We played this game for several days before he decided to teach me a new one. My sister was in the bathroom when he climbed out of bed and said, "I have a new game for you."

I was chewing on a piece of candy when I said, "Okay…"

He took a piece of candy and unwrapped it. He said, "I'm going to have to take your panties off for this one."

He started to tug at my panties when I said, "Nooooooo…I don't want to play this game."

He stopped and said, "I'm your friend, right?"

I looked at him and thought about how nice he's been to me and said, "Well, you do give me candy."

He said, "Yes, I do…now, I just want to show you something that I think that you will like."

I waited a minute and said, "Is it fun?"

Salivating, he said, "Real fun."

So he started to pull my panties down. He licked his lips as my panties reached my knees. "Now, I'm going to put some candy down there and I'm going to use my mouth to get it."

I knew something about this was wrong, but he was my friend and a friend wouldn't hurt me. *Right?* "Ummmmm…okay."

He placed a piece of candy down between my legs and began to lick me. It felt really weird. I started to squirm. Then he started playing between his legs. He did that for a few minutes until this white stuff started coming out of him. He moaned and his body went limp. He fell next to me. When he was done, he handed me a bag of candy and made me promise not to tell anyone. My sister entered the room, he stuck a piece of candy between her legs and he used his mouth to get it out.

This went on for a few weeks until he told me that he had another game that he wanted to show me. I like getting the candy so I agreed to play. "Okay."

He said, "Your sister won't be back for a while…it's just you and me. Now…this is going to hurt a little…"

I was sucking on a lollipop when I said, "Like birthday licks?"

Confused, he asked, "Birthday licks?"

I said, "Yeah…it's what people do when they love you."

He said, "Ummmmmm, yeah…I guess…sure I'm going to give you some birthday licks."

I scooted away from him. "I don't like birthday licks. They hurt."

Looking more confused, he said, "Ummmmmm, they are a new kind of birthday licks…I promise…it's going to only hurt for a little bit, but you're going to like them…you're going to like them a lot."

I hesitated and said, "Nawwwwww, I heard that before…nope, I don't want any more candy and I don't want to play anymore." I handed him the half-eaten lollipop. He pushed it away and said, "Look you little tease…you gon' take care of this dick. Whether you want to or not." He grabbed for me.

"Noooooooo," I said, jumping up and running towards the door. He grabbed me by the leg and pulled me towards him.

"Nooooooooo!!!" I screamed.

He pulled at my panties until they were down around my ankles.

"Noooooooo…" I said, kicking and screaming. "Come here you little bitch," he said, pulling me underneath him.

"Nooooooooo!!! Stop it!!!!" I said, kicking and screaming.

He pried my legs open.

"Noooooooooo…stop…I don't want to be your friend anymore!!!!"

"It's too late," he moaned.

Suddenly, everything went black.

The next thing that I remember, I was lying in a hospital bed. The police was talking to my parents. My Mama was crying and my Daddy was cursing. I tried to sit up, but my bottom was so sore. I removed the sheets to find dried blood on my legs and on a big white thing that looked like a diaper.

The doctor walked into the room. "We did a rape kit and we're going to send it in for analysis. We are going to give her some medications…this should stop pregnancy…"

"Pregnancy!!!!" my mother, shouted.

The doctor continued, "We're also going to give her something to prevent the transmission of infection."

"Infection!!!" my father, shouted.

The doctor continued. "While she is still very young, we still need to protect against these possibilities."

My mother sighed and said, "I understand."

"I will kill that son-of-a-bitch…do you hear me? Kill his ass," my father said.

"Look sir…we don't recommend that you go looking for the assailant. I promise you, we will find him…I promise you."

When the officer left the room, my dad turned his attention on my sisters. "How could you let this happen? Where were you? How did that man get in the house?"

Ivy said, "I was sleeping."

Raven said, "I was studying with my headphones on." They both dropped their heads and began to count the floor tiles.

My father turned to Regan. "I left her with you. Where were you?"

She looked him straight in the eye. "I was in the shower." She glared in my direction.

"Girl, what kind of shower were you taking that keeps you in there so long that someone had enough time to come in the house, rape your baby sister, and then leave out of the house without you hearing her screams." He paused and looked around the room. "Damnit…how in the hell did not one of you…not one of you…hear this child's cries for help?"

Ivy and Raven didn't look up. Regan stared in my direction.

My Daddy walked over to the side of the bed and looked me "dead" in the eyes and said, "Baby Girl, who did this to you?"

I looked at him and then back at Regan. She stared at me. "Nobody, Daddy...," I answered.

His eyes grew wide. "What do you mean, nobody? Little girl, if you don't want your ass-whupped, you better tell me who did this to you."

"Daddy, you can't whup her...she's already hurting," my mother said.

Frustrated, he said, "I'm sick of this shit with these kids...shit happens and nobody seems to know nothing...folks don't just get raped...You expect me to believe that this shit just happened?" He threw his hands in the air and continued. "Maybe a ghost raped her? That makes as much sense as y'all not knowing what the hell happened to her...Now, somebody better open their mouth or somebody gon' be occupying that empty bed next to her."

I thought about what that meant and while I was afraid of Regan, I knew what my Daddy was capable of, so I told him. "It was a man in Regan's room who gave me candy...he was my friend...he put candy in my mouth and then took it out with his mouth...and he put candy down there..." And I pointed between my legs, "...and he used his mouth to take it from down there...and then..." They were completely mortified by this revelation. They both turned to look at Regan so fast and hard, I heard their necks crack. My father's eyes were bulging so far out that I thought they were going to pop out of his head. My mother made a weird sound before collapsing at his feet. He didn't even bother to pick her up and my sisters didn't dare move to help her. They all, excluding my mother who was still lying on the floor, turned to look at Regan, who was walking towards the door. I continued, "He did the same thing to Regan...didn't he, Regan?"

Before I could finish my story, my Daddy stepped over my mother, ran towards Regan, and wrapped his hands around her throat. He was banging her head against the wall when the police came running back into the room. They pulled him off of her. They were holding him by his arms when he said, "She knows who did it. The bitch knows who touched my baby." The officer grabbed her by the arm and dragged her out of the room.

One of the officers said, "Look, we can take you in for assaulting your daughter, but I'm going to give you a pass because we know that you're upset, but if you don't calm down, we are going to have to take you in." They forced my father into a chair. "Are you going to calm down?"

He shook his head, "No," but then "Yes" came out of his mouth.

"Are you sure?" the officer asked. He sighed and said, "She better be glad that you guys were here…'Cause I was gon' kill that motherfucker."

At the police station, they asked Regan over and over again for the man's name. She lied and gave them three different stories. The first one involved me falling and hurting myself and that I lied about the man, the next story entailed a burglar who broke in, raped me and then left the house, and finally, she told them that she was seeing the man and while she was taking a shower, he raped me.

After getting the man's name, the police went out and picked him up, but he had a completely different story to tell. He claimed that Regan wanted him to do it and that's why she kept leaving the room – leaving him with me. He also said that she offered me to him for extra money.

When the officers asked, "Why would she do something like that?"

The man responded, "Because she hates her."

They were both prosecuted for the rape. Even though she consented, she was still a minor when he was having sex with her, so he was given several years for raping the both of us. She received eight years, for her part in my rape and for prostituting a minor, to be served in a juvenile facility.

One day, we went to visit her in "Juvy." When she entered the room, I noticed that she was getting bigger. When we all sat down, she frowned at me. Sitting across the table, we all stared at her. My father was the only person that spoke to her. He sighed and said, "We don't know why you did what you did…"

She looked down and said, "I'm sorry, Daddy."

"SORRY?!!!!!!" He yelled. Everyone else in the room turned to look at us. He lowered his voice and said, "You are sorry?"

"Yes," she said.

"You stood by...you encouraged a grown man...to violate your little sister and you are fucking sorry?" He was so angry that I thought that he was going to choke her again. "What would make you do something like that?"

Regan looked at Raven. Raven looked away. "I don't know why I did that, Daddy."

"I wouldn't do that to somebody that I hate and you did that to your little sister...who does that shit? What has she done to you that you would want something so horrible to happen to her?"

Regan looked at Raven again before saying, "She didn't do anything."

He threw his hands in the air and said, "Then why, Regan...why?"

She didn't answer.

"I asked you a question, child...why?" he asked.

She sighed. "I don't know why."

He shook his head, took a deep breath, and then looked at her stomach. "And that makes it even worse...you did it and don't know why you did it?" He stopped and shook his head.

"He gave her candy and money..." I mumbled.

My father looked at me. "What did you say?"

I looked at everyone sitting around me and said, "He gave her candy and money."

Ivy and Raven shook their heads and proceeded to stand to walk away.

Through clenched teeth, he said, "Sit your asses down." He looked back at Regan. "He fucking paid you...he fucking paid you..."

You could hear my mother praying, "I'm going to kill her, Lord...I know that you say, 'Thou shalt not kill', but does that apply to her?...Lord, please send me a sign...and if you're too busy to do so, I understand but I'm gon' need you to turn away, Lord...close your Godly eyes...'cause I'm going to kill her...I'm going to kill her...Amen."

My father spoke. "That's so low-down that I can't even wrap my mind around it...this requires a level of thinking that I'm not even capable of...are you, Mama?"

My Mama was still praying. "Jesus, Lord Jesus...touch my heart, Lord before I stop hers..."

My father turned back to Regan. "And now you're knocked-up by a rapist...who gave you candy and how much money did he give you to rape you and your sister?"

"He gave me $50," she said, proudly.

My father closed his eyes, inhaled, and then exhaled slowly. "$50...for the both of you...Damn, that's all you're worth?"

"Well, he gave me $40 for me and $10 for..."

Raven looked at Regan and shook her head.

"You have got to be the lowest, dumbest, and dirtiest Bitc…" he stopped.

She looked at my father and said, "Daddy, he didn't rape me…"

My father balled his hand into a fist. My mother grabbed his arm. "What the hell is wrong with you? Are you smoking something because you have to be high or really freakin' stupid? I ain't raising no dummies, so you must be high. That grown man had sex with you and my baby…You are a child…my child…it was wrong, Regan."

She looked away.

He continued, "Don't you know that? Don't you know that it was wrong?"

She didn't answer.

He continued. "And now you're carrying his baby."

She rubbed her stomach. "Yes, Daddy, and it's a boy too."

My father covered his face to hide his tears. He tried to compose himself. He wiped his face and said, "I'm done…That baby will not come into my house."

"But Daddy, he's my baby," she said.

"You're right…he's your baby…you and that rapist's…that pedophile's baby…you nor that baby…will never step foot in my house," he said.

My mother leaned over and whispered, "Daddy, you don't mean that."

He looked at her with tears in his eyes and said, "That girl and that baby will never step foot into my house!!!" He stood to walk out of the room. "Let's go," he demanded. We all stood and followed him.

Regan yelled out. "Daddy, I'm sorry. Daddy, pleeeaaaaasssseeee!!!"

My father grabbed my hand and began to drag me towards the door.

I looked back and Regan was standing there with her hands reaching out to him, but he didn't stop until we were in the car. Then he pulled off and never looked back.

Chapter 8

*T*hen the letters and the phone calls started. She called me every day from "Juvy". I was still young when this happened so when the calls turned "crazy", I used to just hang-up on her or hand the phone to my parents and let them hang-up on her. When my mom and dad refused to let her speak to me, the calls turned dark and threatening. The phone calls had gotten so bad that my parents blocked the number.

Next, the letters started. Now, remember she was evil, but she wasn't stupid...well, not real stupid. She wrote things that she knew would upset me, but she made sure to stay close enough to the "line" without actually crossing it. She didn't want to end-up with more time.

Dear Peaches,

My sweet little sister. I don't blame you for sending me to the "home." What that man did to you was wrong. I know that now and it's not your fault that they took away my baby. My one and only baby. Nope, it's not your fault and when I get out, I'm going to prove it to you. You know how much I love you and you remember how we used to show each other love? Yeah, when I get out, I'm going to love you all day and all night. I promise you that. Just me and you.

Love your big sister, Regan

Since I hadn't told my parents about the other abuse, they would see the letters as harmless, but I knew what it meant "to be loved" by them "all day and all night." Raven and Ivy knew what it meant too. Now, how can you look at that letter and think that love meant pain? How do you tell people that your sister wants to "love" you to death? You can't. It was at that moment that I knew that I needed to grow-up and get out of my parent's house and soon before that evil girl was released for good behavior.

After a while, there were no more phone calls and no more letters. My parents said that we needed to deal with her with a "long-handled" spoon, so they cut her completely off. We had no more contact with her and I'm sure that this really pissed her off. She needed to be mean to me like she needed to breathe, so not having access to me must have felt like death to her.

For years, my parents blamed themselves for everything that happened. First, they blamed each other for working too much and not spending enough time at home with us. They blamed it on TV and rap music. They blamed it on the lack of "God" in our lives. After blaming it on everything but the kitchen sink they finally settled on the fact that she was just plain crazy and that's how my parents dealt with stuff. If they couldn't get things to fit in a certain mold, they'd just file it under "just plain crazy."

Chapter 9

With Regan out of the house, Raven seemed to direct her energies elsewhere. In the beginning, she seemed lost without Regan – "like a chicken with her head cut off." She wandered around for months clueless as to what to do next. It was clear that she wasn't the brains behind their madness. Without Regan, Raven had no idea what to do with herself, let alone me.

For a long time, she was depressed. Every day, she walked around sad and then one day, as if someone had slipped her a happy pill, she snapped out of it. She took the gloomy look that she'd been wearing for a while and traded it in for a smile. At least, I think it was a smile. With Raven, it was kinda hard to tell. Her frowns and smiles looked the same to me.

She became focused – on what? I don't know. I was just glad that it wasn't me. She graduated from high school with Honors, but she didn't move out of my parent's house. She got a job at an animal clinic and seemed to be very happy. And Ivy? Interesting enough, Ivy blossomed into a beautiful young lady. She graduated from high school and moved out of my parent's house. She was attending a college in the south and was doing extremely well. At least, that's what they told me.

For me, I was getting used to being a teenager. As traumatic as the incident was, I learned that it takes a sick individual to do nasty things to little girls. While I hated the man who raped me, I was not angry at my sister. No matter how much I tried to, I couldn't hate her. My mother believed that my forgiveness was due to my age – because it happened at such a young age that I had more time to heal, both mentally and emotionally. I don't think that that was the case at all. When you've been hurt by someone that you love and trust – hurt by them over and over again, it's like being stuck with a knife over and over again – after a while you just don't feel the pain anymore. You just go ahead and die inside. And that's what I did. I died inside.

While Regan was still in "Juvy", I still lived with one of the Wicked Sisters of the Southside, so the horror wasn't completely over. Freshmen year was pretty uneventful. Everything was good for a long time. We actually seemed normal for a while, whatever that meant. My parents were home most of the time. I went to school, did what I had to do and came home, but then there was Raven. Like I said, normal for a while, but things started to get weird, again.

There were nights that I woke up to find her standing over me. When I asked, "Why are you in my room?" she would just smile and walk out. One morning, I was getting ready for school. I had the radio playing while I was taking a shower. "Ooooooooo, baby, baby, ooooooooooo, what you dooooooooo, baby, baby, ooooooo…" I was so loud, I didn't even hear the bathroom door open. "Hello," I said. "I'm almost done." No one said anything. I stuck my head under the running water to rinse the soap out. When I came from under, out of the corner of my eye, I saw a flash of light. I rubbed my eyes because I thought that I was seeing things. I rubbed my eyes again but there was nothing there. I threw the shower curtains back and saw the door, closing. I knew that it wasn't anyone, but Raven. I thought about confronting her, but that wouldn't do me any good. The consequences of saying anything were too great, so I decided to ignore it.

After school, I arrived at home to find Raven locked-up in her room. When I got up to get something to drink and to use the bathroom, I could hear her talking to someone. I didn't really think about it because she was an adult and really? Who cared who she was talking to? As long as she wasn't talking to me.

Over the summer, I noticed that she was starting to bring some of her "work" home. Since she worked at an animal hospital, that meant that sometimes, she would bring home a bird, sometimes a cat, or maybe even a puppy. Sometimes, she would let me play with them. I enjoyed it but usually the next day, whatever she brought home was usually gone. I didn't really think about it because I never had a chance to really get attached to them. They left as fast as they came. This went on all summer. Every day a new animal would come in and then the next day, they were gone.

One morning, Ivy called. When I answered, she immediately asked to speak with Raven. I walked in the living room and asked my mother if Raven was still home and my mother said, "Hand me the phone…let me talk to Ivy." I handed her the phone, went and sat next to my dad, on the couch, to watch TV.

"So how's school?" I heard my mother ask before knocking on Raven's door. There was no answer. My mother knocked again and still there was no answer. "Whew…what is that smell? Hold on for a second, Ivy." I heard the door open. Suddenly, there was a blood-curdling scream and the phone hit the floor. My dad and I ran down the hall and when we arrived at her room, we just stood with our mouths hanging open. My mother dropped to her knees in the corner of the hallway. She rocked back and forth as my dad and I entered the room.

The pungent smell waffing out of her room was a combination of air freshener, decaying flesh, and old sweaty gym socks. It took everything to keep my breakfast down. We started to search the room to find the source of the smells. We covered our noses and glared around the room. We moved blankets, the computer desk, and we opened the drawers, but we couldn't find the source of the smell. We were about the walk out of the room when something told us to look up. We stopped and slowly followed the walls that were slashed with droplets of blood. Hanging from strings attached to the ceiling were the carcasses of dead animals. My father walked over to the window and threw the curtains back. He was frozen as he looked up at the ornaments of death that hung from the ceiling. I rubbed my eyes so hard, they were starting to burn. I couldn't believe what I was looking at. In the distance, I could hear Ivy's voice calling through the phone, "What is it? What's happening? Will somebody say something?"

My mom and dad spent the whole afternoon packing-up all of her belongings and cleaning up the room. My father packed all of the dead animals up into a box, carried them out back, and buried them. During the digging, he unearthed some of the baby dolls that Raven had buried out there. He just looked at them, tossed them to the side, and shook his head.

For the first time, Raven didn't come straight home and that was a good thing because our Daddy was on fire. He was so hot, you could see smoke coming from his afro. He was pissed. "This is one of those moments when I wish I had something to drink," he said.

My mother didn't respond.

"What the hell is wrong with these kids?" he asked.

My mother remained silent.

"I think their asses are possessed. That's it."

My mother held her tongue.

"Or it's something in the damn water…I mean, what are the odds that we end-up with two crazy-ass kids? What are the odds? Usually, there's only one per family, but we got two of 'em…TWO…it's got to be the damn water."

Finally, my mother responded. "I have to agree, but if it's the water…why aren't we crazy?"

For the first time in an hour, my father stopped pacing and wearing a groove in the hardwood floors. He said, "You're right…it's got to be something else…don't you have some crazy folks on your side of the family?"

"What?" my mother asked, frowning.

"Yeah…remember that fool that used to hump trees? Yeah, Uncle Tree-Humper…you know that ain't no normal shit…that's some crazy shit…who goes around humping trees? Yo' crazy-ass family."

"What about your damn family?" my mother asked. "It's a loooootttt of crazy folks on that side…shit, you shake your family tree and watch how many nuts fall out."

My father started pacing again. "Look, whatever it is, we need to figure it out. I can't take no mo' of this mess…who do you know does this shit? This ain't no Black people shit, is it?" He stopped pacing to hear her answer.

"Well, you know that Black people do crazy shit too."

He started pacing again. "I didn't say that Black folks don't do crazy shit. I KNOW that Black folks do crazy shit…I'm asking do they do THIS kinda shit?"

"Well, crazy people…no matter the race…if they are capable of crazy…they are capable of this kinda crazy."

"I just never heard of this mess happening in the hood. This is some stuff straight out of the suburbs."

"I know, baby…it's crazy."

He stopped pacing and examined her. "We've already established that it's crazy…"

Suddenly, the front door opened and then it closed. I walked out of my room and hid in the kitchen so that I could hear and see everything.

My father started right away. "Have you lost your damn mind?"

Raven started taking off her coat. "What are you talking about, dad?"

He walked over and pulled her coat back up onto her shoulders. "Ummmmmmm…there is no need for you to take that off."

She adjusted her coat. "What are you talking about?"

My Mama interrupted, "We went into your room."

Raven's eyes widened. "What are you doing in my room? Did Peaches go into my room?" She glanced over in the direction where I was hiding.

My Daddy responded. "First…you forgot RULE NUMBER 1…didn't I tell you that this is my house…MY HOUSE…don't be asking me no questions about what I do in my house. Now, you need to answer my question. Why were there dead animals hanging from the ceiling…in my DAMN house?"

Raven responded, "First of all…"

My Mama and Daddy eyeballed each other and said, "Did she say, 'First of all…?'" They both looked back at her.

She continued, "I mean…yes…it might have looked strange…"

My Daddy glared at her. "Might? Might? Nawwwwww, that mess was definitely strange."

Raven sighed. "I didn't kill them. I brought them home because they were sick and they died on their own and I didn't want to bury them. I wanted to keep them close by hanging them from the ceiling and that way, I could look at them every day…sort of my way of honoring them."

My Daddy threw his hands in the air and said, "Now, that makes so much sense...doesn't it, Mama?"

My Mama looked confused. "Ummmmmmmm sure...," she said. "I guess..."

He continued, "Yeah, it makes perfect sense to hang dead fucking animals from the gaddamn ceiling. You see, most people bury dead animals, but noooooooooo, I got a daughter who hangs hers from the ceiling...and buries her dolls...dolls that we paid good money for...dolls that she was supposed to be playing with... in the backyard...dead animals on the ceiling... perfectly good dolls buried in the backyard...yep, makes perfect damn sense..."

She looked shocked. "How did you know that those were my dolls?"

"I can look at your room and see who buried those dolls...doesn't take no Forensic Analyst to figure this one out."

My Mama was still confused.

"Any-who, I'm glad that you told us because we didn't understand."

Raven studied the room and said, "Ummmm, okay?"

He continued. "Yeah...yeah...now, we gon' need you to take your stuff and your 'hanging-dead-animals-from-the-ceiling' ass and go find you another place to live. I got enough damn problems than to have the police looking for your 'Hannibal' ass all up in my house."

My Mama interrupted him. "I don't think he hung animals from the ceiling."

My Daddy stared at her and shook his head. "I don't care if he shoved them up his ass, okay? I'm trying to make a point." He turned and looked at Raven.

"Okay…proceed," my mother said.

They both examined her. He sighed and he turned his attention back to Raven. He shoved some bags in her face and pushed some boxes at her feet and said, "I love you…but you got three choices. You can leave, I can call the police and they can lock you up for killing animals, or I can call the "nuthouse", have them bring you one of those 'special jackets' and pick you up…but I don't care where you go…you gots to get up out of here."

Before she could say anything, he was pushing her towards the door, but before she made it to the threshold, he said, "Peaches, say goodbye to your sister." I didn't say anything. I just stuck my hand out and waved.

My father mumbled the same thing, over and over again, all through the night and into the next day. "I got one in "Juvy" for helping rape her little sister and another one hanging dead animals from the ceiling…what's next?"

Chapter 10

I was able to get over some of the stuff that they did to me, for the most part. While many of the physical scars healed, the emotional ones still left a mark and I was sensitive – sensitive to looks, remarks, and to touch. I didn't want anyone coming near me – for any reason. I didn't want to be hugged, I didn't want people whispering in my ear…nothing. I wanted people to stay as far away from me as possible.

It really took a long time to warm up to people. They tried to befriend me, but I was uninterested. I just couldn't trust anyone. I learned early that if family could hurt me, a stranger could hurt me – there was nobody left, so I just built a wall around myself to protect me and my secrets. It would take a "special" kind of person to be my friend – someone as dysfunctional as I am. During sophomore year, I met that person.

Her name was Nicole. The best way to describe Nicole is "interesting." She stood out because she wasn't loud like most of the girls in school. She was quiet like me, but there was only one difference. While I spent most of my time being invisible, she stood out – like a sore thumb.

Nicole wore all black. No matter what day of the week, no matter how hot or cold it was outside, she was always covered in black. She called it "Goth," but I called it being in perpetual mourning – like getting up every day and dressing to go to a funeral. Interesting enough, under all of that dark makeup, jet black hair, black clothes, and enough piercings to keep her grounded in any airport was a truly beautiful girl.

She was so cool. Everything about her was cool. She had a presence that was strong and fearless. She hated authority figures, but what teenager doesn't? Teachers, parents, police, didn't matter, she hated them. She only respected people who respected her. I really liked her and I wanted…needed…someone who could just accept me for me and I desperately wanted her to be that person.

We hung out all of the time. We would talk for hours about things that absolutely made no sense to the average teenager. We talked about everything from politics to Nicole's hatred and disdain for girls who thought they were the "shit", her hatred for racists, her hatred for all of the actors on every Reality TV show, and how she wished that they could all be shipped to an island far away from everyone else and take their bullshit with them.

Again, we talked about everything, but not once did we talk about what happened to me. She knew that I was "wounded", but I don't think that she was really interested in how I got that way. She was just interested in who I was when we spent time together. I never told her anything about my childhood, but it was something about me that according to her, "Wreaked of pain and fear." She said that that is what led her to befriend me. She told me that we were "kindred spirits" drawn to each other by the Universe or some dark force with a sick sense of humor. Of course, as a teenager, that kind of stuff was too deep to comprehend, but that's what made her different.

Sometimes, we'd go to the park and lie out on the grass and look at the sky. She'd light a joint, take a puff and say, "Do you see that, Peaches?" Still holding the joint, she'd point towards the sky and say, "Right there...do you see it?"
I'd look up at our sky-blue surroundings and say, "What am I looking for, Nikki?"
She'd take another puff and say, "Right there...those cluster of clouds...you know what they look like?"

Still searching the sky for what she was looking at, I said, "I don't, but okay…"

She inhaled. "They look like angels."

I tilted my head from the right to the left and said, "Angels? I don't see any angels…"

She pointed again. "You don't see it?"

"No, I don't see any angels," I said.

"Here, try this and look," she said, handing me the joint.

I took it, looked at it, and handed it back. "Naw, I'm good…I'll just have to take your word for it."

She took another puff. "This is what you need…it'll fix some of that shit that you got going on in your head."

I smiled and asked, "And what happens when I'm not able to get high? What happens to the shit in my head then?"

She took a long drag, exhaled and said, "That's why you have to stay high." She laughed and inhaled again.

"Naw, I can't mess with no drugs. I got so much I want to do with my life and I can't do it if I'm high all of the time."

She sat up, took another puff, and exhaled the smoke into my face. I coughed and fanned the smoke away.

She laid back down next to me. "First thing, weed ain't no drug. It's some natural shit that grows out of the ground whose purpose is in making you feel good. God put it on the planet so that mankind can have a natural way of dealing with all of the messed-up shit in the world. What's not natural is that poison that human beings make…that mess will have you all messed-up. The worst thing to happen after smoking this shit is I'm going to go home, eat, and take a damn nap. That stuff that mankind makes will have you walking around selling your ass to get the next hit. You ain't NEVER heard of somebody selling their booty for weed," she laughed again.

I thought about it for a second. "Does that fall under Crackhead logic?"

She finished the joint and said, "Don't mess with the crack, at least not yet, but never say never…right now, my friend, it's just me and the Chronic. The bigger the "demons", the bigger the drug. Small "demons" small drug. We all need something…I choose weed and you do…" she looked at me and continued, "….whatever it is that you do…but we all need something."

I thought about what she said and went back to looking at the clouds.

I met her mother. We were going to the park one day and she needed to pick up her stash of weed from her home. As I walked up the driveway, I expected the door to open and a bunch of bats to fly out of the house. I expected a big door that creaked when you opened it, eerie music playing in the background, darkness, lots of darkness, and I expected everyone to be dressed in "Goth," but that's not what happened. When the door opened, I was greeted by the most beautiful woman I'd ever seen except for my Mama. She was dressed in a beautiful pink-floral dress, she was wearing heels, and her hair was done-up like one of those women from the 60s. Their home was bright and smelled like homemade pie.

"Come in," her mother said and as Nicole tried to walk pass her, she grabbed and kissed her.

Nicole wiped the kiss off of her face and said, "Don't you have a husband?"

Her mother laughed. "I do, but your kisses are sweeter."

"Gross," Nicole mumbled. "People go to jail for that...you know that right?"

She laughed, nervously. Then she turned to study me. "Come in and have a seat."

I hesitated.

She walked into the room and motioned for me to sit in a chair that sat near the kitchen door. She extended her hand. "I'm Nicole's mother…"

I figured that out when I walked up to the door. I thought to myself. Nicole was the spitting image of her mother just creepier.

"What's your name?" she asked.

I walked in, extended my hand, and said, "My name is Grace, but people call me Peaches."

She smiled. "Oooooooo Peaches…how urban."

Urban, I thought to myself.

"Would you like something to eat…drink…Ms. Peaches?"

"She don't want nothing!!!!" Nicole shouted from down the hall, but I was a little hungry so I said, "Yes, I would like something." I smiled and looked away, but then I noticed that she was still standing there. I looked up and she was still smiling. There was a moment of uncomfortable silence.

Then she asked, "You would like something…?"

I studied her and said, "Yes, I would like something." But she still didn't move.

She said it again, "Yes, you would like someTHING??????"

Nicole yelled from down the hall. "Say please…say please!!!!!"

I looked up and said, "Ohhhhhh...Yes, I would like something, PLEASE."

She smiled and if I had just hit an ejection button, she sprung out of the room. Seconds later, she was standing in front of me with a plate of warm cookies and a glass of milk. I took the items from her hand and said, "Thank you." I bit into one of the cookies. "Oh...these are really good."

She smiled. "Thank you...it's one of my mother's recipes."

Nicole came rushing down the hall. She scooped up the cookies in her hand, shoved them in mine, and said, "Let's go before she tells you how grandma had to walk 900 miles, barefoot in the rain, to get flour and eggs..."

"Don't be rude, Nicole," her mother said.

"Drink the milk and let's go before she tell you how granddad spent all day grabbing on some cow's tits for the milk..."

I could see that the tension in the room was building, so I drank the milk in one gulp. Nicole was dragging me out of the house. I glanced back. "Thanks again, Mrs....Mrs...." I looked at Nicole and asked, "What is your mother's name?"

When we got to the door, she pushed me out of it and said, "You don't need to know her name."

I wiped the milk moustache from my mouth and said, "You weren't nice to your mother...she seemed like a really nice lady."

Nicole stopped and said, "Look...we cool, right?"

"Yes." I said, still chewing on the cookies.

She said, "So I'm going to teach you something...'cause it's better that you learn today...and that you learn it from me." She paused and looked back in the direction of her house. "Because a person looks nice doesn't mean that they are. Looks are deceiving...if I pour chocolate over shit does that change anything? No, it doesn't. You pull back the layers of chocolate and all you got is chocolate covered doo-doo. That's it. It still stinks because it's still shit. Everything that looks good ain't good for you. When people look at me, they think that I'm weird and scary..."

Because you are kinda weird and scary. I thought to myself.

She continued. "...but I'm not. When people look at her, they see nice shit...'cause her ass is covered in 'chocolate'...I get to see what she looks like without it and it's scary. The kind of stuff that nightmares are made of. I know the truth and ain't nothing about her that's nice...you hear me? Nothing..." She waited for me to answer.

135

"Yeah…I hear you." I took her comments about her mother with a "grain of salt" because most kids hate their parents – no matter how nice they are.

She grabbed my arm and started pulling me down the street. "Now, let's go because I need to get high."

When we got to the park, someone was waiting for us. He was listening to his headphones so he didn't see us walking up behind him. Startled, he jump back and said, "Gurrrrllll, you almost got jacked." Nicole smiled, but I laughed.

"Where are you from?" I asked, looking him up and down.

He frowned and said, "Why you asking about my 'hood?'"

When he said it, I fell out laughing.

"What's so funny?" he asked.

Nicole answered the question for him. "His pale ass is from Naperville."

"Naperville???" I laughed so hard, tears filled my eyes until I couldn't see. "Naperville? That's your 'hood'? That's some funny shit."

He frowned. "It's not where you come from, but where you end-up."

I stopped laughing and wiped my eyes. That made a lot of sense. "You right…you right," I confirmed.

Nicole scanned us both and said, "Can we now get this buzz on or do y'all want to stand here and bump gums all day?"

We walked over to the merry-go-round and they proceeded to roll some joints. I sat and watched as they poured the "weeds" into some papers and licked them. They wrapped the ends tight and lit one up. They took a puff, inhaled and exhaled. They did this several times until they both broke out in laughter.

"What's your name?" he asked.

I pointed at myself and asked, "Me?"

He looked at me and smiled, "Yeah, you...who else do you think I'm talking to?"

I frowned and said, "People call me, Peaches."

He exhaled and said, "Well, Peaches...do you taste like a peach?"

Nicole punched him in the arm. "What did I tell you about that shit?"

He took a puff, blew the smoke in her face and said, "You know that you're my sexy-chocolate." They both smiled. He kissed her, gross-like, like she had food all over her face and he was trying to lick it off. I didn't think that she was going to have any skin left when he was done. When they finished what resembled a poor attempt at Mouth-to-Mouth Resuscitation, they both glanced up to find me frowning.

"What's wrong with you?" Nicole asked.

"If that's what you call kissing then I don't want to have anything to do with it," I said, looking down.

Nicole laughed.

He frowned. "What you need is a boyfriend, so you can have somebody to kiss instead of watching us," he said.

"What makes you think that I don't have one?" I asked.

"Well, if you did, you would know that there's only two wheels on a bicycle."

Confused, I asked, "Huh...what...?"

"Huh, is right...I wouldn't expect the third wheel to understand...," he laughed.

"What did you say your name was?" I asked, becoming disgusted with him.

"I didn't," he said.

"Well, whatever your name is...I don't need or want no boyfriend."

"What...you like girls?" he asked.

I frowned. "No, I don't like girls. I just don't want no boyfriend."

He laughed. "She's gay."

"I'm not gay...I just...I just..."

Nicole punched him. "Leave her alone...she said that she's not gay and she don't want no boyfriend."

"Okay, but it sounds kinda gay to me."

"You're an idiot," Nicole said.

"But I'm your idiot," he said.

Nicole looked at him and said, "She's waiting for Mister Right."

He adjusted his collar and said, "Yeah, you need a man like me."

I frowned and said, "She said, 'Mister Right', not Mister Right Now."

He frowned. "What do you mean…Mister Right Now?"

"Do you need an interpreter, Mr. Schaumburg? Oops, I meant Naperville."

Nicole tried to assure him that I was joking, but I wasn't.

While they talked to each other about my decision not to have a boyfriend and why he was Mister Right, I reflected on what that man did to me when I was a little girl; his mouth all over me. His face between my thighs, my legs sticking together from the stickiness of the candy, his pawing and grabbing at me – it was too much. I looked back at them and said, "Hand me that."

Nicole's eye's widened. "Well, lookie here… Sister Peaches wants to taste the 'Ooooooo-Weeeeee.'"

I reached out and took it from her. "Shut-up and just hand it to me." I stared at it.

"Gurl, it ain't gon' jump into your mouth…now, puff it or pass it."

I placed it to my mouth and inhaled – hard. I started to choke but was determined to "get the shit out of my head," so I placed it to my mouth again and I inhaled. I held it and exhaled. I did this several times.

"Gurl, you better slow down…"

I puffed and inhaled, puffed and inhaled until the world started spinning. Suddenly, I exhaled and threw-up all of the milk and the cookies that her mother had given to me.

They both laughed. "Told you."

After I finished throwing-up, I looked up and saw them – angels. I smiled.

Chapter 11

*N*icole's parents weren't home so we all decided to hang-out over there after school. Nicole and her boyfriend were smoking, as usual and I decided to use this as an opportunity to do some homework. Nicole leaned towards me with her hand extended. I glanced at her hand and said, "Nawwwwww, I ain't ever doing that stuff again."

She leaned back and took a puff. "Why? What happened?"

"That mess made me sick as a dog," I said, turning the pages of my Algebra book.

Her boyfriend took the joint from her hand and said, "That just means that there's more for us. I ain't gon' ever beg somebody to smoke my bud."

I looked at him and just shook my head. "Whatever," I said.

He exhaled and said, "What you reading anyway?"

I turned towards him and said, "I'm doing my homework."

He laughed. "Homework is for squares."

I eyeballed him and looked at Nicole who seemed to be hanging off of his every word. They started laughing. Then he started to do something that he thought was rap. He started making these weird sounds with his mouth while Nicole rocked back and forth.

"My name is Kevin, people call me "K" as in AK-47 and if you mess with me, I will send your ass to Heaven…in a box, with Goldilocks… and…the Three Bears and I swear…"

Nicole took a puff and said, "Go 'head, baby…that's the shit." She waved her hands in the air.

"What the hell?" I shook my head and said, "That's some shit, alright…some bullshit…"

He threw a pillow at me and said, "You just hating."

I blocked it and laughed. "Drop that "G", Street…it's hatin'… not hatinG… Mr. Naperville." I sat up and asked. "Where's yo' bathroom…not YOUR…bathroom?"

He frowned and she pointed towards the door. Before I walked out, I glanced back and saw that they were trying to swallow each other's tongue again. I frowned. "That's all kinda nasty."

She threw another pillow at me.

I was walking down the hall and turning the knob on the doors to each room to find the bathroom. I opened the door to five rooms until I finally walked into a room where someone was lying on the bed, reading. "Oops, I'm sorry," I said, trying to get out of the room. I don't know why I did what I did next, but something in me said, "Go back." I walked back into the room. "Hi," I said.

"Hi," he said.

He struggled to put a smile on his face.

I stood there for a second before saying, "Well, I'm really sorry."

He sat up on the bed and said, "No, don't be sorry."

"What's your name?" I asked and before he could answer, Nicole shouted from over my shoulder. "His name is Nerd-boy...Geek-a-licious...freak boy..."

He interrupted her. "Stop Nicole."

She walked passed me and said, mimicking him, "Stop Nicole." She jumped on his bed and proceeded to put him in a headlock. They were wrestling on the bed when she said, "You want to see me make him cry?"

I watched.

They wrestled for a minute and he became angry and pushed her off of him. She rolled off of the bed and onto the floor.

"Look who's trying to be a man. Where were your balls, yesterday when I was kicking yo' butt?"

He fixed his hair and clothes and said, "Get out."

She mimicked him again. "Get out...Or what?

143

You gon' tell yo' Mother?" She waited for an answer and said, "I didn't think so." She stood and walked passed me. But then she walked back and grabbed my arm. "Let's go."

When we walked back into her room, I could see Master "K" was asleep on her bed.

She could see that I was angry. She kicked me. "What is your problem?"

I responded. "That wasn't nice. You were so mean to him."

She laughed and said, "Gurl, you and that nice shit."

I turned to face her. "What's wrong with being nice?"

Nicole could tell that I was being serious so she stopped laughing. "Look, I love you like a big girl loves cake…but you and that nice shit…it's getting old….fast."

I shook my head.

She continued. "That's my little brother. I don't have to be nice to him."

"Why not?" I asked.

She laid back on the bed and said, "That's what siblings do…they are mean to each other." She closed her eyes.

I thought about what she said and I felt like I needed to get something off of my chest, so I said, "Do they help their boyfriends rape them? You know…siblings?" I asked.

Nicole's eyes opened as she slowly sat-up on the bed. "Huh? What did you say?"

By the look on her face, I could tell that I'd made a big mistake. I turned away and said, "I didn't say anything."

She said, "No, no, no...I heard what you said...I'm high...not deaf."

I looked at her and said, "Just forget it."

She crawled next to me and said, "Siblings are cruel to each other because they love each other...believe it or not. That's just what they do, but raping or helping somebody rape somebody...that's something else...that's not love, that's hate..."

I thought about what she was saying and didn't respond. She waited for me to say something. She was staring so hard that she was burning a hole in the side of my head. I turned to face her. "Ummmmmm...what are we talking about? I don't know anybody who's been raped."

Nicole's eyebrow went up and she said, "Like I said, that's not love...that's hate."

I opened my book and went back to reading.

Chapter 12

Another sleepless night. For the past month or so, I've spent every night staring at the ceiling. It's been a year since my last nightmare, but lately I couldn't get him out of my head. His breath, the smell of his saliva on my skin, the heat from his body as he laid on top of me – and Regan, who made it all happen. Why would she do something like that to me? That question has haunted me every day since it happened.

The next morning, I dragged myself down the hall to the kitchen, I plopped my butt into the chair so hard that I almost hit the floor. I gazed around the room, but I didn't see anyone. Faintly, I could hear a voice coming from the living room. Then I heard, "You have to stop this. You need help." Her voice dropped to a whisper again until she said, "Leave her alone!" Next, I heard the "beep" indicating that she'd disconnected the call. She walked into the kitchen, wringing her hands together.

"Who was that, Mama?" I asked.

She turned to me and said, "No one."

I could tell that she was hiding something.

"Mama, is everything okay?"

"Everything is fine." She walked over and grabbed a package of waffles, removed two and threw them into the toaster. "You need to hurry up and get ready for school...I'm taking you today."

I rubbed the crust from my eyes and said, "Why are you doing that? I like riding the bus."

My mother frowned and said, "You're going to eat and get ready so that I can take you to school."

"Awwwwwww man, Ma'...I don't want to be seen being dropped-off at school by my mama."

She took a deep breath and said, "Did I ask you what you don't want?"

I was too tired from lack of sleep to keep fighting with her, so I said, "Fine...whatever."

The waffles hadn't even popped out of the toaster before she reached in, grabbed them, and threw them onto a plate. She handed me the syrup. "Now, let's move like you have a purpose."

I slept in the car all the way to school. I was so tired when we arrived at the school that I didn't want to get out of the car. I had a really foul attitude. Today was not the day to mess with me.

As I walked down the hall, I could see people staring at me. When I arrived to class, people were staring, pointing, and shaking their heads. I stared back at them.

"What are you looking at?" I asked, frowning. They all turned around and proceeded to walk down the hall.

After being in class for a few minutes, I raised my hand to get a pass to leave the room to go to the bathroom. After getting it, I slowly walked down the hall thinking about the day that I would graduate and finally be done with these jerks. When I entered the bathroom, I checked my hair to make sure that it wasn't out of place, checked my nose for boogers, and checked my teeth to make sure that I didn't have anything stuck in them, but everything looked good.

I walked into one of the stalls. The bathroom door opened and I heard two girls talking.

"Did you see that picture of her?" one said.

"Yeah, I saw it. You can't 'unsee' that shit if you tried," the other one said.

Then the first one said, "Man, if she didn't have breasts, I would have thought that she was a dude."

"Yeah, and she had enough hair under her arms and between her legs to be considered an endangered species," the other one said.

They started cracking up.

As I wiped myself, I thought about the things that they were saying about that girl and thought, *How cruel and insensitive? I'm glad that I'm not that girl.* When I exited the stall, the girls looked at me and laughed. I frowned. *Bitches.* I washed my hands and went back to class. The rest of the day was spent watching the clock, counting every second until it was time to go home.

After school, we went to Nicole's house to hang out. Her brother heard my voice and came into the room to say, "Hi."
I smiled and said, "Hi."
We stared at each other. Nicole noticed our interaction with each other and said, "Why don't you too get married already."
We both laughed.

We hung out together that afternoon. He was so smart, just like his sister. He had a way of looking at me that made me feel special, safe, and wanted. What I liked about him most of all was his way of just listening to me. He wouldn't say a word. He just looked at me and listened.

When I was around him, I always felt uncomfortable and sick to my stomach. I wasn't sure if it was due to something that I ate, so I purposely avoided food when I knew that I was going to see him to see what would happen and like clockwork I became "sick as a dog."

I wasn't sure what I was feeling because I'd never felt that way before. I wanted to talk to my mother about it, but wasn't sure how to even approach the subject. I mean, what do you ask? "Ummmmmm, Mama...I met this boy and ummmmmm, every time I'm around him I feel like throwing up? What do you think that's about?" No, I couldn't do that, so I decided to ask someone who I thought would understand better.

One afternoon, Nicole and I were sitting on the swings at the park. We were quietly enjoying each other's company when I decided to break the silence. "Nicole...I know that this is going to sound weird, but your brother makes me sick."

She frowned and said, "What?"

I shook my head and said, "No, no, no...wait a minute...not sick as in sick-sick...I mean, he makes me want to throw-up, but not in a bad way, but in a good way...I think."

With one eyebrow raised, she said, "You sure that you're not smoking?"

I sighed. "No, I'm not."

Then it looked like she was processing something in her head when she asked, "You got feelings for my brother?"

I tried to play it off and said, "Naw, girl..."

151

She laughed and said, "You got a crush on my brother."

I waved at her and said, "Girl, you trippin'…your brother makes me nauseous."

She smiled and said, "When you feel nauseous does it make you want to stop seeing him or does it make you want to see him more?"

I smiled and surrendered. "It makes me want to see him more."

She pushed the swing that I was sitting in and teased, "Girl, that's love."

I stopped the swing and said, "Love?"

She laughed. "Girl, yeah…that's love alright… makes you want to throw-up."

Confused, I asked. "Love makes you want to throw-up?"

"Yep, love will make you do a lot of stuff that you don't want to…have you all messed-up…love will make you see and do things…it is insane what love can do," She stopped for a second and began to laugh. "Girl, I am telling ya'…love will turn a mole into a beauty mark, turn a receding hairline into a 'fade'…will turn a grown man with no job and a lot of baby-mamas with a bunch of kids, none of which are carrying his last name, into marriage material…love will turn a grown man who still lives with his mama, who walks around with his pants hanging off his ass...," She paused and continued, "You get my point."

"Got it," I said, pretending to write it all down.

"Love will have your butt looking for folks in broad daylight with a flashlight...just crazy..."

Still confused, I said, "That makes absolutely no sense."

"That's love and love makes no sense... Look...that's the only way that you know that you love someone because love makes you crazy...it keeps you on your toes. Once you stop feeling that way, you've gotten comfortable and then it becomes something else."

"What? What does it become?" I asked.

"It becomes boring or you can look up one day and realize that you've made a big mistake...and if that happens, it can turn into hate. You heard about that 'thin-line?'"

I frowned. "Thin-line?"

"Yep...the line between love and the desire to choke the shit out of somebody. Both will give you great pleasure, but only one will get you 'three hots and a cot'...get you one of those bright orange jumpsuits...have you sleeping with your ass against the wall...have you..."

I interrupted her again. "Got it." I shook my head. "Love seems complicated and gross."

"It is, but it's worth it," she said.

I shook my head. "I guess."

"Look…don't try to figure it out. You're just going to end-up with a headache…another symptom of love."

I shook my head.

She punched me in the arm. "Love will make some folks think that nerds are sexy."

I smiled and hit her back. "Nerds are sexy."

"My point, exactly," she said, shaking her head.

We laughed and spent the rest of the afternoon swinging and trying to see who could go the highest.

That evening, Remy walked me home. I wasn't feeling very well, so he allowed me to rest my head on his shoulder. We didn't say a word to each other all the way there. When we got close, we stopped under a big Weeping Willow tree that stood in the middle of the block. "Well, we're here," he said.

"How much do I owe you," I said, trying to smile.

He looked deeply into my eyes and said, "A hug would be payment enough."

I smiled and leaned in to hold him. He pressed his chest gently against mine and slowly wrapped his arms around me. His heart was beating so hard, I could feel it beat against my chest. He held me tight in his arms and I was locked in his embrace. I nuzzled my face into the side of his neck and inhaled his essence. He smelled so good – like fresh baked apple pie. He was warm and I didn't want to let him go. We both began to smile and laugh as we held each other. Minutes had passed, when he began to loosen his grip and his arms left mine. When I opened my eyes and looked over his left shoulder, I saw him. My father looking back at me. He didn't say anything. He just turned and walked towards the house. "Daddy, Daddy!!!" I called out to him, but he just kept walking.

When I walked in, I said, "Daddy…Daddy????" I found him sitting at the kitchen table. He looked up and said, "You're trying to be a whore too?"

"What are you talking about? All it was, was a hug," I said.

He looked at me and said, "A hug today and then tomorrow you'll be on your knees for some home-boy."

"What the hell are you talking about? Because your oldest daughter is a tramp, you think we all are?" As the words rolled off of my tongue, I saw it – my life flash before my eyes. I covered my mouth and stared at him. For a moment, we stared at each other then he just walked out of the room.

As I watched his back disappear down the hallway, I dreaded what just happened and wished that I could take it back, but it was too late. It was done, so immediately, I ran to my bedroom and put on five shirts, three pair of pants, three pair of socks, a ski mask, a coat, a pair of shoes, a pair of gloves and I waited – waited for him to "lay hands on me." After about five minutes, I wrapped myself in a blanket and waited and waited and waited, but nothing happened. I was sweating to death in those layers of clothes but I wasn't going to take it off because with my luck as soon as I do, he would be all over me with a belt like a hot breeze in the summertime. So I waited a little bit longer, but still, nothing happened.

Suddenly, I stood and walked over to the door. I peeked around the corner, but there was no one there. I slowly walked down the hall. I really didn't have a choice because it was hard walking in all of those clothes. When I arrived at the kitchen door, I saw my mother standing over the sink. I surveyed every corner and slowly walked into the kitchen. "Mama, where's Daddy?"

My mother sighed and said, "He left…"

Looking around the room to make sure that he wasn't hiding and just waiting for me to take off all of the clothes that were protecting my skin, I asked, "So he just left?"

She shook her head. "Yep...just left."

Damn, why did she have to say that? I thought to myself. My Daddy never "just did" anything. He never "just left" anything that needed to be dealt with. He didn't like unfinished business. That is not who he is. This was big. He had to be thinking of something good to punish me with.

"Yep, he just left, Peaches...without saying a word," she said.

I looked at her and thought to myself. *He just left.* Even thinking it sounded weird. "Wow...and he didn't say anything?"

"No, he didn't...he's tired...you and your sisters don't know what you do to that man. He loves you all so much and every time he looks up, y'all give him a reason to be unhappy."

I walked towards her. "Mama, I didn't mean to yell at him or disrespect him, but..." I paused for a second and then continued. "Mama, I was just tired. That's all."

"Well, that gave you no right to yell at him," she said.

"I know, Mama...I promise...when I see him, I'm gonna apologize."

"Okay," she said. I sat down at the table and she poured me a bowl of cereal. I ate it as sweat dripped from my forehead into the bowl.

I waited for him in the living room. When he walked in, he took his coat off. "Where's your Mama?" he asked.

I answered. "In bed."

He stopped and looked at me. "Don't you have school tomorrow?"

"Yes," I said.

He was about to walk pass me when he stopped and said, "You know that I love you, right?"

I was taken aback. I didn't know how to respond. That was the first time that I ever heard him say the "words." I mean, I remember him saying it in passing, but he never took us to the side and said, "I love you." He might have slipped it in while cursing us out, but he never did it like this...this felt "personal." I knew that he loved me because he was always there for me, he put a roof over my head, and he made sure that there was always food on the table, but I couldn't remember actually hearing him say "it." I questioned, "You love me, Daddy?"

He smiled. "Every day, Baby Girl."

I smiled. "Every day?"

"Every day, Baby Girl, and twice on Tuesdays," he said.

"And twice on Tuesdays?" I asked, laughing.

"Yep…twice on Tuesdays," he confirmed.

And for the first time, I said "it" to him. It had always been something that was just assumed until that moment. I thought that by being a good little girl and not getting on his bad-side, was enough, but saying "it" gave something that I held inside of me, "life"…gave it a "voice"…gave it "meaning."

I walked towards him. Standing in front of him, I gazed into his eyes. He looked so sad. Looking at him was like looking at a male version of myself. I said, "About the things that I said earlier…I'm sorry and I love you too, Daddy."

He smiled. "Stop acting weird and take your ass to bed."

Chapter 13

*T*he next day at school, the "staring" was worse and the laughter was louder. It was really getting on my nerves. I couldn't understand what the hell was going on. I was thirty minutes into my Biology class when the classroom's phone rang. I was deeply emerged in "Chemical Reactions" when the teacher said, "Grace...the Principal wants you to go down to the office." I gazed around the room, confused, because I knew that she had to be talking about someone else. I've never been called to the office. I pointed at my chest and said, "Who me?"

She nodded. "Yes, you...now, hurry back."

As I grabbed my books and book-bag, I began to wonder what I could have done wrong that warranted a visit with the principal. As I walked out, everyone stared at me.

On the way to her office, I felt like a prisoner walking the "last mile." The halls felt like they were closing in on me.

When I entered the office, I could see the back of the heads of two extremely angry adults. One of the assistants told me to sit down and to wait until the principal called me. I sat there. I could hear the female adult say, "What the hell are you teaching these degenerates?"

"Yeah, degenerates," the man said.

"I send my child to school to learn," she said.

"Yeah, learn," the man said.

"Now, one of these little losers took pictures of my baby and passed them out...who does that shit?"

My eyes widened. I knew that voice.

"Yeah, who does this shit?" the man said.

What are they talking about? I stared at the assistants sitting behind the desk who were now staring at me too.

The door opened. "Grace, could you come in here?" the principal asked. I slowly walked towards the office. I looked in to find my mother and father sitting in there holding something in their hands. I studied the pieces of paper. I dropped everything in my hands.

Suddenly, everything moved in slow motion. "Grace..." the principal began "...we found these circulating around the school." She handed me the photos. After she said that, it was like everything around me went quiet. Their mouths were moving but nothing was coming out. I looked at them and back at the photos, at them and then back at the photos.

"Peaches... Peaches...PEACHES!!!!!!"

I looked at her. My mother said, "Get your books and let's go home."

The ride home which normally took fifteen minutes felt like days. I sat in the back seat while my mother and father argued back and forth. I listened as they accused each other for raising messed-up kids. I listened as they swore that they would never have anything else to do with her. *Her? Who is 'her'?* I thought.

When we pulled up into the driveway, they both jumped out at the same time, leaving the car's doors wide open. I slowly climbed out and closed all of the doors. I was walking behind them when SLAM!!!!! The front door almost took my nose off. *Damn.* I opened the door and walked in. "What did I do?" I said, closing the door. No one was there to respond. No one was in the living room and no one was in the kitchen.

When I glared down the hall, I saw my mother standing in front of my bedroom holding one of the photos. My father was standing in front of the bathroom holding the other photo. I walked up and said, "What is going on?" My father handed me one of the photos. I carefully studied it. Then I looked at the bathroom. I looked at the photo and then back at the bathroom. I did that several times before it set-in. Then I ran to my mother's side and did the same thing. "Wha…wha…what is this? What does this mean?"

My father stared down the hall at Raven's old bedroom and said, "We had a rat in this house."

After that incident, my Daddy raised a "Holy" war against Raven. He was so angry and disappointed. If he could've taken the semen back that helped make her, he would've, but as angry as he was with her, he loved her. She was still his baby, but she was too old for him to put his hands on and too old for a "time-out." So he told her that if he ever saw her again, he would do something that he might live to regret. I don't know if he would have done that, but the threat alone kept her at a distance – at least for now.

Chapter 14

I couldn't go back to school after that incident. I spent the rest of my junior year at home. I did my homework and asked Nicole to give it to my teachers. After school, she dropped off any new assignments. I loved seeing her every day because she became my link to the outside world and it beat facing those vultures at my school. You would think that after being away from school for so long, that people would have forgotten about it by now, but teenagers are not quick to forgive or to forget.

"Girl, I don't know why you're tripping...I thought that they were cute. I'm sorry, let me change that...those baby pictures were cute, but that picture of you, butt-ass-naked, in the shower? That'll be with me for a loooooooong time." She laughed, but I didn't find that funny. She saw that I wasn't laughing with her so she said, "Look girl...it could have been worse and believe me...I've seen worse...But it ain't that bad."

I frowned. "That was a violation of my privacy...she shouldn't have done that to me." Curious, she asked, "Who did that to you?"

I sighed, "My sick-ass sister."

She shook her head. "Dang, she must really hate you. What did you do to her?"

I frowned and asked, "Do to her?"

"Yeah…I mean, that's low for even me. There's a lot of things that I could think of doing to Remy, but that? Naw…I draw the line at that stuff."

We were still talking when I heard a tapping sound on my bedroom window. I glanced out and there was Remy, smiling and waving. I opened the window to let him in. When Nicole saw him, she grimaced. She walked over to the window and stared at him. Once he entered, she stuck her leg out of the window to exit and said, "Remy…" She reached out to him to steady herself.

He frowned. "Nicole…" He jumped out of the way, causing her to stumble and almost hit her face against the window.

She frowned back. "Asshole…"

"Bitch," he fired back.

"Fuck you…," she responded. She frowned and stuck up her middle finger.

"I don't 'do' family members, you freak," he said.

She smiled and said, "Are you sure?"

There was a moment where you could tell that she'd said something that she wasn't supposed to. Trying to clean it up, she joked. "That's cause you too busy doing you, you perv…I see you with those nasty magazines and that jar of hair grease."

He walked over and closed the window almost crushing her fingers. She began to shout and curse but he closed the curtains and walked away.

He walked towards me and plopped down on the floor next to my bed. I crawled down to join him. We were sitting next to each other. Our skin touched. It gave me goosebumps. He reached over and grabbed my hand. Our palms began to sweat. "When are you coming back to school?" he asked.

"Next year," I responded.

He cleared his throat. "I heard about the pictures."

Releasing his hand and wiping the sweat on my shorts, "Well…" I began.

He interrupted me. "Look…I didn't see them and don't want to."

I said, "Really?"

He smiled and said, "Look, I don't know who did that…"

"My sister," I said, interrupting him.

He shook his head. "Family can be so messed-up."

"I know, right?"

There was an uncomfortable moment of silence, then he said, "Let's make a deal...we will never talk about those pictures as long as we never talk about the nasty magazines and hair grease." We both began to laugh. He reached back over and held my hand. I looked down at our fingers – embracing each other. He blew a puff of air in my ear and when I glanced up to see what he was doing, he kissed me. When he did it, he pushed his mouth against mine so hard that his tooth cut my top lip.

"Ouch," I said, grabbing my mouth.

He grabbed my hand. "I'm so sorry...so sorry."

He began to inspect my lip. Our eyes met. I touched his face and he touched mine.

"You're bleeding," he said.

I licked my mouth and he licked his. Slowly, he leaned in and his lips met mine again. His tongue slid inside of my mouth and I flinched. I looked at him and he smiled. I took a deep breath, closed my eyes, leaned in, and pressed my lips against his. You could taste the metal of the blood in our mouths. I exhaled. He began to moan and wrapped his arms around me. I was lost in his embrace, but the kiss took me back to a place of fear, pain, and darkness. I pushed him away – turned and wiped my mouth. He grabbed my chin and turned it back towards him. He looked me in the eyes and said, "It's going to be okay."

I shook my head because I'd heard those words before and remembered the pain associated with them. When people said that things would be okay, I knew to trust and believe that they wouldn't.

Chapter 15

I didn't leave my house during the summer, but I told myself that I wouldn't spend my senior year in hiding. Oddly enough, when I returned to school, no one cared about me or my pictures. Kids had other things to think about like what they were going to do once they graduated and I was thinking about the same thing. Contrary to popular belief, no one wanted to spend twelve years in school only to graduate and end-up becoming a permanent pain in their parent's ass. At least, I didn't. My goal was getting out of my parent's house and moving as far away from the "hood" as I possibly could. I continued to see Remy, but I spent more time researching colleges and scholarships – trying to figure out a way to pay for school. I was focusing so hard on school that I forgot about the most important part of senior year – Prom night.

When Remy walked up to me, he had a serious look on his face.

"What's wrong?" I asked.

"You know that prom is coming up...and...I bet you wanna go don't you?"

I turned towards him and said, "To be honest, I'm not really interested in having a bunch of fake-ass people smiling and pretending to like me because I have on some makeup and a pretty dress."

He was surprised by my response. "Wow…why don't you say what you really feel?" He laughed.

"Naw, I'm just saying…these people don't like me and I don't like them, so why would I have my parents spend all of that money so that I can hang with them for a night…just so we can go back to not liking each other the next day?"

He scratched his head and said, "Wow…okay…."

"The only way that I would go…Remember that movie about that girl who the students picked on and she took revenge by killing every last one of them? I want to be her…with the special power that allows me to take revenge on all of the people who treated me like shit…the perfect evening would consist of blood, guts, fire, and folks screaming?"

His eyes widened.

I continued, "I'm just joking, but am I?" I smiled. We were quiet, but then I broke the silence. "I'm joking…really, I am…but hey, if you want to go don't let me stop you."

He looked like he was having a hard time believing that I was joking, but then he said,

"Now, why would you say that? I'm not going without you. What I look like going to prom without my girlfriend?"

"Girlfriend?" I asked. "When did that happen?"

He laughed. "It happened when you wasn't looking."

We both smiled. The bell rang. "You want me to walk you home?"

"Sure," I said, handing him my books.

Instead of going to prom, Remy, Nicole, Kevin, and I decided to hang out at their place and watch movies. I wanted to watch "Chick-flicks" but since I was outnumbered, we had to watch scary movies. We settled on a movie whose content consisted of a masked-hatchet wielding zombie who had an infinity for young ladies with blonde hair who couldn't seem to run without falling. After watching him slice-up people who couldn't seem to turn on the lights in the house when they heard creaking sounds, I fell asleep.

I don't know how much time had passed, before I was awakened to the sounds of people screaming and telling me to hurry up and get dressed. Clumsily, I struggled to find my shoes and we ran out of the house. As we ran, I kept asking them to tell me what was happening – what was going on, but they just kept telling me to run and to run faster. As we approached the street where my house sat, I was bombarded by sounds of sirens. When I moved towards the end of my driveway, I was met by an officer who asked me if I knew anyone that lived in the house.

"Yes, yes, my mom and dad…and me…I …I…live in the house." When I said that, out of the corner of my right eye I saw them rolling a stretcher to an ambulance. On top of it was a black bag. I looked to the left and another stretcher rolled passed containing the same thing. I gazed at the officer. "What is that? What is that?!!!!!!"

He said, "I'm sorry to say that your mom and dad…your mom and dad didn't make it."

It felt like I'd been kicked in the chest. All of the air left my body. I fell to my knees. "What do you mean? What do you mean?" I reached out towards them. "Mommy…Daddy…Mommy… Daddy…noooooooooo…Mommy…Daddy…noo oooooo…."

They took me to the last floor of the hospital. I stared at the two black bags, lying on tables next to each other.

"Do you have anyone with you?" the coroner asked.

In a daze, I said, "No."

"Well, we need someone to come down and identify the bodies."

I looked at him with eyes that were filled with tears and said, "Those are not bodies…that's my Mama and Daddy and I know what my Mama and Daddy look like…"

The coroner looked at me and said, "But you may not be able to handle this. We normally reserve this…"

I interrupted him and said, "Unzip the damn bags."

He hesitated for a second, but began to unzip them slowly – one bag at a time.

The sound of the zipper sent chills through my body. I watched as the first bag opened slowly, revealing the most beautiful long jet black hair that was now stained with blood. Her face was cut-up, covered with blood, and there was a hole where her eye once rested. "MOMMY!!!!!" I

175

yelled as the floor disappeared from underneath me. I kneeled on the side of the stretcher trying to catch my breath when the corner asked, "Would you like to stop?"

I took a deep breath and said, "No, I wanna see my Daddy."

He zipped the first bag up and then slowly unzipped the other one. My Daddy's eyes were still open – looking up at me. "DADDY!!!!! Oh my Gawd…I'm so sorry, Daddy!!!" The coroner walked over and zipped the second bag. I fell down on the floor next to them and cried until I couldn't cry anymore.

By the time that I arrived at the police station, there was nothing left. Everything that mattered was now gone. I didn't have the energy to deal with them, but I knew that I had to.

After several hours of questioning, they asked me if I had somewhere to go. I asked them if they had a phone and I called Ivy. Within minutes, she was there to pick me up.

Crying, she said, "Who would do this?"

I glanced at her and said, "I don't know…they are investigating it."

"Investigation? They think someone murdered them?" she asked.

"Ivy, I don't know what they think. All I know is, my Mama and Daddy are gone…they are gone." I placed my face into my hands and began to cry again. Then I heard her voice – grating against my eardrums.

"Oh my Gawd…oh my Gawd…what happened?" she said, with the driest eyes in the building. Even the death of my parents made the police cry. This bitch must have been conserving water for a "rainy day", because there wasn't a tear to be found. She put her arms around me. I pushed her away. The police officer who was watching the whole interaction began to take notes.

Raven noticed that he was watching us. She sat down next to me and held my hand. "Oh Peaches, I'm so sorry."

I snatched away from her and said, "They were your parents too."

She stood and fixed her clothes. "Ummmmm…yep, you're right...my parents too." She glared over at Ivy and said, "Ivy…"

Ivy said, "Raven…" They both frowned and looked away.

"Well, isn't this nice," she continued. "A mini family reunion…it would be complete if Regan was here, but you fixed that, didn't you Peaches?"

"Don't start no shit, Raven," Ivy said.

Raven leaned into Ivy's face and said, "You don't want me to stick your ass in a closet, do you?"

When she said that, I turned so fast that I almost broke my neck. Ivy pushed her and said, "Try that shit now and you're the one that'll be locked in a closet." They both stared at me and then they looked at the police officer who was writing everything down.

Raven cleared her throat and laughed. "Awwwwww, you are so funny, Ivy…" She began to pat Ivy on the head. "I loved when we played Hide-and-Seek too." She stopped to reflect. "Good times…goooooood times…"

Ivy slapped her hand, frowned, and said, "Yeah, right…Hide-and-Seek…if that's what you wanna call it…Now, come on, Peaches… let's go."

I stood and walked towards her.

Raven walked up behind us and said, "We must get together soon…bury our parents…walk down memory lane…talk about the insurance money, you know, sister shit."

Ivy stared her up and down before saying, "Go fuck yourself."

Chapter 16

*W*hile making funeral arrangements, we found out that my parents left everything in my name but due to my age, my sister, Ivy, handled the arrangements. After she paid all of the expenses, she set-up an account for me, so that when I was older, I could have the rest of the money to start my "life" with. This really pissed Raven off. I mean, I've seen her mad, but this was "mad times 1000". She made sure that you knew it every time she opened her mouth.

"I can't believe this. They had four daughters. Why in the hell would they leave everything to her?" she asked, Ivy.

"Raven...I don't know and don't care."

"You don't care because you're doing okay, but I could have used some of that money. I got bills and other stuff that needs to be paid for."

Ivy responded, "They die and you think that you've won the lottery...they are dead...don't you know that? Only you, Raven...Only you."

"What do you mean, 'only you?' And of course, I do...I was there."

Ivy and I stopped and looked at her. "What do you mean...you were there?"

She swallowed and said, "I meant that I was at the police station…with you guys…remember?" Ivy and I didn't buy that for one second. We suspected that she had something to do with it but now our suspicions were confirmed.

Ivy studied her. "Did you have something to do with their death?"

"No, of course not," Raven insisted. "Why would I do something like that? I loved them too." She said that like she was trying to win an award for Best Lying-ass Actress of the Year. I knew that she wasn't telling the truth, but I had to admit that while I was proud that Ivy was finally standing up to her, I was still afraid of her, so I didn't say anything.

Ivy continued, "You better pray that you didn't do this, because if you did, I will make you suffer every day for the rest of your sad and sorry ass life."

Raven chuckled. "Look who had a second helping of balls this morning. Do you take yours with whole milk or 2%? With sugar or that artificial stuff?"

Ivy frowned and mumbled under her breath. "Shut-up bitch."

"And why would I kill them? 'Cause they tossed me to the side like a used paper towel? Or is it because they had my twin locked up?" She paused and continued, "It could have easily been one of you. They didn't like you either, Ivy…and while Peaches looks innocent, she could have shot and killed them."

Curiously, I asked, "How do you know that they were shot? They haven't told us how they died."

Raven smiled. "I just took an educated guess."

Ivy grimaced. "There's nothing educated about your dumbass." She turned and spoke to me. "She don't know what she's talking about."

Raven smiled and took pleasure in Ivy's new found voice. She wasn't at all intimidated. She was amused.

She leaned across the table. "Cute little, Ivy…how quick we forget…don't let me remind you..."

Ivy looked at her. She became scared. Her mouth began to tremble.

"I thought so…now, remember your place," she said, slowly leaning back into her seat.

Nothing else was said.

The room dropped 10 degrees as soon as she entered it. I was surprised to see Regan at the funeral. I wasn't sure why or how she was there and I didn't ask. I assumed that they'd given her a pass or something. She didn't look happy to see me and the feelings were mutual.

The funeral was so beautiful. My mom and dad laid side by side, together, as they did in life. Several people stopped by to pay their respects. It was really nice until they closed the caskets and we had to say our final "goodbyes."

After laying them to rest, we all decided to meet at a seafood restaurant to discuss who was going to keep the kid who inherited all of their parent's money. Regan couldn't join us because she had to return to the facility right after the burial. I was glad because she made me very uncomfortable; staring at me with those cold dark eyes. She didn't say anything during the whole service. Even when she and Raven sat together, huddled in a corner; Raven talked and Regan just nodded her head. They watched me and Ivy like they wished that it was us lying in those caskets.

We were all sitting around the table; staring at each other. The waitress walked up and placed the dishes of food in front of us. Raven had ordered a shot of Jack and swallowed it in one gulp. "So…who's going to keep the twerp?" she said, tearing into one of the biscuits.

"She's going to be eighteen in a couple of months and she plans to go to college. She only has a couple of months until school is over. I think that she should stay with me until she graduates..."

Raven interrupted, spitting chunks of biscuit across the table. "Now, isn't that nice...you would love for her to move in with you...her and the insurance money."

"Is that all you think about?" Ivy asked.

Raven responded. "No, it isn't. I think about rainbows, leprechauns, and the Easter Bunny..."

Ivy interrupted. "We know what you think about bunnies, with yo' crazy ass."

I looked at Ivy and wondered how long THIS moment of courage was going to last before Raven beat it out of her.

Raven scowled. "You better press 'pause and rewind' on that shit before you get your feelings hurt."

Ivy didn't respond.

Raven picked up another biscuit. "Anyway... they just didn't understand me and they didn't have to put me out because of that...that's why..." Raven caught herself.

"That's why what?" Ivy said.

Raven frowned and said, "Nothing...anyway...I just don't think it's fair."

Ivy was breathing heavily. She looked like she was going to explode and then suddenly, she did. Ivy slammed her fork on her plate – crabmeat flew everywhere – getting some in my eye. The people sitting around us began to stare. She took a deep breath and said, "You know what's not fair? You and Regan…and the crap that you did to me…that's not fair…" she paused and looked at me. "…and Peaches…and then you sent those pictures of her to that school. That was dirty and you are too old for that shit."

Raven slammed her fork down. "That wasn't me and I told Daddy that it wasn't me. Why would I do that? What do I have to gain from doing that?"

Ivy responded. "What did you have to gain from doing any of the crappy shit that you did? The beatings, sticking me in the closet, putting shit in my food…you did that mess."

Raven laughed. "Remember when we made those cookies out of shit? You loved them. I mean, who puts peas and corn in cookies? That should have sent up a red flag. You were so stupid. I watched you eat two of them before you figured out what they were, but by that time it was too late. You ate my shit…my shit."

Ivy was fuming. "You are such a loser…you and your look-alike…a bunch of miserable old bitches. You thought that you were so special until you realized that you weren't. It must have been a shock when you found out that God didn't like you as much as you thought He did."

Raven said. "Stop it."

Ivy continued. "No, you need to hear this…look at you…you are a broke-ass carbon copy of a lunatic…that's what you are…being born five minutes after Regan must have really pissed you off. I can imagine you two fighting in Mama's womb trying to see who would get out first and if Mama had known that you two were going to turn-out like you did she would have pushed your asses back up inside her and not let you out until your asses were right in the head."

Raven said, "Stop…" her eyes begin to fill with tears, not because she wanted to cry. She was mad and those were tears of a person who wished that she could stab Ivy with every butter-knife that was sitting on the table.

Ivy continued, "She should have aborted your asses…"

Raven stood, grabbed the fork, and said, "You bitch…"

Ivy struck a nerve. She smiled.

Raven was breathing heavily. "You're going to regret that, Bitch."

Ivy smiled and said, "Like you made Mama and Daddy regret it?"

She took a deep breath, gained her composure and slowly placed the fork back onto the table. She looked around at all of the watching eyes and said, "Lunch is on you and this ain't over." She threw her napkin on the table, smiled, and walked out.

Chapter 17

I cried every day. People told me that it was going to be hard, but who could have imagined that I would lose them so suddenly and so tragically. I missed them so much. People talk about how hard it is to lose a child, but what about Mamas and Daddies? I began to believe that it didn't matter. It hurts no matter who dies. There were days that I picked up the phone to call them, only to realize that there would be no one there to answer. No more "I love you, Baby Girl." No more "It's going to be okay." No more anything. Just like that, tomorrow came, and they weren't a part of it.

In the beginning, we visited their graves every day. I used to sit on their graves and tell them about my day and all of the mundane stuff that it contained. I would cry and tell them how much I loved, missed, and needed them, but I knew that they didn't want that. I knew that they wouldn't want us to mourn them – they would want us to find their killer or killers. We spoke to the police about it, but they claimed that they didn't have any suspects. We asked them to look at Raven, but they said that she had an alibi for the night that they were killed. I knew that she did it or at least she knew who did.

I've always hated Raven, but this whole situation with my parents took it to a whole 'nother level. It wasn't okay to hurt me, but, and I know that this is weird, but I understood it – got used to it, but my mom and dad? I just couldn't fathom that she would be that heartless and cruel.

There were sightings of Regan all over town. You would think that she was 'Bigfoot' the way that she kept popping-up and disappearing into thin air. She didn't try to contact us and we didn't try to contact her. We decided to keep our distance from the both of them – it was for the best. I didn't even invite them to my graduation. When I marched across the stage, only four people shouted my name, and that was okay. I knew that my parents were up in Heaven cheering for me.

That night, we celebrated like adults. Nicole found some bottles of wine in her parent's refrigerator. We poured it into paper cups and proposed a toast. I held my cup up in the air,

"This is for my Mommy and my Daddy," I said, putting the cup up against my mouth.

Nicole held her cup up. "This is for all of the losers who thought that I wouldn't graduate." She put her cup up against her mouth and sipped.

Remy said, "Yeah, it only took you two tries."

Nicole frowned. "I got yo' two tries...water boy."

"You are such a bitch," he said, frowning.

"I got your bitch, freak," she retorted.

He frowned. "Don't call me that."

She looked at him. "If it walks like a freak, talks like a freak..."

They looked at each other for a minute and then he turned and looked at me. I held my cup up and teased. "Children...children...play nicely."

They gave me a look that indicated that I'd just struck a nerve. I thought that I did a good impersonation of their mother. Clearly, they didn't appreciate it. "Sorry..."

Nicole put the cup up against her mouth and emptied it.

Remy looked at me. He looked like he wanted to say something, but decided against it.

We continued to drink all through the night. When I woke up, I found myself resting comfortably in Remy's arms. I sat-up to look at him. He was snoring. His breath smelled like someone had took a 'dump' in his mouth, so I turned to look away. He must have felt me moving because he woke up and said, "Good morning."

I covered my nose and said, "Good morning."

He smiled.

"Look...," I said. "I need to get out of here before Ivy gets upset."

He sat up and said, "Let me go use the bathroom and when I come out, I will walk you to the train."

"Okay...thanks."

He stood to walk out of the room. As he stood, my eyes couldn't help but follow the bulge that was hiding behind his zipper. He caught me staring. I turned and looked away. He smiled and strutted out of the room. When he was done using the bathroom, he came back into the bedroom holding his toothbrush. It was dripping with water. "Here, you want to use this?" he asked.

I pushed his hand away. "Ewwwwwww...didn't you have that in your mouth?"

He frowned and said, "You can kiss me, but you can't use my toothbrush?"

Frowning, I said, "That's different."

Annoyed, he said, "I'm going to ask you why, but I need you to keep your explanation brief. I have a headache."

I smiled and said, "Because, it's gross."

192

He frowned. "I'll have to remember that the next time that you stick your tongue in my mouth and I hate to say this, Sweetie, but your breath doesn't smell like you fell asleep with a peppermint in your mouth either."

I could tell that his feelings were hurt. I felt so bad and even though I was still against it, I grabbed the toothbrush and followed him into the bathroom. He stood in the door watching my every move. I slowly squeezed the toothpaste onto the wet toothbrush and began to brush my teeth. He smiled and walked out of the room. As soon as he left, I spit and rinsed my mouth. I was wiping my face when I heard, "What the hell?" I walked out of the bathroom and ran into Nicole who was stumbling out of the bedroom. We both walked into the living room where Remy was standing and staring at the door. I walked around to the side of him and in big red letters were the words, "Peaches is a whore" sprawled across the white painted door. He turned to me. I didn't know what to say.

The police came and took a police report. Even though I didn't do it, I knew that one of my sisters were behind it, but I didn't know which one. I was so embarrassed and apologetic. I didn't know what to say to their family other than "I'm sorry." Your home is your sanctuary. You should feel safe and then this happens. To have someone vandalize your home is like an attack on your "self." It is wrong especially when YOU didn't do anything to provoke the attack.

I was so hurt and torn-up about it that all I wanted to do was get out of there. I called Ivy. When she pulled-up, she found me and Remy sitting on the curb. When I stepped in the car, I looked back to find Remy's mother standing in the door with a bucket of water and a sponge. Remy dropped his head and walked slowly to the door.

Chapter 1.8

I went to the police station the next day to request an *Order of Protection*, but it is hard to fill out one when you are not sure who your stalker is. I didn't have any proof that Raven was behind any of the things that were happening to me. I was frustrated because I knew that it had to be her, but without proof, I had nothing. After that, I decided to stay out of my neighborhood for a while because what she did to me was one thing, but I couldn't have her messing with my friends.

I realized that what drove Raven was the power and control that she felt she had over me. Her and people like her feed on fear. Although, I was still afraid, I knew that I had to move on with my life. She would have loved to see me locked-away somewhere – living in the shadows, depressed and afraid, but I refused to give her the satisfaction. I was going to live, so instead of focusing on Raven and hiding from her, I enrolled in a junior college and focused on my education.

I'd just finished talking to Remy when the phone rang. "Hello, hello?" No one said anything so I hung up. Then it rang again. "Hello, hello?" Again, there was no response. Ivy walked into the room.

"Who was that?" she asked, putting some dishes in the dishwasher.

I shrugged. "I don't know. Maybe it was one of your boyfriend's wives?" I laughed, but Ivy didn't.

"You know that I don't play that. You got me mixed-up."

I apologized. "I'm sorry...I was just joking."

She closed the door of the dishwasher and turned it on. I sat and listened to the water hit the door of the machine.

Ivy touched my shoulder. "What's on your mind?"

Looking at her, I said, "You know that we need to talk about it."

Ivy dropped her head. "Mom and Dad?"

"No," I said. "Regan and Raven."

The phone rang again. This time Ivy answered it. "Hello, hello?" She glanced at the receiver and said, "Folks ain't got nothing better to do." She took the phone off of the hook and said, "Why do you want to bring that stuff up for?"

"Because it bothers me...I have bad dreams about the things that y'all did to me."

Ivy looked away. She took a deep breath before saying, "We are sisters...what do you do?"

I frowned and said, "As my sister, you should have protected me."

She sighed. "I didn't want to hurt you, but they gave me no choice..." Ivy walked over to the window and glared out into the backyard. "The 'closet' changes you. No matter what they've done to you before that...the closet...it changes you...and you are never the same after that..." She paused and continued, "...never the same...you learn to become a predator or you will always be their prey. You realize that you either become a part of their 'crazy' or they will spend every freakin' minute of their lives making you crazy."

Still looking away from me, I could tell that she was crying. She took the washcloth and wiped her face. She continued, "Sometimes, it's easier to surrender...the monsters become less scary when you become one yourself." She dropped her head and closed her eyes.

I knew that something wasn't right. I could tell that she wasn't telling me something. "Ivy...were you raped too?"

She took a deep breath and continued. "They did everything together... everything..."

I asked her again. "Ivy...were you raped too?"

She refused to answer the question.

I thought back to my days of abuse.

Still staring into the darkness, she said, "Think about it…if you paid close enough attention you would have saw it."

I was confused. Now, I wasn't sure what she was talking about.

"They were twins, Peaches…"

I thought back to that night that I was raped. "Wait a minute…you mean?"

She nodded. "All I'm saying is, you never really knew who was doing what…they were both equally dirty."

"You think Raven did that?" I asked, so confused.

"All of this shit is Raven," she confirmed.

"Raven?" I asked.

"Why not her?" She turned and looked at me.

My head was spinning. Remembering what happened that night, I became frustrated. I've been blaming Regan all of these years, but it never dawned on me that it could have been Raven.

She drifted off – reflecting and changing the subject abruptly. "But mom and dad did love you...didn't they?"

"They loved us all," I said, still trying to deal with what she'd just revealed.

She had a really odd look on her face. "Peaches, you don't know what it's like to be the middle child…what it was like to live in the shadows of twin sisters and the miracle baby girl."

"I can only imagine," I said, not because I could imagine but it seemed like the best thing to say. Plus, right now, my head was no longer in the conversation. It was somewhere else.

She frowned. "No, you can't…you can't freakin' imagine." Her eyes darkened and she began to breathe heavily. "You can never imagine… never." She started to look back out into the darkness. "…and you have to think about it, Peaches…they weren't really happy…now, they are both in a better place."

Now, I was frowning. "Who wasn't happy…who is in a better place?"

She interrupted me, "…But now they are."

She was making me crazy. "Who? What?" I asked, scratching my head. *Huh?* I had no idea what she was talking about now.

She turned to look at me. Her eyes were bulging out of her head. I looked at her like she was losing her mind. I couldn't deal with her moment of insanity on top of everything else I was dealing with. I saw this as an opportunity to leave the room. "Well, I guess I'll go to bed now…maybe, do some reading."

"Yeah, you should do that," she mumbled, still staring into the darkness.

The next morning, I was still reeling from what Ivy had said to me. That revelation had me all messed-up. To think that my truth for all of these years could now be a lie. *It was crazy.* The weird thing is, it wasn't like Raven wasn't capable of doing something that horrible to me. Raven would have no problem being that cruel and sadistic, but she just wasn't that type of crazy or was she? I was so messed-up.

Suddenly, my thoughts were interrupted by an urgent need to use the washroom. Groggily, I stood and wandered out of my bedroom and into the hall. "Ivy? Ivy?" I called out, but there was no answer. "Ivy?" I called again, but still there was no answer. I scratched my head and then walked into the bathroom. After taking care of my business, I walked down the hall to check to see if Ivy was in her bedroom. As I approached the door, I heard a whirling sound. "Ivy?" I said, but she didn't answer. I knocked softly, just in case she was still sleeping. "Ivy?" I said again. The sound became louder. I pressed my ear to the door and I heard someone talking.

"Yes," she said.

I continued to listen.

"Yes….yes…"

Still listening, I heard, "Yes…yes…YES!!!!!!"

Then except for the whirling sound, the room fell silent. I was turning to walk away when suddenly the door opened. Ivy walked out of the room. Her face was flush and her hair was all over her head.

"Good morning," she said, as she walked passed me.

"Morning," I mumbled.

Buzzzzzzzzzzz…I turned and looked into her bedroom and sitting in the middle of her bed was a long black plastic thing - still making that sound and bouncing in the middle of her bed.

I approached it slowly, leaned in to see what it was, picked it up, and inspected it. It was vibrating in my hand. I threw it back on the bed, looked towards the door, and then back at the thing that was moving on her bed. I studied it for a minute, waiting for it to stop, but it didn't. It just kept going. In that moment, I decided that I didn't want to know what it was. Sometimes, "ignorance is bliss" and I had too much other stuff to think about.

Chapter 19

When I was younger, I always wanted to be "grown." I couldn't wait to find out what it was like to be an adult, but I wanted to make that transition, gradually – like most kids. My parents being killed sort of threw me into a world that I have to admit that I wasn't ready for. I went from being someone's baby to nobody's little girl. I still had so many questions that needed to be answered, but who do I turn to now?

There were so many things that I needed to learn and that I needed to do. One of the things that I knew that I needed to do was get away from Ivy because to be honest, I didn't trust her. Even though she's always been scary, she was really starting to creep me out.

With me being a new source of animosity between them, I knew that I didn't want to be a part of that. And Raven was on a mission. Every day, it was something new. If she wasn't calling me, she was showing up at my school. I begged her to stop, but she was relentless.

One day, I was walking across campus when I heard a voice. "Peaches…Peaches…" I looked back and saw her running towards me.

"Peaches…Peaches…" I took off running, hoping to lose her. "Peaches…Peaches…"

I ducked inside of the Athletic building and ran into one of the bathrooms. I checked all of the stalls until I ended-up in the one on the far end of the room. I locked the stall door and climbed on top of the toilet. I could hear her shouting, "Peaches…Peaches!!!!"

Suddenly, there was nothing. I lowered one of my feet to the floor, but then the bathroom door slowly opened. I quickly lifted my leg. She threw each door open until she was standing in front of the stall where I was hiding. I could see her feet. She waited a minute before sighing and walking out of the room. At least, I thought she did.

I heard the door open and when it closed, I slowly stepped off of the toilet. I cracked the stall door, but didn't see anyone. I stepped out and walked towards the sink. I turned the water on and lowered my head to splash water on my face. When I came up, I could feel that something or someone evil was in the room. I was afraid to open my eyes. When I did, she was peering at me with eyes that were cold and lifeless. Before I could open my mouth she said, "I could choke you to death…right here…and no one would know it…they would just find you…lifeless and lying on the floor."

I turned and trying to think of a lie, I said, "Hey Raven…it's so good to see you…ummmmm, I was just thinking about you. How are you doing?"

She frowned. She wasn't buying my act.

"I was just trying to get to class."

She smiled. "You were trying to get to class, but ended-up in the bathroom?"

Nervously, I said, "When you gotta go…you gotta go."

She frowned and with one eyebrow raised, she said, "And they thought that you were special."

I didn't say anything as water dripped from my face onto my shirt.

"You know…if I were to kill you…that money would come to me and once again, I would be the special one." She smiled, turned, and then walked out of the room. As the door swung close, I heard her say, "I would be the special one."

Chapter 20

*W*hen I was able to catch my breath and able to process the whole situation, I called Ivy. She answered on the first ring.

"She threatened to kill me."

"Who? Where are you? What are you talking about?" she asked.

"I'm at school…she found me at school." I was pacing back and forth, whispering to make sure that no one overheard the conversation.

"She? She who?" she asked.

"Your evil ass sister…that's who," I said.

She laughed. "That's what evil does…it finds you," she said.

"She's acting a fool...all of this over some money?"

Ivy laughed. "She doesn't need a reason to mess with you…her waking up is the only reason that she needs…money is her way of justifying it."

"I'm tired of this mess. Is it ever going to stop?" I asked, frustrated.

Ivy ignored the remark. "Are you coming home?"

Rubbing my forehead. "Nawwwww…I need a minute. I'll be home in a little while."

"Okay…just let me know."

I hung up. Walking across campus, it became clear that Raven was going to mess with me until she either got too old to chase me or one of us died.

After my classes, I called Nicole and asked her to come and pick me up. When she arrived, there was so much smoke in the car that I couldn't tell who was in it. When I opened the door, the smoke wrapped itself around me like a warm blanket - almost gave me a contact high. "Man, is that all you do all day?" I asked, fanning the air around me.

She giggled. "Nawwwww, I have to stop long enough to go, pick it up, roll it, and light it."

I jumped in. "If anyone is ever looking for a professional pothead..."

She interrupted. "I ain't in the mood for one of your sermons...I'm high and I got a serious case of the munchies." She pulled off – looking for the nearest drive-thru.

"You gon' get enough of driving while high...it's hard enough driving while black...," I said.

"I thought that I said that I wasn't in the mood."

I threw my hands up. "I'm just saying...it's kinda hard to ignore the car with so much smoke coming out of it that it looks like a chimney on wheels."

She turned into a parking lot. "Like I said, I ain't in the mood." She pulled up to the intercom.

"Welcome to Fresh Burger where the meat is so fresh it moooooooos," the voice in the intercom said.

"Do you want something?" she asked.

"Naw, I'm good," I said.

Nicole leaned out of the car window and said, "Let me get a Super Fresh Moo Burger with extra onions and mustard, a large fry, and a large soda and you can hold the hair, the spit, or any other extra shit y'all got going on in there."

We heard a loud "sigh." "What kind of soda?" the voice asked.

"Surprise me," Nicole said, staring at me.

"You do know that NOW they're spitting in your food and sticking some hair on your bun," I teased.

"Not if they don't want their asses whupped," she said, as she looked around her car for her purse. The people in the cars behind us started to blow their horns. She threw her hand out of the window and gave them the "middle" finger.

The voice on the intercom said, "Is that all?"

"Yeah, that's all," she said.

She looked over at me and asked. "What's wrong with you?"

"I don't know...but that voice sounds so familiar."

"Every voice that comes out of that thing sounds familiar…they all sound like they've been inhaling helium."

"Naw, really…I know that voice," I said.

"Okay, your total is $7.59," the voice said.

"Damn, what did I just do? Buy the whole cow?" Nicole said, angrily. "Damn, can you believe that shit?"

Agitated, the voice said, "Drive around to window one."

"They made you pay extra for the spit and hair," I said, still thinking about that voice.

Nicole stared at me and proceeded to drive around to the window. "I swear, my burger better be right or I'm going to slap her ass with the bun." She started snapping her fingers. "Peaches… Peaches…"

I was staring at the person in the window and she was staring at me.

"Well, ain't this a bitch…long time, no see," the person in the window said.

Nicole looked at her and then back at me. "Damn, I must really be high…got me seeing double…y'all look alike."

I frowned and shook my head. "That's because she's my sister."

Watching Nicole eat made me reconsider becoming a vegetarian. Watching the 'juice' roll from the bun unto her mouth was very difficult to watch. With a mouth full of food, she asked. "Why didn't you go in and talk to her?"

"It's a long and complicated story."

"I ain't got nothing but time...and these fries," she said, stuffing a few of them in her mouth.

I didn't say anything. I was thinking about how my story would sound to a person who has never been through it, but it's been an anchor that has been weighing me down for such a long time. I really needed to talk about it. But she was just like my sister. She tortures her brother. Opening my heart to her would be like a lamb crying on the sleeve of a wolf. She wouldn't understand what I've been through, because people like her are never the victim. And while she's been my friend for a long time, I spend most of my life protecting myself from people like her. So I decided not to talk about it. "Again, it's a long story and I have to get home."

Nicole spoke. The smell of the onions and mustard on her breath was an attack on my senses – made my eyes water. "Look...I don't know what's going on between you and your sisters, and I'm sure the story is good enough to make the 'movie of the week', but at some point, you're going to have to talk to somebody…me, a therapist, the crackhead on the corner, God…somebody…or it's going to eat you up inside."

"I thought that we weren't doing sermons today?" I asked.

"I SAID that you couldn't give me one…that didn't have nothing to do with you."

I turned and stared out of the window.

"I saw Regan, today," I said, throwing my book-bag onto the counter.

"You did? Where did you run into her?" Ivy asked.

"She works at Fresh Burger."

"I bet that was interesting," Ivy said, handing me a glass of lemonade.

"I didn't say anything to her."

"You didn't? You're better than me. I would have broken a record cursing her butt out."

"Really?" I knew that she was talking crazy. It's one thing to stand-up to Raven, but she wasn't no fool. Regan would break her butt in half, glue her back together and then break her ass in half again. I dismissed that comment as fast as she said it. I took a sip from the glass and said, "And then what? Give her and her clone another reason to be annoying? Plus, what would I say, 'Thanks for messing up my life?'"

Ivy thought about it for a second. "Yeah, you got a point. Did she follow you here?"

Sticking my finger in the glass and fishing for one of the ice cubes, I said, "Nope…plus, I was with Nicole."

"The Stoner?"

"So she smokes weed, and?"

"I'm not judging her. I don't care what she does."

"Good, because she's my friend and I'm not dropping her."

"I never said that you should," she said.

"Good…"

"Good," she agreed.

There was a moment of silence when it was quickly interrupted. The phone rang and we both looked in its direction. "I'm going to get the number changed."

"Good idea," I said, before leaving the room.

Chapter 21

*H*e understood me and that wasn't an easy thing to do. He never judged me, because he too was broken. I used to wonder if the only reason why he was in my life was because he had a sister that was a lot like mine. I often wondered if our journeys were brought together because we were both in pain. Whatever the reason, I was glad that he was in my life.

It was weird. We knew what each other were going through, but when we were together, we never talked about that stuff. We were just Peaches and Remy - two young people, who cared about each other, and two young people who were trying to get out of the 'hood.' We were not our experiences. We were not our pain and he did everything that he could to remind me of that.

One day, I stopped by to see Nicole and he was home. When he opened the door, he looked like he'd been working-out. He was soaking wet. I couldn't help but notice how the wet t-shirt embraced his body.

I asked for Nicole, but I really wanted to see him. I wanted to play it "low-key." Didn't want to make his head big.

"Hey Peaches…," he said, wiping water on his clothes.

"Ummmmm hey…where's Nikki?" I asked.

"Ummmmm she's not here, but I am," he said.

"I can see that…well, when I get back, please let me know…" I said, nervously.

"Huh? I and me?" he asked, confused.

Shaking my head like I was trying to shake myself from a daze, I said, "You know what I meant."

He laughed. "Yes, I know what you meant. I'm just playing with you."

I wanted to stand there and talk to him all day, but instead, I turned to walk away. "Well, let her know that I came by."

"What are you 'bout to get into?" he asked.

I smiled, but I didn't want him to see it, so I wiped it off of my face before I turned to look at him. "Ummmmmm nothing…what are you up to?"

"Ummmmmm nothing," he said.

And we stared at each other for what felt like a lifetime. Then a voice came from over his shoulder.

"Hi Peaches," she sang.

How Urban, I thought to myself.

He glared over his shoulder. His mother walked passed wearing a robe.

"How about we do 'nothing' together?" he asked, closing the door.

I smiled. "I would like that…" I looked at his wet clothes. "Would you like to change your clothes first?"

He looked at the door and said, "Naw…I'll let the sun dry 'em."

We spent the afternoon walking down by Rainbow Beach. He had a wild fascination with airplanes and we spent the whole afternoon talking about them. Suddenly, a plane flew overhead. He looked up and pointed at it.

"Did you know that the risk of being killed in a plane crash is less than the risk of being killed in a car accident?"

"Nawwwww, I didn't know that."

"Did you know that 'research shows that the first three minutes after takeoff and the final eight minutes before landing are when 80% of plane crashes happen'?"

"Nawwwww, I didn't know that," I said, wondering if watching paint dry was more exciting.

"Did you know that 'the oxygen in an airplane's emergency oxygen masks lasts for only about 15 minutes'?"

Yawning, I said, "Nawwwwww…but what I'm learning is that the best way to get around is by walking."

He laughed. "But then how would you see the world? You don't want to be stuck here all of your life."

The thought of that was scary. "Nawwww…I'll figure out a way to get around that won't involve me falling out of the sky." I smiled and yawned again.

He could see that I was bored so he tried to switch it up. "What would you like to talk about?"

I yawned again. "Let's not talk about anything. Let's just sit here and enjoy each other's company?"

"Sure," he said.

I watched him as he tilted his head back to take in the sun. It looked like fun, so I decided to join him. I closed my eyes and enjoyed the breeze as it embraced my face. Blindly, I reached for his hand. When I did, I immediately noticed that his hand was unusually soft and his fingernails were extremely long. I opened my eyes and looked at his hand. "What the hell?"

"Boy, if mom and dad could hear you curse," she said.

"Damn, Raven, really? What are you doing here? Why are you following me?" I snapped.

Her face frowned-up like she was having a bowel-movement. "You think too much of yourself. I was just passing through."

"How were you just passing through? I believe that like I believe in Santa Claus."

She threw her head back and said, "I don't care what you believe. I like the beach too. The way that you're acting, you would think that you owned it." She glanced over at Remy and said, "And who might this be?" But before I could answer, she'd wedged herself between us. "Hi...I'm Raven."

"And WE are leaving," I said, preparing to walk away. "You know what, Raven? You should really consider getting some friends...or maybe a better hobby than stalking me. You know that there are laws against this stuff?"

She grabbed my shirt. "I don't need a friend when I got you and how can I stalk my own sister? Now, don't be rude...you don't want to make your Big Sister angry, do you?"

I shook my head and sat back down beside her.

"Now, let's have that name," she said, purring.

"I'm Remy."

She licked her lips and said, "I bet you are."

He frowned and said, "So you're her sister?"

She leaned in, so close that she could tell me how many blackheads he had on his nose. "I'm one of the family's best kept secrets."

He raised one of his eyebrows and said, "And often time things are a secret for a reason...and should be kept that way..."

219

She scowled but caught herself. She reached down and touched his knee. She wanted to hurt me by trying to hurt him, so she decided to tell him about a part of my life that I wasn't quite ready to talk about. "Did she let you fuck her yet?"

We were both in complete shock. My heart stopped beating for two minutes. A heart attack, a tornado, or any other calamity would have been better or easier to deal with than having her tell him about the most traumatic aspect of my life and in such a horrible and raunchy way.

"EXCUSE ME?!" He turned his body to face her. "What did you say?"

I stood up. "Let's go, Remy." I tugged at his arm, but he wasn't budging.

"What did you say?" he asked, again.

Her eyes squinted and she said it again. "Have you fucked her yet?"

Oh my, Gawd! Oh my, Gawd! I can't believe what's happening.

Remy stared at her. He had a look on his face like he was weighing the possibility of jail-time in his mind against his desire to slap the mess out of her.

It was a lot to take in all at once…my sister…my crazy sister…the crazy sister who just told my boyfriend that the girl that he was crushing-on wasn't a virgin…that was a lot to process, but then all of a sudden, as if he had just got a sign from God, he smiled.

"Clearly, you haven't taken your meds, so I'm going to go easy on you. Me and my girl's sex life is our business." He sighed and continued, "There is nothing less attractive than some old chick trying to live vicariously through her younger sister. It must be pretty sad that this is who you are. Look at you…rubbing on the leg of a complete stranger…so desperate for attention that you don't care how you get it…even if you have to get it from a stranger. I feel sorry for you." He pushed her hand away and said, "Messy people do messy shit…you need to clean-up your act."

I studied Raven's face and it looked like all of the blood had been drained from it. She was deflated – the wind had been knocked out of her. For the first time, she actually looked sad.

"Let's go, Peaches." He stood and grabbed my hand. When I glanced back, she was standing and watching us and she continued to do so until we were completely out of sight.

"Do you want to talk about it?" he asked, wiping the tears from my face.

I tried looking away, but he grabbed my face.

"Which part? My messed-up sister or what she said?" I tried looking away again.

"Both," he grabbed my face again.

"They both require a lot of time…"

He pretended to look in a Day-Planner, flipped some fake pages and said, "Looks like I'm free." We both smiled.

"Where would you like for me to start?"

"Whatever is less difficult…less painful."

I thought about it and sadly, they were both equally difficult and painful. So I started with what I thought would be important to someone who said that they wanted to be a part of my life.

"Well, I was raped by a man when I was a little girl and one of my oldest sisters was behind it."

The only thing that moved were his eyes that were blinking at least 100 miles per minute.

"Please say something," I pleaded with him. "Please…"

"Damn…that is really messed-up…I'm so sorry that that happened to you."

When he said that, I felt weird and angry. I thought that when I finally opened up to someone, that I would finally feel better, but that was not the case. Hearing him apologize felt empty because while it was "nice", it didn't come from the asshole who violated me.

He rubbed his forehead and said, "I don't think I can take anymore 'sharing' today...that's big."

I was actually glad that he said that because I was done 'sharing' for the day.

"That's crazy...that your sister would do that to you."

"Yep, and she's a twin."

"Damn...there's two of them? That's 'double-ly' messed-up...and they're your sisters?"

"Yeah, it's messed up." I sighed and said, "We may have the same Mama and Daddy, but we're definitely not sisters."

Chapter 22

"Time flies when you're having fun...or NOT!"
I was always on edge. From the "Heavy-breathing" phone calls to the impromptu visits, Raven was really becoming a "fly in my ointment." I was so tired of her and I know that people say that all of the time about the "pains in their asses", but she was really getting on my nerves. They say that some victims of abuse, any form of abuse, almost always develop a close bond with their abuser, but that is not the case at all. I was tired of looking over my shoulder and tired of her mess. I don't wish bad things to happen to people, but if her ass was on fire, I wouldn't even spit on her to put it out.

And you would think that she would be bored by now, but she was just turning the "dial" up on the madness. It was insane and unnecessary. I used to find reasons to justify her mess, but at some point, you just have to acknowledge that something is broken so that you can begin fixing it. And they...we...were definitely broken.

In spite of all of that I've been through, I knew that if I remained focused, I could get away from her - graduate from this life and into a new one. I hadn't really thought about my future yet. I just knew that I wanted one that didn't contain them and I worked really hard to make that happen.

Things became a lot easier when Remy started college too. It was really a blessing because he was able to help me get through the really tough courses. I enjoyed his company and I felt a lot safer having him around.

The weird thing is, lately, I hadn't seen Nicole. She was always 'out' when I went to visit, both physically and mentally. Most of the time, she was with her boyfriend and when she was at home, she stayed in her room – out of sight. Every once in a while, she would emerge from her cave, grunt something in my direction, and then she would disappear again, unless her and Remy were arguing about something. She'd changed so much. She wasn't the Nicole that I used to know.

I can't say that I didn't miss her because I did, but just recently, the fights between her and Remy were becoming more volatile. I hated to see it because it reminded me of my awful childhood and I was trying to get away from that "life." It always placed me in an awkward position – between my friend and my boyfriend and it was usually over something stupid.

One day, his mother walked into his room and told him to wash the dishes. He didn't feel like doing them, so as soon as his mother walked out of the room, he told Nicole to do them.

"Go wash the dishes," he said, standing at the door of her bedroom.

"Ummmmmm, I thought that I just heard Mama tell you to do them."

"Ummmmmm, you did, but I did them yesterday and the day before. So go and wash the dishes." He came back into his room where he grabbed a book and began to read it.

She came stomping into his room.

"Hi Nicole," I said.

She frowned and turned her attention back to Remy. "No, I don't want to and I'm not going to." She walked over and slapped his book out of his hand. "Now, you go do 'em." she demanded. He reached over and picked the book up and was flipping the pages to find his place when she slapped it out of his hand again. "Now."

Things quickly escalated.

"Bitch, you got one more time…" he leaned over to pick up the book again. He was flipping through the pages when she slapped it out of his hand again, but this time her finger grazed his face. He grabbed his face and when he looked at his hand, there was blood on it. Before I knew it, he'd pounced on top of her. I moved out of the way to avoid their blows. She slapped him and he grabbed her hands in an attempt to stop her from hitting him until she kicked him, hard, between his legs. He let out a high-pitch squeal, grimaced, buckled over, and started crying. "I'm going to kill you when I get up."

She brushed her hair out of her face and said, "What? I can't hear you…it must be those balls that are stuck in your throat….all up in your vocal cords."

He glanced over at me like he was looking for permission to kick her ass. I'm a true believer that "all is fair until you kick a man in his junk and then all bets are off," so I turned my head and closed my eyes and waited for someone to scream, "Dial 911!" But before that could happen, their mother walked in the room.

"What in the Sam-Hill is going on here?" she asked, wiping her hands on her apron.

"He started it," Nicole said, choking on the lie that her smile was hiding.

With his hands between his legs trying to rub the pain away, he said, "Are you freaking kiddin' me? Look at me, I'm the only one holding his balls."

His mother frowned. "Because you're the only one in the room with balls, Remy."

He continued. "I'm the only one in this house washing shit too…"

228

"Watch your language, Remy…and the problem is?" She tapped her feet impatiently.

He took a deep breath and then looked down. "There's no problem…"

Nicole stood to walk out of the room. Before exiting, she stuck out her tongue. Remy stuck his foot out and Nicole went flying across the room. His mother caught her before she hit the door. Nicole turned with fire in her eyes. "You want some more, don't you?"

Their mother held her by the waist. "Nicole, get out of here."

"I'm going to hurt your damn son…you should have had two because that one is going to end-up with his face on a milk carton."

"You wish, pothead…," he said.

"Remy, don't say mean things to your sister," his mother said, but in a way that made me feel uncomfortable.

"Are you kidding me? She started it…"

Nicole wasn't done. "It's a good thing that you have a girlfriend…you can finally give your fuckin' hand a much needed vacation."

Their mother looked at her. "Nicole…language."

Nicole waved her off.

"Look who's talking? Nasty heifer…" he fired back.

"NASTY???!!!! Did you say, 'nasty'? You know I did laundry the other day…sweaty drawers are one thing, but unless you're sweating SHIT, somebody is not washing his ass."

"Are you talking about underwear? Really? You went there? There's so much blood, semen, and fingerprints in your panties that they are not even considered underwear, they are considered a damn crime scene…tramp," he retorted.

"I got your tramp and you can go and fuck yourself…"

The next thing I knew, they were clawing and scratching at each other. Their mother stepped in the middle of them and said, "You better look up and see me." They stopped and looked at her. Fixing her clothing, she smiled, and pointed in my direction. In the most eerily sweet voice, she said, "Children, you two need to stop it…we have a guest."

Everyone turned to look at me. I smiled, uncomfortably.

"You need to do something with your daughter," he said.

"Remy, she's a lady. This isn't how I raised you to treat a lady." She walked over and began to rub his cheek.

Suddenly, there was a weird silence between them. They just stared at each other.

Remy broke the silence when he mumbled "Yes, mother," quietly under his breath.

"Women are special…We must remember that…now, go and wash the dishes," she said, smiling. She kneeled down and kissed him; watching me the whole time. "Mother is going to bed at 9pm…do you understand?"

He looked away and said, "Yes, mother."

Nicole and their mother walked out of the room with his mother watching us the whole time.

He looked diminished – like something had been stolen from him. I felt that something weird was going on, but didn't want to ask. But we were just sitting there, so I decided to break the silence. I touched his shoulder. "Parents are…" I started but stopped to think about what I was going to say – choosing my words carefully.

He finished my sentence, "…are fucked up."

I waited to see what was going to follow that statement, but he didn't say anything else. He stood, still holding his balls as he walked down the hall to do the dishes.

Chapter 23

"Thank you for standing in for mom and dad," I said as I was looking at the reflection of a young woman wearing a cap and gown – getting ready for the next phase of her life. I was thinking how it felt just like yesterday when I'd graduated high school and here I was, graduating from college

"It's the least that I could do…considering," Ivy said, as she helped me with my dress.

"Considering what?" I asked, adjusting the tassel on my cap.

"Oh it's nothing…let's go before we're late."

When we walked out of the door, Remy was there waiting with a camera.

"Hey gorgeous…say 'cheese'."

"Cheeeeeeeessssssseeee." I was smiling so hard, my face hurt. I noticed that someone was missing. "Where's Nicole?"

"She couldn't make it," he said.

"She couldn't make it to my graduation? My graduation? What was so important that she couldn't make it?"

"She wasn't feeling well."

Her absence hurt me, but I couldn't do anything to change it and I wasn't going to let it ruin my day. "Oh okay…well, I hope that she feels better."

"Ummmmm, yeah…let's get you to that stage."

Pomp and Circumstance was playing as everyone filled the room. I stared at the bleachers and watched as family and friends packed the seats. There was so much chatter around me that I could barely hear myself think. We all sat down and I quietly said goodbye to everything that would remind me of this place. "Goodbye bleachers. Goodbye walls. Goodbye nasty-ass cafeteria food…"

One of the long and drawn-out speeches was interrupted by someone snoring in the first row. The speaker joked about it. "Well, I guess that's my que…" We all started laughing. After more drawn-out speeches, we stood to receive our diplomas.

When they called my name and I stepped up to receive my diploma, I could hear someone calling me. I moved my tassel to the other side of my cap and looked up to where the sound was coming from and saw Remy standing and waving his arms. I waved back.

After the ceremony, we all threw our caps into the air, congratulated each other, and then piled out of the building – row by row.

When we got outside, everyone opened their robes and took pictures with their friends and family members. We were all so excited that it was all over and were having a really good time. Slowly the crowd started to thin-out. I thought that it was a good time to remove my robe. I'd been in it long enough.

Initially, I didn't hear it, but then it grew louder. I looked around to find people laughing and pointing at me. I was trying to figure out what was going on when I felt it. A summer's breeze wrapped itself around the neon pink thong panty that I was wearing. I glanced back to find my dress, stuffed inside of my slip and all of my ass was hanging out. Remy ran up behind me and started to fix my dress.

"Oh my, Gawd...Ivy...why didn't you see this when I was standing in the mirror? Ivy? Ivy?" I looked for her, but Ivy was nowhere to be seen. She'd already walked to the car. I was so embarrassed that I didn't even think; I ran towards the car and almost broke a nail trying to open the door. "What the hell, Ivy?" I asked, climbing in.

"And what the hell to you too...what is your problem?"

"My problem is you...you were helping me get dressed..."

"Soooooooooooo?" she asked.

"AND MY ASS IS SHOWING!!!!!" I shouted.

"Why are you walking around with your ass hanging out, Peaches?" she asked.

"Are you kidding me? You were helping me get dressed." I tried pulling the rest of my dress out of my underwear.

Ummmmmm, you're an adult. Don't blame me for your wardrobe malfunctions."

"Are you serious, Ivy? Today of all days, you would pull this shit..."

"Gurl, you better check your tone and remember who you're talking to." She started the car. "You're making it a bigger deal than it is. So you showed a little ass. Who doesn't? Now, let's go."

I wanted to wrap my hands around her damn throat. I was so mad. I had to slow down my breathing to keep my head from exploding. All I could think about were the things that they did to me over the years and I'd had enough. They couldn't pull this mess on me today. I deserved a reprieve for at least one day.

I snatched the keys from the ignition. Her eyes widened and before I knew it, I was tasting the backside of her hand. There was a puddle of

blood forming in the bottom of my lip. My eyes filled with tears. "That's it. THAT'S IT!!!!!"
I jumped out of the car and threw her keys across the parking lot.
She jumped out and demanded. "Go get 'em!"
As I walked away, I glared over my shoulder. "Go and get 'em yourself."

Remy and I walked for more than four miles. The whole time, we barely spoke to each other. Well, he spoke and I gave him dirty looks. After giving him three dirty looks, he stopped trying to talk to me. I wasn't in the mood for anything that he had to say.

I wore my cap and gown all the way to his house. Cars were blowing their horns at me as they passed, but I was too pissed to care. By the time we made it to his house, my feet were cursing me out in eight different languages and I was cursing back.

Everyone was asleep, which made me happy because I didn't want to have to explain the dried-up mascara streaming down my cheeks. When we entered the room, I begged him to keep the lights off. I didn't want him to look at me and I couldn't look at him right now. I just couldn't. I sat at the foot of his bed and started to cry. He crawled across the bed and pulled my arm.

"Come here," he said.

"No."

"Peaches…come on."

"No, I can't…"

"Peaches…please…"

Gently, he tugged on my arm again. "Come on up here and lie down next to me."

"I've had such a messed-up day…please…just give me a minute."

"Come on, Peaches…we both had a long day and I don't know about you but after walking more miles than I've done in a lifetime, I could really use some sleep. Now, come on…"

I gave in, crawled to where he was sitting, laid down beside him, and we fell fast asleep.

In the middle of the night, I turned over and noticed that he wasn't lying next to me. In the darkness, I found him changing his clothes. I was

238

about to close my eyes again when I heard the door open. I looked up to find his mother standing in the doorway. Remy looked at me and then slowly exited the room.

Chapter 24

"*H*ave you ever been to a club?" she asked, exhaling. Nicole was having a crisis. She wouldn't tell me what was going on, but by the amount of weed she'd been smoking, I assumed that it had to be major. Clearly something was going on because now we were talking again. I didn't want to question the sudden desire to talk to me. I just shut-up and let it happen.

"No, I'm too young to go to a club," I said, with my face hanging out of the bedroom window to avoid a "contact" high.

She inhaled and then exhaled. "I'm going to take you out."

I laughed. "You must be really high. How are we going to do that?"

She blew some smoke in my face and said, "You let me handle that."

"Ummmmmm, okay…whatever you say," I said, not taking her seriously.

She stood and walked over to her closet. She started pushing the clothes around until I saw something red. "What is that?" I asked.

She laughed. "Girl, every woman has to have that one thing that she can throw on to remind her man who's really in control. I call this my

'Slippery when wet dress.' You put this on and a motherfucker who has forgotten his place will quickly remember it. You don't have to say a thing…the dress will do all of the talking for you."

I was in shock. I thought that she'd cornered the market on black clothing and then she pulls this out of her closet. And I thought that I knew her, but clearly, I didn't. Then she reached way in the back of her closet and pulled out a pair of matching red pumps. "I call these my 'Bitch Please' shoes." She laughed again.

"Do yo' Mama know you have that dress?" I asked.

She frowned. "Who knows what she knows and who cares what she knows?"

I left that alone, quickly. She was becoming agitated. She reached back into her closet and pulled out another dress and some shoes. It was a slinky form-fitted dress and some pumps. "Here…you wear this…this dress is for beginners…you'll be okay in this." She threw the dress at my head and said, "Let's get ready to party.

I tried on the dress. It was a perfect fit – hugging all of the important parts. When I slipped into the shoes, I felt really warm inside. I ran my hands over my body – admiring every aspect. Looking at myself, I realized how grown-

242

up I was. I was no longer a little girl. I looked at my hair, pulled the rubber-band out of it, and watched as the curls sprung out and wrapped themselves around my face and my shoulders. I was dancing in front of the mirror when the door opened and Nicole walked in wearing nothing but a towel. She locked the door and then dropped the towel. From the reflection in the mirror, I could see her body. She was spreading lotion on her skin when I noticed that she didn't have any pubic hair. When she caught me staring, I looked away.

She laughed. "Girl, you ain't never seen a vagina before?"

Still looking away, I said, "Yeah, I look at mine's every day."

She put down the bottle of lotion and walked over to me. I put my hands over my eyes. She grabbed my hands and said, "Look at me."

I closed my eyes tighter. "No way, weirdo...put some clothes on."

"I'm not putting any clothes on until you look at me."

"Nicole, I'm not gay," I said.

"And I'm not trying to come out of anybody's closet either...now, look at me."

I hesitated but then slowly opened my eyes. I looked at her. She was so beautiful. Then she grabbed me and hugged me. "Stop, Nicole...I like my fruit hanging."

She laughed. "I wanted to show you that two women can be close without being gay."

"Okay, okay, now, can you and your tits go over to the other side of the room?"

She laughed and then released me. "You're the weirdo."

I wiped the front of the dress like I was trying to remove any traces of breast or vagina residue that she may have left behind.

She laughed again. I looked at her and said, "Nicole...where is your hair?" I asked, trying not to stare.

She looked down and touched herself. "I cut it off."

"Why?" I asked.

She smiled, coyly. "Some men don't mind hair in their food...my man does."

Confused, I asked. "In your food?"

She laughed. "Ummmmm, you know...when your man wants to lick from the honey pot?"

Still confused, I asked, "The honey pot?"

Frustrated, she said, "Oral sex...when your man goes down and..."

Before she could finish, I stuck my hand up and interrupted her. "I know what you're talking about."

She frowned. "Damn, girl…you are 'green' as hell. Sometimes, I wonder about you."
Little did she know, but I was extremely familiar with oral sex – more than she would ever know.

That night, we went to a club on the south-side of Chicago, right off of Stoney Island. After we got dressed and put on some makeup, we did look older, but not old enough to get in a club. I was curious to see how she was going to pull this off. In the meantime, I was enjoying being an adult for the night.

When we arrived at the door, the bouncer stopped us and asked for ID. I knew that our charade was up, so I prepared to turn around and walk away when Nicole whispered something in his ear. He looked at her and smiled. She looked at me and said, "Wait here."
She took his hand and they walked around to the back of the building. Fifteen minutes later, they returned. They were both smiling. He looked at

me and said, "You can go in." He smiled as I walked passed.

"What did you do, Nicole?" I asked.

She raised one of her eyebrows and said, "You don't ask me my business and I won't ask you about yours…we got in, didn't we?"

"Yes," I said. "But at what price?"

"A price that you didn't have to pay…so why worry about it?" She reapplied her lip gloss and continued, "Now, let's do this…"

We walked across the club until we found a booth. Shortly, the waitress walked over with two drinks and said, "Joe said 'thank you'."

Nicole smiled and said, "Tell Joe that he's welcome."

I just stared at Nicole. I didn't know who I was sitting next to. This girl was completely different from the girl that I've grown to love.

And the drinks kept coming. After the first one, I couldn't remember where I was and by the time the second one came around, "I'd forgotten my name. Nicole was putting them down like she was drinking water. The DJ played a song and then everyone hit the dance floor. She wanted to dance, but I couldn't move let alone try to shake my butt, but she was in her element. She got up and was rubbing herself on every man on the dance floor. This went on for a few hours when she walked up to me holding Joe's hand.

Slurring her words, she said, "I'll be back," and before I could protest, she was gone.

I was sitting at the table, trying to work off my buzz when a man, wearing all of the gold in Africa around his neck and a gallon of cheap cologne, walked towards me.

"Is this seat for me?" he asked.

I was hoping that if I ignored him, he would just walk away, but after a few seconds, I looked up to find that he was still standing there. I guess that he got tired of waiting and decided to sit down.

"Hey lovely lady…" he said.

"Hey," I said, looking away.

"Girl, are you the tiger from the Frosted Flakes box, because you are looking Grrrrreat!!!"

I looked at him to find him smiling – teeth were so yellow that they glowed in the dark. "I'm sorry, but I want to be alone."

"A woman like you should never be alone," he said.

I kept praying that when he spoke, he didn't accidentally spit on me. "I appreciate that, but really…I would like to be alone."

"Look…I'm alone…you're alone…let's be alone together…would you like another drink?"

"Naw, I'm good, but thanks."

He looked at me. I could tell that he was lonely and I didn't want to be mean to him, so I asked, "What's your name?"

He smiled. "It's Edgar."

You look like an Edgar. I thought to myself. "Well, Edgar, I'm Grace."

He smiled and said, "It's nice to meet you, Grace."

After talking to him for a while, I realized that he was a really nice person. We laughed and talked until they turned the lights on letting us know that it was time to go home. When the crowd dispersed, I didn't see Nicole. Me and Edgar said our 'goodbyes' and then I went to look for her. I looked all over the club, but I could not find her. I went outside and searched the parking lot and still could not find her. I was about to call the police when I saw Joe walking towards me dragging Nicole along-side of him.

"What is wrong with her?" I said, taking her from him.

"She just had too much to drink," he said.

Nicole mumbled something and then looked at me. She had a really weird look on her face. "Nicole, I swear to Gawd...you better not throw up on me. She opened her mouth and after a few dry heaves, she leaned over and kissed me.

I wiped my mouth. "NICOLE!!!!"

She smiled before closing her eyes. *Damn, now I have to carry her heavy ass home.*

Chapter 25

*T*he next day, I was seeing double. When I sat up, it felt like someone had just kicked me in the stomach. I tried to stand, but decided that crawling would be the best way to get to the washroom. All the way there, I was praying to the "Porcelain Gods" to put me out of my misery, but they ignored my prayers. I was throwing up foods that I couldn't even remember eating. I was lying on the floor trying to forget the night before when I heard a knock on the door. With every knock, it felt like someone was kicking me in the face. "I'll be out in a minute," I whispered, hoping that they would hear me and go away. I stared at the ceiling wondering why I keep letting her talk me into this shit. I was in desperate need of a "Come to Jesus" moment. I couldn't keep allowing myself to succumb to this stuff and while it sounded so convincing in my head, I knew that something inside of me needed to be addressed. I have to figure out why these things keep happening to me. As I continued to have a conversation with one of the many voices roaming around in my head, the weakest one, convinced me that I did it because I loved her and this is what friends do, but as I continued to

251

justify the crazy, I could hear my Daddy saying, "If a friend jumped off a bridge, would you follow them?" *Hell no.*

There was another knock on the door. "I have to use the bathroom."

"Okay…okay…I'm coming." I sat myself up on all fours, crawled to the door, and opened it. I looked up to find Remy standing over me. Tapping his feet, he said, "Did you have a good time?"

"Good morning, Remy…how are you? I'm fine…thanks for asking."

He frowned. "You don't look fine."

I crawled passed him, down the hall to Nicole's room. I looked up at her bed. "Where's Nicole?" I asked, crawling back to my position on the floor and throwing the throw-rug over my head.

"She left out of here early this morning."

Blindly, I searched for my purse. When I opened it a piece of paper fell out. Remy picked it up. He read it and asked, "Who is Edgar?"

"Remy, if you care about me, you would stop talking."

"Ummmmm, you need to tell me who Edgar is." I threw the carpet back and through squinted eyes, I said, "A lot of things happened yesterday, but becoming your wife wasn't one of them. Now, again, please…let me just close my eyes for a minute. He walked out and slammed the door. "Asshole," I mumbled as that minute turned into the next day.

The next morning, my feet were still throbbing from the night before. High-heels are so sexy until you have to walk halfway across town carrying a drunk person. I started to rub my feet hoping that that would help, but the more that I rubbed them, the more that they said, "Fuck you," so I stopped trying.

I looked around and I noticed that I was by myself. As I laid there trying to figure out what I was going to do next, I heard a commotion down the hall.

"Nicole…wake up…NICOLE…WAKE UP!!!!"

I got up and limped down the hall to find Remy in Nicole's bedroom shaking her limp body.

I limped to his side. "What's wrong with her?" I asked.

"She was with you," he said. "You tell me."

I hobbled out of the room, to the kitchen to grab a cup of cold water and on my way back to her room, I hit my pinky-toe on the corner of the doorway. "Son of a Bitch!" I screamed as I

253

dropped the cup on the floor. I stood to go back to retrieve another cup, when I heard her mumbling. I turned and hopped back to her room. Nicole threw up, everywhere.

"Dang, Nicole...aim that mess," I said, looking at my feet.

Frowning, he asked, "What happened last night?"

His tone was starting to get on my nerves, but I decided to be nice because of our current situation. "Nothing happened...we went to a club and she hooked up with the bouncer..."

"Were you with her when she was with the bouncer?"

"No...she told me to wait for her."

"And just like that, you did?" he asked.

"And exactly, what-else should I have done?" I said, still wiping the vomit off of my feet. "You know how your sister is AND it looked like she knew him. They were...friendly....very friendly."

"Friendly?" he asked.

"Yes, friendly?"

She began to stir.

"Nicole...wake up. Can you hear me?" I said.

She opened her eyes, smiled, and started to sing a demented version of a children's song. "I love you...you love me...we're one fucked-up family...with a fucked-up Mama...and a fucked-

up Daddy too…won't you say you love me too."
She laughed.

I liked the lyrics, so I started to sing it with her, but Remy decided not to join in. "I love you…you love me…we're one fucked-up family…with a fucked-up Mama…and a fucked-up Daddy too…won't you say you love me too." She smiled before passing out. I was still snapping my fingers when I looked over to find him frowning at me. You can tell that Remy was disgusted by the situation.

I looked at the cup. It had a few drops left in it. I poured it into my hand and rubbed it on her face. She started to mumble.

"Remy…we should call your mother."

He looked up. For a minute he didn't respond, but then he said, "We won't be doing that."

"But Remy…she looks like she could use a doctor."

Still looking at me, he said, "She'll be fine…we're not calling my mother."

Something about the look on his face told me that his decision was final, so I didn't ask again. "Let's get her clothes off," I directed.

Without hesitation, Remy began to remove her clothes. I thought that this was kinda odd. Most boys would rather shoot themselves than to see their sister's naked body, but he was extremely comfortable with the request. I thought that this

255

was truly interesting, but I couldn't focus on that at the moment.

I pulled her shirt over her head. "We need to turn her over so that she doesn't choke on her vomit." Curiously, he asked, "And you know this how?" "I've watched enough TV to know and believe me...I've watched a lot of TV."

He accidentally touched one of her breasts. He hesitated for a second and stared at it. He looked up to find me staring at him. We glared at each other for a moment before he covered her with a blanket and walked out of the room.

Chapter 26

"*A*wwwwwwww…look at her. She's sleeping like a baby."

Remy looked at her and frowned. "Yeah, like one of the Devil's spawn."

I shook my head. "How long has she been this way?" I asked.

"What way?" he asked.

We both were standing over her – watching her sleep.

"Look at your sister…this is abnormal…even for her."

"I have to admit that I don't know…I usually stay away from her…as far as I possibly can. She doesn't ask me about my business and I don't ask her about hers. She and D.J. "K", or whatever his name is, come in this room and smoke that stuff…that's all I know."

"That stuff don't do this to people…she has to be doing something else," I said.

He shrugged his shoulders.

"Let's look around her room while she's asleep."

"Man, I'm not doing that…I'm not giving her a reason to be up in my face acting a fool."

"Then I'll look…" I looked on her dressers, in her closet, and I looked in her purse. I found a small bag with some rocks in it. "This looks like crack."

He frowned. "How do you know?"

"I saw it on…"

"TV…yes, of course, that's where you saw it…why did I even ask?" he said, finishing my sentence.

I ignored his attempt at sarcasm. "When did she graduate to crack?" I asked, holding the bag up to inspect it.

"Ummmmmm, you know better than I do. She was with you, remember?"

Frowning, I said, "I know that you're not blaming this shit on me."

"All I know is, she wasn't a crackhead a few days ago…"

I was becoming angry. "How do you know, Mister I Mind My Own Business? She could have been doing this right under your nose…"

"Maybe and maybe not," he said.

"And maybe this is the stuff that she got from Ol' boy…don't put this on me."

He walked over and stood in my face. "Women…"

"What do you mean by that?"

He huffed. "I meant exactly what I said."

"You didn't say anything or maybe I missed it."

He stared at me.

"Well?" I asked.

"Well, what?" he asked.

"Remy…you're her brother…"

"And that means what exactly?"

I was picking up a different vibe from him – like there was something else going on. "Remy, are you mad that I went out or are you mad that your sister is doing crack?"

He hesitated. He opened his mouth to say something when Nicole began to mumble.

Groggily, she looked around the room. "What are you doing in my room?" she asked.

Remy stood to leave. "Ask your friend…"

"Don't leave me in here by myself," I insisted.

Before I could finish talking, he'd already left the room. *Damn.* I sat down on the bed next to her and handed her the bag. "Nicole, what are you thinking? This mess will kill you."

"What are you doing going through my stuff?"

"You weren't feeling well…," I said.

"And you go through my stuff?" she asked, becoming agitated. "What the hell is wrong with you?"

"I was worried about you," I said.

"Worry about your damn self…" she said.

"Damn, Nicole…," I began.

She interrupted. "And if you were minding your own business…"

"If I hadn't been minding YOUR business you'd be in here lying in your own vomit."

"Whatever…as you can see I'm fine…" she said.

"So…is that what you did with Joe?" I asked.

"What are you? The fucking police?" she asked.

"I'm just worried about you."

"Joe showed me that I was doing it all wrong," she said.

"A man that you met a couple of days ago is now an expert on what you need to get high? You let a stranger introduce you to crack?"

She interrupted me. "And where exactly do you expect me to get it…at your local drug store?"

"What about D.J. What's His Name?"

"What about him?" she confirmed.

"Nicole…I have seen and heard some of the dumbest shit…this, by far has to be the dumbest."

She frowned. "You sit there with your fucked-up ass life and fucked-up ass family and you try to judge me?" She paused for a second and then said, "At least, I'm not walking around trying to pretend that my life is fucking perfect when I know damn-well that it isn't…my shit is real."

"Real stupid…" I said.

She fluffed her pillow and said, "Fuck you…now, get out."

Nicole…"

She sighed. "Peaches…when we were younger…"

"We're still young, Nicole."

"Anyway…like I was saying…when we were young, we were cool, but like training bras…at some point you grow out of shit…at least some of us do."

I looked down at my chest. Hearing her say this, broke my heart. "So that's how it's gon' be? Just like that? I was your girl, a couple of days ago."

"Yep," she said, pressing her head into her pillow. "Out with the old…"

"Damn, Nicole…that's cold," I said.

She adjusted herself under her blankets and said, "Then grab a sweater on your way out."

I stood to walk out. "Well…Okay…I'll pray for you."

"Save your prayers for somebody who believes in that shit. Now, bye."

I walked towards the door. With tears in my eyes, I looked back and said, "Bye Nicole."

Chapter 27

I stood outside, looking at the door. I dreaded dealing with what was waiting for me on the other side of it. I hadn't spoken to my sister since my graduation. I would rather get a root canal then to have to hear her mouth, but unfortunately I had to hear it. I didn't want to do it, but I didn't have anywhere else to go. I took a deep breath and walked towards the door. I started to open it, but it was already open. Slowly, I walked in. I didn't want to say her name, but I wanted to make sure that I wasn't walking in on a crime scene. "Ivy…Ivy…" I called out, slowly moving from room to room. I stopped by the kitchen and grabbed a knife before moving further. When I entered the living room, she was sitting there – alone in the darkness. I turned on the light. "Didn't you hear me calling you?"

"I heard you," she said.

"Then why didn't you answer? You almost got cut." I placed the knife on the table.

She studied it. Then, I looked at it. Now, we were both staring at it. Slowly, she looked up. "Where have you been?"

"I decided to stay at a friend's house?" I plopped back onto the couch.

"When you're staying at somebody's house, you should respect them enough to at least call them." She smiled. "Love the lip."

I rolled my tongue over the bump that I'd received when she hit me in the mouth. "First, respect is earned…because you took me in after somebody killed our parents, doesn't make you a surrogate and that mess that you pulled on the day of my graduation…"

"First, let me say this again, you are an adult…you walking around 'mooning' people is your fault…not mine…and second, I didn't do half of the stuff that they did to you."

"You know what, Ivy…it seems like every time that I talk to you, you are always going back to our childhood and what happened to us and don't get me wrong, I feel that we need to talk about it, but the stuff is just random. I'm talking about one thing and you are talking about something else. It's confusing. Please stop or at least give me a heads-up, so that I can keep up. I'm going left. You're going right…confusing…I'm just saying."

She stared at me, blankly. "Like I was saying…It was horrible what they did to us."

"Yeah, but you didn't stop them either."

Her eyes widened. "Shit…I was scared too. At least, you had somebody to take the blows for you. Who did I have? Nobody…and you think that you had it bad? Man, please…who do you think that they practiced on? They were pros by the time you came around. Remember, until you were born, I was the baby. I was the baby…"

I listened. I'd never thought about it like that.

"And do you think that Mama and Daddy did anything about it? No, they didn't."

"Did you tell them, Ivy?" I asked.

"Did you?" she questioned.

I couldn't respond.

"Anyway, what would they've done? Not a damn thing." She said and continued, "And you know what? Sometimes, some shit…some shit happens for a reason."

"What are we talking about now, Ivy? Are we still talking about the abuse or are we talking about something else?"

"I'm talking about everything…shit happens for a reason."

Chapter 28

I was invisible to her. I missed her so much, but she didn't want me in her life anymore, so I had to learn to love her from a distance. Even when I visited Remy, she walked passed me as if I was a part of the décor instead of treating me like someone who still cared about her. If she could walk through me, she would have. Instead, she walked around me and refused to acknowledge my existence. It hurt and she knew that it did, but she didn't care or maybe, because of the drugs, she was unable to care. Whatever the case, I was hoping that things would change so that we could become friends again.

One day, we were looking through the *Want Ads* and she walked in the room. Her hair was disheveled, she looked like she'd stopped bathing, and even though she was "present"; Nicole was gone. It broke my heart to see her that way, but I didn't know what to do or how to help her. Remy didn't even look in her direction. He lifted the newspaper that he was reading to block his view of her. Being a victim too, I understood why he ignored her. Sometimes, it's hard to love someone who has done nothing but hurt you. And to be honest, they both were right. This was none of my business, so I didn't ask any questions and decided to stay in my "lane."

Remy decided that he was ready to move out of his parent's house - even though, he had it good. He felt like a man who needed his own.

"They are looking for a cook," he said, pointing at one of the ads.

"Is that what you want to do with your life…cook?"

"There's nothing wrong with being a cook."

"I'm just saying that there's a lot more out there."

"Maybe, but if being a cook would help me get the hell out of here then hand me a damn spatula. Plus, I'm almost done with school. This will hold me until graduation and then I can look for something else."

I was so happy to hear him say that. Most young people…young men…were looking for that 'fast-money' and nothing was good about fast-money. My parents taught me that anything worth having is worth working hard for.

"Well, you know that I still have the money from my parent's life insurance policies. We can use that to get on our feet and then you can look for a job."

His eyes darkened. "A man doesn't get a woman first, use her money, and then get a job. There's an order and that is out of order. What kinda loser do you think I am?"

I was taken aback. He had never raised his voice to me before, but I guess that it was better that he got angry standing up for his manhood; feeling like I was questioning it and not just sitting back and letting me insult it.

"I'm sorry…I didn't mean anything by it."

He took a deep breath, and then reached over and touched my hand. "I want to be your man…not your boy…I'm sick of being somebody's boy."

"I never called you a boy," I said.

"As long as you know that I'm not one…I'm a man…a grown-ass man."

"Ummmmm, okay…a man…got you."

We stared at each other. I grabbed his hand and smiled. "I'm sorry." I said that not really sure what I was apologizing for, but I wanted to eliminate the tension that was growing between us.

He took my hand and kissed it. "Apology accepted. Now, I'm going to see if they still need that cook."

I left his house late that night. He wanted to take me home, but I needed to be by myself. I had a lot to think about and I had to admit that when I was with him, I couldn't think about anything else but him.

It was beautiful outside. The moon was so bright that it lit the streets. I wasn't afraid of the darkness at least not on that night. I welcomed it. The streets were completely empty and quiet. There was nothing but me and the music that was coming from my headphones.

I was almost at the bus stop when I noticed out of the corner of my eye, a vehicle slowly approaching me. I started to walk faster and the car approached faster. I started to run and the car drove until it caught-up to me. The driver rolled down the window. He started to say something but I ran away.

There was a liquor store, open, on the corner. I ran inside. When I went in, I looked outside to see if the car was still following me. It wasn't but I decided to wait a while before going back outside.

Suddenly, a man walked up to the door. I ran and pretended that I was looking at the different types of potato chips. He walked in, surveyed the room, and slowly approached me. I pretended not to see him. He leaned in and asked, "How much?"

I looked at him like he was crazy. "How much for what?"

He looked around as if he was trying to make sure that we weren't being watched. "How much?" he asked, again.

Confused, I said, "They usually run between $1 and $4 based on what you got a taste for."

His eyes lit up. "Really? Damn, is it on sale? That's almost like getting it for free."

Still confused, I said, "I don't know if it's a sale. I thought that they always ran for those prices."

He smiled. "Shit, for those prices, I'll take a little bit of everything."

I stepped away from the chips, so that he could get what he wanted, when he said, "You want to do it in the car or would you rather get a room?"

"Do what in a car and a room for what?"

"So you can give me what I have a taste for?" he asked, flashing the five teeth that made-up his smile.

Have you ever had something so crazy happen to you that it takes a minute for your brain to catch-up? Well, that's what happened. I actually stood and stared at him for a couple of minutes before I went off. "Man, if you don't get out of my face."

He seemed confused and shocked. "What are you talking about?"

"Do I look like a prostitute to you?"

He looked me up and down and said, "Well, maybe not, but those are the kind that I like…those undercover-hoes…Look all smart and classy but a freak in the streets and under the sheets."

This is one of those moments when I wish that I could go back in time to the day that he was conceived and hand his mother a birth control pill. "Why would you think that I was doing that?" I asked.

"Your pimp…told me that you were available…said that you were the best hoe she had."

"My pimp?"

"Yeah, she's right outside," he said, pointing towards the door.

I followed his finger to a figure that was standing in the darkness across the street. "See…over there."

When I started to run across the street, the figure started to run. By the time I got across, they were in the wind. I walked back to where the man was standing. "What did my pimp look like?"

He said, "I wasn't paying attention to your pimp…she couldn't do anything for me but point me to the 'goods.'" He looked me up and down. "So ummmmm does this mean that you're not working?"

I sighed. "No, I'm not working, fool." I was pissed.

"Do you know anybody who is? I got to hurry up...get home to the wife and kids...and ummmmm, I would like to get 'one' off before I do."

I started to walk away, but then Nicole's words began to play in my head. *"You and this nice shit...it has to stop..."* Something in me snapped. It was time for this shit to end. I stopped, turned, and said, "You know what...I'm not working, but I know someone who is."

All the way there, I kept telling myself that this was wrong, but I was so angry that I didn't care anymore. Plus, I wasn't really doing anything. All I was doing was taking the man to meet my sister and let "nature" take its course. I couldn't predict that anything would happen. All I could do was put one and one together and let Regan do what she does best.

We sat outside of the restaurant until closing. When she walked out, I pointed in her direction.

"Her?" he asked.

I said, "Yep..."

He began to lick his lips. "Something about that uniform is really turning me on. How much?"

I looked at her, thinking about what she did to me and said, "$10."

His eyes almost popped out of his head. "$10...that's all...for all of that? Shiiiiiiiiitttttt, for that I would have easily given you $200. What's wrong with her?"

"Nothing's wrong...she just likes it...a lot."

"I like that she likes it...," he said, biting on his bottom lip. "Yeah..."

"Yep, $10 is enough. The only thing I ask is that you don't tell her that you've already paid me. You also have to pretend that you like her. She performs better when she thinks a man likes her...and you have to also promise that you don't tell her that I sent you. She likes to think that she's in control..."

He started rubbing himself. I frowned. "Save all of that for her."

"Yeah...yeah...yeah...for her..." He reached into his wallet and handed me a $10 bill. He looked in the mirror, fixed his hair, threw a piece of gum in his mouth, and then jumped out of his car.

I walked across the street to watch the whole "transaction". He walked up to her. They began to talk. She smiled and then he smiled. He touched her hand and she laughed. An hour had passed, before he pointed at his car. Without hesitating, she followed him to it. She jumped in and they pulled off. *Damn, old habits die hard.* I shook my head and then walked away.

And then there were two.

Chapter 29

I thought that they stopped looking. I hadn't heard anything about my parent's case since the night that it happened, so I was thrown-off by the phone call. "Ummmmm, hello?"

"Hello…is this Grace Davis?"

"Yes, it is."

"This is Detective Graham."

"How can I help you, Detective Graham?"

"I was calling about your parents," he said.

"Do you have any updates on their case?" I asked.

"Well, we've interviewed a few people…which led to us questioning a few people of interest, but nothing panned out…we haven't charged anyone with the crime yet…but we're still looking. I called to ask you…who do you think could be behind this?"

"My parents had no enemies…they worked and they came home…that's it."

"Did your parents owe anyone any money?"

"No…"

"Were there any problems in their marriage?"

I thought about it for a second and said, "Their kids were their problems."

"What do you mean?" he asked.

"My parents have some 'odd children.'"

"What do you mean by 'odd?'" he asked.

"I mean...that if you looked under the word 'odd' in the dictionary, you would find us." I took a deep breath and continued. "We weren't your typical kids."

"Typical in what way?" he asked.

"Well...think about what you think is typical...we were the complete opposite of that."

"Was there abuse?" he asked.

"My parents? No, no, of course not...we were disciplined when we did wrong, but not abused."

"Did any of you resent your parents?"

"What kid...do you know...doesn't hate their parents...doesn't think that they are mean...doesn't think that they aren't fair? We're kids...we feel that way about all adults, but I could see my sisters resenting them. My sisters did some things that would make my mom and dad do and say some things that as parents, I'm sure that they regretted, but they were our mom and dad...they did what they felt they had to do, but murder?" Then I thought about who I was talking about. Murder wouldn't be a reach for any of them. "Now, that I think about it..."

"Is there one in particular that we should be looking at?"

"I have three sisters...pick one..."

He laughed. "I take it that you don't like them."

"Let's just say that I don't feel much of anything either way."

"Well, that says a lot."

"Well...they aren't the nicest people in the world," I said.

"Wow...that probably made your parents very unhappy."

"It did..."

"There's a saying that goes, 'a parent is only as happy as their unhappiest child'," he said.

"Then my parents were miserable."

"I hate to hear that. I'm a father, myself."

"Well, pray that you're kids turn-out better."

There was a moment of uncomfortable silence. Then he said, "Well, thank you, Ms. Davis...we'll keep looking and if we have any additional questions we will contact you."

"Well, like my parents used to say, 'If you want to find the nuts, just shake the family tree, Detective...just shake the family tree..."

Chapter 30

*N*ow, that I've graduated, I've been thinking more about living on my own. It was time to move on. I wasn't sure how to broach the subject with Ivy, but I knew that it was time to have the conversation. I just needed to find the perfect moment to do so.

That morning, I'd determined that the right moment was now. I got up, showered, brushed my teeth, got dressed, took a deep breath and headed down the hall. When I walked into her room, I noticed that she was still sleeping. I figured that this was the perfect opportunity. *She's sleepy, groggy, - yes, now was the perfect time.* I sat at the end of the bed. I took another deep breath and said, "Ivy, I've been thinking…while I appreciate all that you've done for me…I'm an adult now and it's time for me to be out on my own…so Ivy, what do you think? Ivy? Ivy?" I shook her foot. Suddenly, she began to move. "So Ivy…what do you think about that?"

Slowly, the blankets were pushed back. She stretched and said, "Good morning…"

I stumbled onto the floor. I was in shock. "Awwwwwwwwwwwww!!!!! What the hell?"

I ran out of the room and down the hall. When I got to the kitchen, I found Ivy pouring herself a cup of coffee. I was gasping for air by the time I entered the room. "What in the hell, Ivy? What is she doing here?"

Without looking up from her cup, she asked, "Who, your sister?"

"Yes, YOUR SISTER…why is she here?"

"We talked…and she's apologized for the things that she's done…"

I felt like I was having an "out-of-body" experience. This couldn't be real until things suddenly got real.

"Good morning, Peaches…," she said, rubbing her fingers through her hair.

I turned my head to look at her. Everything moved in slow motion. I fell back trying to get away from her. I couldn't believe what I was seeing. "Ivy, how could you?"

"She served her time…she's my…our sister."

I immediately became ill.

"I'm tired of holding a grudge over something that happened when we were kids…all we have is each other…we have to learn to forgive."

Regan smiled.

"Are you kidding me? What did she do to you that was worse than what she did to me?"

Ivy laughed. "So now you want to compare war wounds? We were kids, Peaches…let it go."

I looked at her and then back to Regan. I stumbled backwards until I stumbled out of the door and into the street.

Chapter 31

*M*oments later, I was wearing a groove in the carpet of Remy's bedroom. I was pissed.

"Can you believe it? And under the same roof…," I said, pacing the floor.

He didn't respond.

"…like, how do you not talk to me about it and just assume that it would be okay?"

He avoided my question. Instead, he asked, "So what are you going to do?"

I thought about it for a second and said, "I'm going to get my stuff and the money that my parents left me and I'm going to go…"

"Go where?" Remy asked.

"I don't know, but I'm getting the hell up out of here."

"Okay? I get that, but where are you going to go?" he, asked with a curious look on his face.

And that was a good question. In that moment, reality set in. I knew that I needed to leave, but I really had no idea what I was going to do or where I was going to go. I didn't know my extended family – all I knew were my sisters. This realization was so depressing - to be left alone in this world with no one and nowhere to turn to. Immediately, a sense of helplessness and hopelessness set in. Now, I understood why people end-up staying with the people who hurt them. It's hard when you're face with loneliness, hopelessness, and no other options.

I didn't know much about God, but I knew that I wasn't born to be this damn unhappy. I cannot believe that this is it. That I was born to deal with this mess all of my life. *Why?* What have I done to deserve this? As I pondered all of this, I realized that sitting here talking to myself wasn't getting me anywhere. I needed to figure something out and quick.

An overwhelming feeling of fear came over me. I've been silent for so long that the thought of confronting them left me paralyzed. I didn't want to move from where I was sitting, but the day for all of this shit to end was today. While I was still pissed, I had to muster up the courage to finally stand up to her and HER sisters.

My plan was to walk in, grab my stuff, and say good-bye. *Sounds simple, right?* But nothing about them was simple. In my head, the thought of just walking in and grabbing my stuff seemed easy, but reality would be different. I had to expect the worst and be prepared to fight for my freedom if it came to that.

I took a deep breath and thought that it was now or never. I knew that the smartest thing to do was to stop by the bank first and get the money. Just in case, she wanted to pull something foul, by blocking my access to it. It's sad that I would think that she would do that, but I would be a fool not to.

I walked in the bank. When I walked in, everyone turned to look at me. This made me really uncomfortable, but it wasn't anything that I hadn't experienced before. I was used to walking into places and everyone looking at me – watching me. The guard walked up to me. "Can I help you?"
Stammering, I said, "I need to make a withdrawal."
He looked me up and down and said, "Do you have an account here?"
Now, looking him up and down, I suddenly became agitated. He reminded me of all of the times that I walked in stores to shop and ended-up being accosted or followed by someone who thought that I was in their establishment to steal something. He made me feel like I didn't belong there. Angrily, I said, "Did you ask those other people if they had a damn account?"

He frowned. "No, I did not."

"Then why are you asking me?"

He shook his head and leaned into my face. "If you took that chip off of your shoulder you would see that I was only trying to help you."

I leaned in his face and said, "If you're only asking me 'Do you have an account here?' Then what you think is help is actually reverse racism."

He took a deep breath and said, "First, you asked me if I asked the other people if they had an account, but you didn't ask me if I asked white people if they had an account. If you did, I would have said, 'Yes", because I ask everyone, black, white, brown, yellow, purple, red, green, mauve, lilac, orange…whatever color…who walks in here…especially, folks who look like they've never been in a bank before, if they need some help."

I frowned, "Well, I don't need any help."

"Well, I apologize," he said.

I turned my nose up and said, "Okay." Then I stood there for a second. I looked around and realized that I didn't know what to do. Feeling like an idiot, I turned to him, swallowed my pride, and said, "I guess I do need your help…"

He frowned and pointed towards one of the tellers. "Over there…"

I walked up to the desk.

"Hi, can I help you?" the teller said, cheerfully.

I handed her my ID and said, "I would like to make a withdrawal."

She smiled and said, "Sure, can you fill out this slip and I will pull up your account."

This was a new experience for me. I stared at the slip and decided that $100,000.00 would be a good place to start and that I would get the rest later. The interesting thing is, I had no idea what was in the account. I assumed that the value of a person's life had to be worth at least a million dollars – especially, the lives of two people who had worked hard all of their lives. The funny thing is, is that I actually thought that the bank would just hand me $100,000.00, I would just stuff it all in my pockets, and walk right out the door with it. In that moment, I realized that I hadn't really thought this out. I'm sure that a person who'd been an adult for more than a few months would have had all of that figured out, but I didn't. I began to laugh at myself. There was so much that I didn't know that I desperately needed to learn.

But I was really feeling good about myself – feeling really grownup. You couldn't tell me anything. I filled out the form and handed it to her with a smile on my face that was so big it touched my ears.

She took the slip and said, "I'm sorry, but there's too many zeros on this slip. Would you like for me to correct it?"

"Sure," I said. *It couldn't be that much less.*

Then she said, "Would you like that in $5 and $10 bills?"

"That's going to be a lot of $5 and $10, but sure."

I watched her as she counted, 10, 20, 30, 40, 50, 60, 70, 75, 80, 85, 90, 95, 100, but then a strange thing happened. She stopped counting.

"Ummmmmm, where's the rest?" I asked.

"That's it…and after this, the account will close due to insufficient funds."

I shook my head. "Insufficient funds? There must be some kind of mistake."

She stared at her computer screen and said, "No, that's correct. Your initial balance was $174, 083.01, but you had several withdrawals, leaving you with what you have now."

Confused and trying not to make a scene, I said, "Okay, okay, there must be some type of error because I didn't take out anything."

"Mam, the money isn't here. We can do an investigation, but we check ID before we give out anything…soooooooooo…"

"Soooooooooo, you need to check again," I said.

She sighed. "Mam, that's all that's in there."

My thoughts went to my sisters. I became extremely angry. I put my hand up to stop her from saying another word, grabbed the money, and was stomping towards the door when the guard looked at me and said, "Have a good day." "Shut up," I said as I left the building.

When I got home, I was sweating like I'd just run a marathon. I was breathing so hard that my chest hurt. I didn't even bother putting the key into the doorknob. I lifted my leg and with all of my strength, I kicked the door. I tried to put my foot through it, but the door was a lot stronger than I thought it was. My leg sprung off of the door, causing me to fall backwards, and landing me on my butt. I didn't want them to see me sitting on the ground, so I jumped up, dusted off my clothes, and then turned the knob. I walked in. "Hey, you lousy pieces of shit...I'm home." The noise startled them. They came running to the door.

"Where's my money?" I was ready to take the same foot that I used to open the door and place it knee-deep into their butts.

Ivy responded, "Girl, have you lost your mind?"

"No, but I seemed to have lost some damn money,"

Nonchalantly, she said, "You thought that you were going to get that money? That shit is gon'...gon'..." She threw her hands in the air. *Poof.*

"What do you mean, Ivy?" I asked, breathing heavily.

Laughing, she said, "Did you think that I was putting a roof over your head, providing lights, food and clothing for you for free? The fuck I look like...welfare?"

"No...I mean, yes, you are my sister. You said that you would take care of me."

"And I did take care of you..." She and Regan began to laugh.

She looked at me. "What do I look like? Yo' Mama and Daddy? Sorry, Baby Girl, but they're dead." She continued to laugh, but Regan stopped and looked at her.

I couldn't believe that those words had just rolled off of her lips, "What did you say?"

She folded her arms, twisted her mouth and said, "They...are....dead..." And if that wasn't horrible enough she had the nerve to spell-out the word 'dead'. "D-e-a-d."

"Ivy, why are you acting like this? Why would you say something like that about Mama and Daddy? They loved you."

She folded her arms and frowned. "No, sweetie, they loved you."

"That's not true. Why would you think something like that?"

She didn't answer.

"I don't believe this...Regan, Raven and now, you?"

Again, she didn't answer.

"And you spent all of that money? That money was for me...not you...'

"You know...I thought about it and Raven was right...they had four girls...four...not one...not two...not three, but four...what gave them the right?"

"Ivy, are you serious? You smiled in my face and promised that you would take care of me."

"And I did...didn't I?" she said, smugly.

"I...took...care...of ...YOU."

She walked over and stuck her finger in my chest. I looked down at her finger and then back up at her. Before I knew it, I grabbed her hand and bit the shit out of her. She fell to her knees. "Get this crazy bitch off of me!!!!!"

I let her finger go. Regan ran towards me. "It's been a long time for us to have this moment...but there is no time like the present...it's time to remind you of your place."

Before I knew it, I swung back and then forward, hitting her in the face. *It's on....*

The next thing I knew, we were pulling at each other like animals. We were scratching, slapping, and punching each other. All of that pain, anger, and hatred came out in every swing. In my mind, I thought, *This is for the rape. This is for the lies.*

293

This is for the broken dolls and the messed-up birthdays. This is for being such evil bitches...

Regan hit me and Ivy. Ivy hit me and Regan and I hit the both of them. And we did this until we exhausted ourselves. When it was over, I scanned the floor around us. There was blood and hair all over it. I glanced at Ivy who was holding her mouth and Regan who was accessing how much hair she'd lost. Meanwhile, my face was on fire. During the fight, I didn't feel it but as I sat there for a second, my face started to sting. I reached up and touched it. When I removed my hand, I saw that it was covered in blood. We were staring at each other. We knew that this was it. There was no going back.

I stood and went to the bathroom and splashed my face with cold water. The taste of blood and her finger was still in my mouth. I rinsed with some mouthwash and then I stared in the mirror. My face was red and my hair was all over the place. I tried to fix myself, but I couldn't hide looking like I'd just got into a street fight. I did the best that I could to look normal and then walked down the hall to my bedroom. I put as much as I could into a couple of small bags and a backpack and walked back down the hall. When I walked in the kitchen, they were sitting in a chair, looking like they wanted a 'round two'. I walked right passed them, walked out of the door, and didn't say goodbye.

"Gracie…where are you going?" Remy asked, looking at the scratches and bruises on my face.
"I'm going as far as $100 will take me."
"Sweetie, one hundred dollars will get you to 95th street and that's walking…you can't get nowhere with one hundred dollars."
"Remy…look at me…I don't have a choice. Where else am I going to go? They took everything…EVERYTHING!!!...I don't have anything but the stuff in those bags. My whole life is in three freakin' bags."
Remy looked at me. Then he proceeded to pack a small bag. "Okay, but I'm going with you."

Chapter 32

*A*nd there we were, standing in the middle of somewhere with nowhere to go. Just like that, we were both homeless. Well, I was homeless, but Remy had a home to go back to, but he just didn't want to. It was nothing for him to say 'goodbye' to everything. He didn't even tell his mother that he was leaving because he knew that she wouldn't let him go. He promised that he would call her after a few days to let her know that he was okay, but he didn't act like he was looking forward to it. He looked more happy to be "free" than me.

I was so grateful that he decided to come with me because I was really scared and lost. He assured me that everything would be okay, but if that first night on the street was any indication of what the rest of the journey would be like then things were looking bad – real bad.

We spent the first night on the "L". Before getting on, we grabbed some chips and soda for dinner from a local grocery store. We knew that once we got on the trains, we wouldn't have access to any washrooms, so we knew that we needed to "go" before we got on, but where, we had no idea. Most of the restaurants were closed and most of the establishments that were open didn't have any public restrooms. At this point, I was doing the bathroom "dance". I told myself that I wasn't riding a train all night without first relieving myself.

We were walking down an alley when Remy said, "How bad do you have to use it?"

"I have to use it bad," I said, now crossing my legs.

He pointed at a dumpster and said, "You first."

I looked over to where he was pointing and said, "Me first what?"

He smiled and said, "You gotta piss, right?"

I frowned. "You could have said that better, Remy."

"Orrrrrrrr, I could let you pee on yourself."

I took a deep breath and said, "Damn…"

I looked around before pulling my pants down. It was awful stooping on the side of a dumpster trying to relieve myself. I couldn't help but wonder how many people were looking out of their windows staring down at me. This was so humiliating. When I was done, I realized that I didn't have anything to wipe myself with.

Remy was becoming impatient. "How much longer?"

"I don't have any toilet paper," I said, still looking around.

"Use your hand," he said.

I wasn't sure if he was joking or being serious, but I still needed to wipe myself or I'll be walking around like this all night. I kept looking around and he was growing more impatient. The thought of picking something up off of the ground to clean myself with was terrifying. I looked inside of my book-bag and grabbed a shirt. I wiped myself, but now I didn't know what to do with the soiled shirt.

"Peaches…," he said.

I didn't know what to do. I didn't want to throw it on the ground and I wasn't sure if I was going to need it again, so I decided not to throw it away. I balled it up and stuck it back in my book-bag. I pulled up my clothes and we walked away. I kept looking over my shoulder at the puddle of urine that I'd left on the ground. Something about that moment left me feeling "different". Although, I've had a lot of bad experiences, pissing in a dark alley sits right up there on the list of messed-up shit that has happened to me. Yep, it was really messed-up.

The walk to the train was a long one. While waiting for the train, I tried to process my current situation. I wanted to cry so bad, but the tears wouldn't come. I'd cried so much for so long that as much as I tried, nothing happened.

When the train stopped and the doors flew open, we looked to find two seats in the back of the car. We took out the food, but I realized that I'd just used the washroom on the side of a dumpster. "Damn, I need to wash my hands."

Remy looked at me. Frustrated, he said, "You need to come to terms with what's happening…toilet paper…soap and water…let it go. You hungry, you eat…you gotta piss, you piss…"

I frowned and then the tears that wouldn't come earlier decided that this was a better time to reveal themselves. Remy wrapped his arms around me. "I know that this is hard…and it's not easy for me either, but…" He paused for a second and then continued. "You are going to have to let some shit go. It's hard enough…"

He was so callous. I knew that I had to let some things go, but I needed time to adjust. I've never known this "life." A few hours ago, I had a roof over my head and now, I'm riding a freakin' train because I didn't have a place to rest my head and using the bathroom in alleys. *Is it too wrong to have a minute to take it all in?*

While we were coasting through downtown, I thought about my "bathroom" experience. I couldn't help, but think about all of the people, all of the women, who must do that every day. I couldn't even imagine what I would have done if I'd been on my period. The thought of me "menstruating" on the ground in some dark alley was disturbing, depressing, and horrifying. I tried not to think about it, but I knew the day would come that I would have no choice but to think about it. Especially, if our circumstances didn't change.

We rode the train back and forth until sunrise. By the time we got off, I was tired of looking at Chicago, even though the streets that make it what it is was now my home.

That morning, it was raining. I was glad because now Remy couldn't see my tears. I could tell that he was scared, but he wouldn't let on that he was. He was determined to be strong or at least look like it, but I was falling apart inside.

We walked and walked. We had no idea where we were going. Sadly, while we saw signs and billboards that advertised everything from liquor, to cigarettes, to who to call if you're in a car accident, there were no signs that said, "Homeless people go here," "If you're hungry there's help," or anything along those lines, but if we needed to find hair weave and the best "Yaki" in town, we knew where to go.

After walking for hours, we decided to stop and get something to eat because the little food that we had was now gone. When we walked in, the heat from the vents kissed our faces, but the rest of our bodies could not enjoy it, because we were freezing from the soaked clothing that we were wearing.

We were looking at the menu when the waitress walked up. "Are you ready to order?"

"Yes…I'm starving…I would like a stack of pancakes, some hash browns, and a spinach omelet with extra spinach, please" I said, excitedly.

"And you?" the waitress asked.

Remy looked at her and said, "Could you give us a minute?"

She said, "Yes," and walked away.

In a whisper, he said, "What you have is all that we got. We need to make it last."

Hearing him say that saddened me, but I knew that he was right.

"So we are going to get what you ordered, minus the extra spinach and share it. Is that okay?" he said.

I studied him for a second and said, "Yes…it's okay."

After eating we hit the streets again. As we walked, we tried to see what other people on the streets did to make money. We saw some of everything and none of it looked appealing, but we knew that if we were going to be out there, we were going to be doing a lot of things that weren't appealing and we needed to accept that realization and quick.

It was weird. Normally, when I spent time with Remy, he always had something interesting to talk about, but these past two days, he'd been quiet. I felt terrible – like I'd stolen his joy. I knew that he was doing all of this for me and I felt extremely guilty because of it.

The only time that he spoke was when he was giving suggestions on what we were going to do next. Other than that, there was nothing. He was becoming distant. This was difficult – for the both of us. It was easy to say that I wanted to walk away from everything wrong in my life until I actually had to do it. Now, look at my life. I'm sure that this was not the life that my parents wanted for me, but here I was walking pass park benches trying to find one comfortable enough to call it my bed for the night. I'm sure that they were in Heaven looking down at me and shaking their heads. Before, I became displaced, I used to walk passed the homeless, walk around them, as if they weren't there with their hands stuck out asking for help, but now, in an instant, I'd become one of them.

304

Chapter 33

We stopped by a local shelter and they allowed us to use the phone. Remy took a deep breath and then dialed the number. Remy's mother was yelling so loud that everyone within two feet could hear her. There were a few "insanes", "what are you thinkings", a few "you barely know that girls", a few "you are ruining your life(s)", and quite a few "why are you sleeping on the street when you got a homes," then he finally said, "I'm not coming back," before hanging up the phone.

They offered us a place to rest out heads for the night. We could have said, "No," but what was the alternative? So we accepted the next stage in this journey and took them up on their offer. We ate dinner with everyone else. It wasn't the tastiest stuff that I've ever eaten, but I ate it like I was at a 5-star restaurant. I sucked my teeth trying to get every little bit of it because I wasn't sure when I would get it again.

Then they led us to a room where cots were lined-up from wall to wall. We grabbed two of them, pushed them close together, and then sat on top of them. As I watched Remy fluff his backpack, turning it into a pillow, I said, "You don't have to do this."

He laid down and said, "Stop talking stupid… they want us out of here by 6am, we need to spend every minute sleeping…we have a long day ahead of us."

I put my bags under my head and I stared at him until we both fell fast asleep.

It was about 4am when I heard a crunching sound. I opened my eyes to find someone trying to go into one of my bags. Still half-asleep, I said, "What are you doing?"

The person was still tugging at my bag.

I said it again, "What are you doing?"

This time, I woke-up Remy.

They pulled some toothpaste from my bag and said, "You have to share."

Sleepily, Remy asked, "Wha…what's going on?"

I snatched the toothpaste from their hands and said, "This is mine…don't touch my stuff."

They snatched it back from me and before I knew it, we were in a tug-of-war over toothpaste.

We were tugging and squeezing the tube so hard that it squirted all over the place.

The man began to lick the spilled toothpaste from his hands and began to suck it from his shirt. As I stared at him, I was mortified. *Is this the life that I've chosen for myself?* I handed him the rest of the toothpaste. He scurried away - sucking the remaining toothpaste from the tube.

I grabbed my bag and held it tightly. Remy turned over and fell back to sleep. I couldn't go back to sleep after that. I couldn't stop thinking about the desperation in his eyes and what he was willing to do for something as simple as toothpaste. That man was once someone's son, probably someone's brother, someone's husband, and now, he would become the main character in one of my nightmares.

And we did that for the next couple of weeks, walked from shelter to shelter, buying our time until the little money that we had ran out. There were a few days when Remy wanted to call his family, but he refused to.

One night at the shelter, I removed my shoe to find my feet were covered in blisters. I cried, because I didn't think that I could go on. He took my feet and began to rub them. "I'm going to find a way for us to get out of this...I promise you." I tried to believe him, but our circumstances were looking grim.

The last night at the shelter, while we were sleeping someone went into my backpack and took the rest of our money. I was unaware that it was gone until the next day when we were out in the summer's heat and I reached into the bag to find that it was gone. This made Remy angry, but what could we do? Blame each other for the loss? Check the pockets of every homeless person on the street until we find it? It was me who screwed up. I took my eyes off of my bag for one second and that's all it took for someone to take it. Now, we couldn't do anything but wander around until the shelter let us back in.

We were able to find a public water fountain to quench our thirst, but by noon, we were starting to get hungry. We stopped people and asked for money, but the donations weren't enough to get anything to eat. We walked behind one of the restaurants and knocked on the doors to see if they would give us anything to eat.

Knock, Knock, Knock

The door opened. I didn't know what to say to the person who answered it, because I wasn't used to asking a stranger for anything. I took a deep breath, swallowed, and said, "Hi, we're hungry. Do you have anything to spare?"

The person looked at me, pointed towards the dumpsters, and said, "It's in there." They closed and slammed the door in my face.

Remy and I walked over and stood next to the dumpsters. I don't know if Remy was paying attention, but here we were again, back at the dumpsters. Our bathroom was now our kitchen. My heart sunk as I listened to the sound of the flies swarming around it. The "buzzing" was almost deafening. We looked at it and then at each other. We just couldn't do it.

Remy finally broke down and called his mother again. This time she didn't scream at him. When they were done talking, he looked at me and said, "This is our last night out here." That night we decided to rest on a park bench. We held what we had left close and we took turns falling asleep. A couple hours later, Remy woke me and said, "Come on..."

We got up and started walking. It was still dark out. We wandered from block to block as the smell of fresh coffee and fresh baked donuts filled the air. My stomach began to growl. I was so hungry that it felt like my stomach was trying to eat itself.

We walked passed a corner and a voice called out, "Do you have any change?" I looked in the direction of the sound. Again, I heard it. "Do you have any change?" I pulled away from Remy to find out who was speaking.

"What…come on, Peaches," he said.

"Give me a second, Remy," I said.

Then I found the source of the sound. A man sitting on a stoop with a cup, a sign, and a cane, asked again, "Do you have any change?"

I looked at him. He was wearing a jacket covered in medals. "Ms…do you have some change?"

I reached into my pocket and found two quarters, a dime, a penny, and some lint. I picked the lint out from among the coins and threw it on the ground and said, "All I have is this." I placed the change in his hand.

The man looked at me and said, "Thank you…may God bless you."

I walked back towards Remy.

"Why did you do that?" he asked.

"I don't know…maybe it was the right thing to do."

After about thirty minutes of walking around, a dark blue BMW pulled up. The window came down. She popped the locks on the car doors and then looked away. Remy sat in the front seat and I watched the whole interaction from the back.

"Hi…," Remy said.

"Hi what?" she asked.

He sighed and said, "Hello mother."

She was trying to hide her tears. She wiped her face and said, "I don't know why you're doing this. You should come home. We can talk about this…"

"And then what, Mother…you want your little man to just go to his room until you think that it's time for him to leave? I'm too old and I'm tired of dealing with…," he caught himself. "Mama, I'm not coming home."

At this point, she was crying like she just received the news that somebody had died.

He took a shirt from his backpack and handed it to her.

She examined and blew her nose in it. "Can I keep this?" Then she looked at it, placed her nose in it, and inhaled, deeply.

"Yes, you can…you bought it for me."

"Yes, I did…," she said, handing him an envelope. "Here."

He looked at it and said, "Thanks…"

She smiled. "Thanks, what?"

"Thanks mother," he said.

"Do you want a ride?" she asked.

"Naw, I got it from here…"

She touched his hand. "Remember…A bond between a mother and son is very special."

He pulled away. "I know, mother…," he said.

She kissed him for what seemed like forever and said, "I love you…you are MY baby boy…mine."

He didn't respond.

They took one long look at each other and then Remy opened the door to get out. As I pulled the latch, something said look at her. She was staring at me. She had a look on her face that sent a chill through my body. It was a look that I'd seen before and never wanted to see again.

Chapter 34

*I*n the envelope was a key, an undetermined amount of cash, a note that listed an address, and the words, "You are Mama's baby boy." I thought that was weird, but I was just so glad to be off of the streets that I didn't think about it. We walked three miles until we found ourselves standing in front of a house that was just big enough to park a car in.

Remy stared at it and started laughing. For more than five minutes, the air was filled with nothing but laughter. Finally after laughing himself to tears, he turned to me and said, "Mother."

We pushed through the weeds that were the front yard, to a door that looked like it'd been around since the 50s. He inserted the key into the tarnished bronze doorknob. When the door opened, it struggled to remain on its hinges. He had to grab it to keep it from falling on our heads. We stood in the entry way, stared into the darkness, then we turned and stared at each other. I pointed and said, "You first." He pushed the cobwebs out of his face and entered, slowly.

Secluded among the trees on one of Chicago's busiest streets, the 'hut' doubled as a crack-house. As we roamed from room to room, I heard a crackling sound under my feet. I looked down to find pieces of shattered glass sprinkled everywhere. The floor was covered with old syringes and crack-pipes. We pushed through the needles to the bathroom. As we entered, we were greeted by the stench of sewage. I covered my face to prevent from throwing up the remaining traces of any meal that was left in my stomach. The toilet was full of feces and soiled toilet paper. The tub and sink was black from neglect and mold decorated the walls. We shook our heads before backing out of the bathroom and proceeding down the dark hallway. I looked up to see that the light fixtures were dangling – held to the ceiling by a single wire. I was praying that they didn't fall and hit one of us on the top of our heads.

I stared at the back of Remy's head as it shook from left to right in disbelief as we navigated from room to room. Finally, we entered a room that was now our bedroom. We stood in the door as we stared at the urine soaked mattress that was held together by four steel bars. We dropped our bags on the floor. A cloud of dust engulfed the room. We both began to cough and sneeze. Once the smoke cleared, we walked over to the bed that was so lumpy, I pulled the covers back to make sure that a body wasn't hiding under them. We looked at each other and decided that even though we were tired, we weren't going to sleep in that bed.

We walked over and cleared a spot on the floor. We grabbed our bags, made some make-shift pillows, and stretched across the cold floor. Lying there, we found ourselves staring at a hole in the roof that was so big it could have doubled as a skylight. There were water stains in the remaining parts of the ceiling. In that moment, I was starting to miss the shelter. He pulled the envelope from his pocket. He looked at it again. He counted the money, shook his head, and said, "Home sweet home."

That night in our new home was scary. We kept hearing and seeing shadows. I spent the whole night making sure that some fool in a mask, yielding a machete wasn't going to pop out of the closet while Remy and I slept. Then, I thought about it. *The closet.* Finally, I found myself looking over in its direction. It was dark and empty. Suddenly, I saw the face of a little girl sitting on its cold-hard floor, playing with her dolls, waiting for it all to be over, and waiting for someone to say that it was okay to come out. Then I saw him, the man with the bag of candy, crawl over to her, she was so happy that someone wanted to play with her that she didn't see the monster who wanted to hurt her. I closed my eyes trying to erase the image, trying to silence her cries, and when I opened them, she was gone and the screams had stopped.

While I lay awake, I thought about the journey that led me here and where it was going to take me. While I could visualize my past so vividly, my future was still an illusion. I could look at this moment as a set-back, but somehow I knew that this was where I was supposed to be.

Chapter 35

We had no idea what to do next. We were sitting in this cold, dark, damp place, with an envelope full of money, and no instructions. We knew that we had to figure something out quick or we would die from our stupidity or from being eaten alive by the critters that roamed the house at night.

We figured out that electricity would cure the darkness, heat would cure the cold, and food would fix the hunger. That was the easy stuff. We purchased some cleaning supplies and started cleaning the house. After a while, it almost seemed livable except for the big ass hole in the ceiling.

Remy was determined to prove that he was the "man of the house." He picked up a "How-to" book from the library and read it like he was studying for his ACTs. After about a week, he caught the bus and started bringing home one box of shingles a day. By the end of the month, he had carried home everything that he needed to fix the hole in the roof – except for the most important tool of all, a ladder.

One day, I saw him staring at the roof trying to figure out how he was going to fix it without a ladder.

"Baby, maybe we should call somebody?" I asked, rubbing his shoulders as he contemplated his next move.

He shook his head. "Naw, you see…that's what she wants us to do…call somebody like we had to call her. She wants to prove that we can't do this on our own…she wants me to run back to her. Plus, this is all of the money that we have. We have to make it last."

I knew that he couldn't do it without help, but I didn't think that anything that I would say would keep him from making this happen. So I decided to support him, whatever the decision, but I would soon find that that would be one of the worst decisions of our lives.

The night before, Remy stared at that hole so hard that I thought that via mind control, it would fix itself. The next morning, Remy jumped up and with his chest sticking out, he strolled out of the house. I was so proud of him until I saw him climbing a big tree that sat close to the house.

"Remy, what are you doing?"

He yelled down, "When I get on the roof, I need you to climb up and hand me some shingles."

"Huh…? I'm not doing that. That's crazy."

He stopped and slowly came back down. "If you're not part of the solution then you are a part of the problem."

"Frowning, I said, "No…I'm just smarter than that. I'm not going to hurt myself climbing a tree."

"Ain't nobody gon' hurt themselves. Now, go and get me some shingles."

I looked him up and down. "Ummmmm, excuse me…can I get a 'please'?"

"You can grab 'one' while you're in there getting me some shingles."

We stared at each other. I could see that he wasn't going to say "it" even if I stared at him all day, so I gave in and got him the shingles.

He wrapped them under his arm and started back up the tree. Then suddenly, like something out of a "Three Stooges Movie", he screamed and came tumbling down, bringing half of the tree's leaves with him.

I shook my head before running to his side.

He was moaning and screaming like a woman in labor. "Don't touch me…DON'T TOUCH ME!"

"I'll go get help," I stood and ran to the nearest house and called for help. An ambulance came and rushed him to the hospital.

"What happened?" the doctor asked.

I didn't want to say anything because I didn't feel like it was my place. Plus, I didn't think that I could tell the story without laughing, so I kept my mouth shut.

"I fell out of a tree," Remy said, cringing with every word.

"Was there a cat in the tree?" the doctor asked.

"No, I was fixing the roof."

"From a tree?" the doctor asked.

"Yes, from a tree," he said, extremely frustrated.

"You don't need me to tell you that that wasn't a good idea."

"Naw, I got it."

"Because if you need me to, I don't mind telling you…"

Remy interrupted, "I said that 'I got it.'"

They fitted him for a back brace, prescribed him some medication, and sent him home with instructions on how to take care of himself.

While he slept, I went to the store, purchased some garbage bags, some duck-tape, and covered the hole in the roof. I am so glad that I did because that night it rained. I thought that putting the plastic up was a good idea, but it made Remy very unhappy. When he saw the repair, he went completely off. I was in the kitchen when I heard him scream from the bedroom.

"Who did this?!!!"

I ran towards the room. "What's wrong? What happened?"

He pointed at the ceiling. "That…who did that?"

"I did and it's a good thing because it stormed last night."

He tried to move, but couldn't. "I SAID that I was going to fix it."

"Yes, but you hurt yourself and the roof still needed to be fixed."

He looked at me. "When a man says that he's going to do something…you let him do it."

"I understand, Remy, but…"

He interrupted me. "As long as you understand…now, close the door on your way out." Then he closed his eyes, dismissing me. I stood there looking at him for a second, confused, before turning and leaving the room.

I think that the fall bruised more than Remy's back. Not being able to fix the roof and hurting himself left him extremely unhappy. Don't get me wrong, I sympathized with him, but now, on top of all of the other mess that was going on, I had a man with a hurt back. I had too much going on in my life. I didn't have the strength to carry him. He began moping, whining, and complaining, about everything. If I'd taken instruction from my sisters' page book, I would have kicked his ass to the curb, but I wanted so desperately for this to work. Sadly, the only thing that brought me peace was the pills. When he was sleep, there wasn't any complaining and with the silence, I was allowed to focus on finding ways to keep this little roof over our heads.

Chapter 36

I eventually got a job as a Teacher's Assistant at a school close by. I loved having a job. It made me feel like I was making a contribution and accomplishing something. Being around others helped me to forget some of the other stuff that was going on in my life.

While I was away, he was left at home to take care of himself. I don't know what he did all day, but it definitely wasn't trying to find a job or do some chores. Things had gotten so bad that washing his butt wasn't even a priority. He didn't care anymore and if it wasn't in the bottom of a pill bottle, he wasn't interested. He'd turned into something different. He wasn't the person that promised that he would take care of me. I knew that he was in a lot of pain, but the doctors said that he should have went back to "normal" a long time ago, but he never even tried. He sunk deeper into a depression, a place, that I couldn't help him get out of.

It was like living with a person with multiple personalities. He used to take long walks that he called "therapy" - return home, and walk directly into the bathroom without even a "hello." He would spend a few minutes in there and then re-emerge like a completely different person. I never knew who I was talking to from one minute to another, so I avoided talking to him all together.

After working all day, coming home to clean-up and cook, I was too tired to see what was happening right before my eyes, but when we started struggling to pay the bills, I knew that something was wrong.

I confronted him and he wasn't happy about that. "Remy, I need to pay the phone bill. Have you checked the account lately?" I asked, looking at all of the bills that were sitting on the counter.

"Ummmmm, we're going to have to wait until you get paid on Friday," he said, stretching himself across the living room couch.

I walked over and sat next to him. "What happened to the money in the bank?"

He frowned. "Don't ask me…go ask them." He turned his back towards me.

"Remy, does that make any sense." I leaned over, trying to face him.

"What doesn't make any sense is you all up in my face talking about a damn phone bill."

"Remy, I'm not trying to fight with you…I just wanted to know if we could pay the bill?"

He leaned into my face. "Well, I just told you that we couldn't."

I was too tired and frustrated to deal with this. I knew that nothing that I said next was going to put any money into the bank account and continuing this conversation would only agitate him more, so I just stood and left the room. But leaving the room wasn't enough for him. He followed me and continued to argue. I ignored him hoping that he would just go away or wear himself out, but on this particular night, he wanted to make sure that his voice was heard.

I removed my clothes and he said, "You don't know what it's like…"
He was still talking when I went into the bathroom.
"I gave up everything to be with you…"
I jumped in the shower and I could hear him from the other-side of the curtain, "How do you expect me to be a man if I can't take care of you?"
When I was done, he was still talking. I dried myself off.
"It's hard, Grace…it's damn hard."
Once I was dressed, I walked out of the bathroom and was about to climb into bed when he asked, "Grace, do you hear me?"
I have to admit that I was tired of his whining ass and even if I was trying to hide it, the look on my face couldn't. And then it happened…
His hand went up and when it came down, it made contact with my face. It happened so fast

that it left us both in shock. I stared at him while he stood there staring at his hand like he was expecting it to apologize to me. When he realized that it wasn't going to do it, he turned and began to do it himself.

"Grace, I'm so sorry…"

My ear was ringing. I knew that he was talking because his mouth was moving, but I couldn't hear a word that he was saying. I just crawled away from him. He fell to his knees and crawled towards me, but I only crawled further away from him.

"Grace, I'm trying to talk to you…stop moving…I'm sorry…I'm really sorry."

Then I stood and ran into the bathroom and locked the door.

"Grace…Grace…" he said, banging on the door. I walked over to the mirror to look at myself. I saw the red mark that stretched from my cheek to my ear.

"Grace…would you please come out, so that we can talk?"

In that moment, all I could think about was my sisters and the pain that they caused me. I thought that I'd gotten away from that, but now, I was being forced to relive the nightmare with the man that I loved.

I sat on the toilet to think about my next move. I didn't know what to do. For so long, this has been so normal, but I was tired of it. I didn't leave my past behind to start all over again with the person I wanted to spend my future with. I didn't know a lot of things but I knew that I didn't want this.

I knew that I couldn't spend my life in the bathroom. I looked around to see if there was something that I could use to protect myself. I saw a bar of soap, a towel, some toothpaste and two toothbrushes. Unless, I was going to bathe him and brush his teeth, something that he desperately needed right about now, that stuff wasn't going to work. Then I looked down and saw the toilet plunger. I didn't want to use that, but if he hit me again, I was going to "plunge" the hell out of his ass.

As soon as I opened the door, he rushed me; threw his arms around me. He begged and pleaded for my forgiveness. This felt weird. I was used to being hurt by people, but there was never anyone who was sorry for causing me pain. He said that it was a mistake and he promised that it would never happen again, and I believed him because he said the magic words, "I love you."

From that moment on, to keep us from fighting, I cashed my checks and paid the bills myself and any remaining money stayed in my purse. This worked for a while until he started stealing money from me. After that, I never left my purse alone. He'd spent all of the money that his mother gave him and next he went through our bill money. I wasn't going to end-up back on the street and I was going to prevent that at all costs.

Chapter 37

Now, I had another secret... The first slap was just practice. It didn't take much to end-up on the receiving end of another one. If I put a glass on the table without using a coaster, I got slapped. If he couldn't get his medication, I got slapped. If another man looked at me, I got slapped. If I looked at him wrong, I got slapped. If I thought about getting slapped, I got slapped. Just about any action on my part was deserving of the palm of his hand. Sadly, like in my childhood, I dealt with it and even found reasons to justify it. I started to believe that it was my fault because if I had not left my sister's house, we would have never ended-up in this place and he wouldn't have hurt himself; thereby causing him to hurt me. Or maybe it was the pills or maybe it was because he couldn't find a job? I'm sure that he was having a hard time dealing with everything that was going on and maybe this was how he expressed himself – how he dealt with his emotions. I didn't know. I just wanted it to stop.

One day, when I opened the door, she flew passed me. "Hi Peaches...sorry that I can't stay...take care," his mother said before jumping into her car. I walked in to find him sleeping on the couch with an empty bottle in his hand. I took it from him, read the date on the bottle, and realized that the prescription had been filled just a week ago. A month's worth of pills were already gone. I stared at him and saw Nicole. I saw my sisters. I saw everyone who promised not to hurt me, but did. In that moment, I wanted to leave him, but where was I going to go? All I could do was pray that things would change soon.

When he woke up, I handed him the empty bottle. He seemed confused as if he didn't know where he was. After he figured it out, he said, "Hey Baby, where have you been?"

I thought to myself, *I was at work...you know? That's what people do to earn a living.* But I didn't dare say what I was thinking. "Remy, why was your mother here?"

Looking confused, he said, "My mother...she was here? Wow...I must have really been tired."

"She was here and you were asleep," I said.

He looked around the room and continued, "Well she owns the house...sooooooo..."

"That's true, but..." I paused and looked at him. He was "high". The glazed look in his eyes was evidence of that. Talking to him would be like talking to that pillow that held up his head...a waste of freakin' time.

"You know what? I went looking for a job today…yep, ummmmm????" He scratched his head and continued, "What is today?"

My heart sank as I stared at him. "Remy, you need help."

He glanced at the empty bottle and said, "What I need is more pills."

I couldn't believe that he even felt entitled to have an addiction. How can people with no source of income, expect to get high? Spend somebody else's money to get high? Right now, he didn't have 'a pot to piss in or a window to throw it out of' and he's telling me that he needs more pills. He needs to get a damn job.

"Remy…" I began.

"It's just pills for the pain," he said, rubbing his back.

"Remy, the doctor said that you need to get back to living or your back will never get better. No one is ever 'whole' after an injury, but these pills…" I sighed. "They just have to stop."

"I know, I know, and I promise you…next week, I'm going to stop."

"Next week?" I asked.

"Yep, Baby…next week…I promise." He kissed me on my forehead and left the room. I decided to give him until next week and if he didn't change, I would have to do something drastic.

331

Well, 'next week' came and went. Next month came and went. He didn't have a job, but he never seemed to run out of the pills. I didn't know how he was able to pay for them and I was afraid to ask. Every day, I checked the house to see if anything was missing and this wasn't difficult to do since we didn't have much, but nothing was gone.

Now, I was dealing with abuse, lies, and lack of trust and none of this made for a strong or healthy relationship. I couldn't take it anymore. I knew that I couldn't force him to change – he would have to do it for himself, but he had to change or it was over.

I was at work one day when my cellphone rang. I excused myself and went out into the hallway to answer it. "Hello…" the voice on the phone was babbling incoherently.
"What's wrong? Slow down…I can't understand what you're saying."
He took a deep breath and said, "They found her…she's dead."

Chapter 3.8

*T*he loss of Nicole was very difficult for his family. It was really hard for me too. Nicole was the first person that I called my friend. Because of her, I met Remy. At this point, I wasn't sure how I felt about Remy, but I really cared about Nicole. To think that they found her in the park with a needle sticking out of her arm was devastating. That is such a tragic way to go. She deserved better than that. I don't know what made her do it, but clearly she was desperate to get away from something or someone. She was strong, but I guess, not strong enough. Her demons proved to be more than she could handle.

Her death left me thinking about my own life and my own mortality. Nicole decided to suffer in silence. She walked around like she didn't have a care in the world; always putting on a brave "front", but on the inside, she was crying out for help. She was a child who needed someone to hold her and tell her that everything was going to be okay. And while drugs numbed the pain, they couldn't get rid of the source of it. Every time that she came "down", "it" was right there, waiting for her.

One night, I decided to go to the park. I thought that if I went at night, there would be no one there and I could have a moment to talk to her for the last time. As I entered the park, I could see the Merry-Go-Round spinning in circles. As I approached it, I saw a body lying across it. When I got closer, I saw that it was D.J. "K" or whatever his name is.

"What are you doing here?" I asked.

"I could ask you the same thing?" he said, slurring his words.

I looked at his hand and saw that he was holding a bottle of something.

"She's gone, Peaches," He offered me some of its contents.

I put up my hand, "Naw, I'm good."

"Yep...my girl...gone...," he said.

"Yeah, I know," I said.

He looked at me. "What am I going to do, Peaches?"

I shrugged my shoulders. "I don't know."

He put the bottle up against his mouth and swallowed until the bottle was completely empty. He burped. "What am I going to do?" he asked, again.

"Sobriety might be a good beginning..."

He continued. "Why? Why bother? Without her, I'm nothing. She believed in me..."

I didn't respond.

"And then I hear that she's been cheating on me with some other nig...," he paused. Even though he was drunk, he was smart enough to know that if he finished that "word", he was getting his ass whupped. The look on my face confirmed that. He fixed it right away. "...with some other brotha."

I stared at him.

He continued. "I know that you think that I'm a joke...another white boy acting black...but that is not the case at all..."

Confused, I said, "It's not?"

"No, being "Black" is a state of mind...a level of consciousness...if I think it, therefore I am."

More Crackhead logic. I thought to myself. "It must be nice...to wake-up and call yourself "black" like you just woke up and put on a hat...wear it as long as it's in style, take it off when it isn't and then you can go back to your life...a life without pain...without struggle...without fear...Your "black" is a mask, a fashion statement, a trend...while mine is real. I can't take mine's off and I don't want to, but what you're doing is not fair to those who are being killed, discriminated against...all because of the color of their skin..." His eyes began to fill with tears. I began to feel sorry for him. It must be so hard to lose someone who didn't see his lies; who didn't see his flaws. All she saw was a man who loved her with all of her lies and imperfections. Then I thought about what she said about love. I laughed to myself then I wrapped my arms around his shoulders. I decided to save the history lesson for another day. I looked up at the sky and said, "Do you see it?"

He looked up and said, "What?"

"Angels…," I said, smiling and remembering the last time that we were all at the playground together.

He laughed and rested his head on my shoulder. "Yeah, I see her."

I couldn't imagine what Remy was going through. He shut down any emotions or hope that he had left. He didn't want to talk and I understood that, but I was afraid for him. He was already dealing with an addiction and I couldn't imagine how her death would effect it. We were already dealing with so much and now this.

One day, he decided that it was best that he went back home for a while to help his parents get through everything. At least, until they laid

Nicole to rest. I had to admit that I was happy. Not because of Nicole's death, but I was glad that he was leaving for a while. He couldn't pack his bags fast enough. All I could think about was the peace of mind that I would have – something that I hadn't had in a very long time. I used this time to heal and to think about what had been going on for the past few years of my life. Being able to do it without all of the distractions or fear of setting him off again helped a lot too.

That morning, after he left, the mail arrived. I was sorting through it when I saw a letter that was addressed to Remy from his mother. I didn't open it because it wasn't addressed to me, but I couldn't say that I wasn't curious. I thought that it was odd that she would mail him a letter when he was staying with her. I sat it down on the table and walked away, but something about it was calling me, begging me to open it. At first, I held it up to the light like they do on TV, but I couldn't see anything. I thought about other ways of opening it without detection, but I knew that somehow he would find out. I walked away from it again, but again, it called me. *Please open me.* Finally, I decided to open it. *Fuck it. All he could do was hit me again.* So I ripped it open. I read it. It was only one sentence.

A bond between a mother and her son is very special.

I held the letter, reading the sentence over and over again, but no matter how many times that I read it, it still didn't make any sense. The words started to sound familiar. I thought to myself. *Where have I heard this before?* I wanted to let it go but something about the words stayed with me. I tried to go on with my day, but I had to know what this was all about. I picked up the phone and called him, but hung up immediately because I was afraid that she may overhear the conversation. So with much hesitation, I decided to go over there. I figured that this would be a good way to pay my condolences too and since we were at her house, he would hesitate fighting with me.

When I got over there, I expected to see the house full of people stopping by to pay their "respects," but there was no one there. I didn't put much into it at first. I walked up to the door and noticed that the house was completely dark. I was going to ring the doorbell, but when I looked at the door, I noticed that it was slightly open. *Who would leave their door open in Chicago?* I thought to myself. Quietly, I called out to him, "Remy...Remy..." but there was no answer. As I walked through the house, I noticed a light coming from under the bathroom door. As I approached it, I could hear water splashing and someone whispering. Again, I called him. "Remy…Remy…" but still there was no answer. I walked up to the door and began to turn the knob. When I opened it, I fell backwards. I couldn't believe my eyes.

His mother saw me and said, "Come in and sit down."

Wait…what?

"Remy, move the towel off of the toilet so that Peaches can sit down," she instructed.

I rubbed my eyes. "What?"

Remy glanced at me. He put some soap on the wash cloth and proceeded to wash her.

I stared at him and then back at her. *What the hell is happening? Am I really seeing this shit?*

"So how do you like the house?" she asked.

Snapping out of my daze, I repeated, "What?"

She asked me again. "So how do you like the house?"

I looked around the bathroom hoping that I was lost or somewhere locked in a bad dream.

She lifted her arm and he washed under it. He slowly ran the towel over her breast.

I looked at Remy. "Remy, what the hell are you doing?!!!"

He gazed at me and then looked away. My eyes filled with tears, but through blurred vision, I

could see them sitting on the floor next to him –
a bottle of pills.

"Remy….nooooo…," I said.

"Don't talk to him…talk to me," she said,
standing and bending over. He placed more soap
on the towel and slid the towel between her legs.
"Make sure that you clean it good, son.
Especially, if you want more of Mama's money."
He cleaned her again. She turned and sat back
down into the water. I slapped myself. After
realizing how much it hurt to slap myself, I
walked up to him and forced him to look at me.
"Remy, what the hell are you doing?!!!!!" He
didn't answer.

I must be losing my freaking mind.
"REMY???!!!!

He didn't respond.

Tired of the freak show, I stood and ran out of
the room.

"Make sure that you lock the front door behind
you!" she yelled.

Later that evening, I heard the front door open.
He dropped his bags and he came into the
bedroom where I was sitting staring into the

340

darkness. He didn't say anything. He didn't remove his wet clothing. He just climbed in the bed and fell fast asleep.

That was the craziest thing I've ever seen and I've seen crazy. I wanted to talk about it, but how do you even begin to approach the subject. "Ummmmmm, hey Remy…how long have you been washing your Mama's ass? "Ummmmm Remy, was it just bathing or did you have to have sex with her too?" And how do you ask a person these questions when they've been hitting you? And what happens next? How do you move on from that? Do you continue to have a relationship with a pill-popping girlfriend-beater who may be a victim of sexual abuse? That's a lot of stuff. I know that I wasn't in the position to judge him, but *damn*. We were both really messed up. This was too much for even me. I was prepared to talk to him that morning, but as I tried to think of the right words to say, he jumped up, walked out of the bedroom, and said, "We have a funeral to go to."

Chapter 39

An over-dose is how she met her demise.
Standing over her body as it lay peacefully in the
casket wrapped in white satin linens, she looked
like an angel. For the first time in all of the years
that I've known her, she actually looked 'happy'
- like she finally found the perfect 'high'. Sadly,
it would be her last one.

I glanced at Remy who wasn't crying as
he stared at her. He had a really weird look on his
face. I touched his shoulder and said, "Remy?"
He looked down at my hand, and said, "Let's
go."

We waited outside for his parents. When
they exited the building, his mother and I
exchanged glances, but didn't speak to each
other. I looked over at the man that was walking
beside her. I'd never seen their father until that
day. I can see why they kept him a secret.

The gap in their ages was visibly
apparent. While she looked like a woman who
was in the prime of her life, he looked like a man
who had been cursed by life instead of blessed
with it. He looked angry and tired. He was stoic
- emotionless. People spoke and waved at him,
but he didn't return the favor. He was cold.

Maybe it was because his daughter had died or maybe he'd seen some of the same things I've seen, but as I looked at him, I couldn't help but wonder if he knew what was happening right under his own roof. I also couldn't help but wonder if he was a willing participant in the "madness" or was he a victim of it too.

I stepped to the side to allow Remy to speak to his parents, privately. They spoke for such a long time that I decided to take off my shoes and sit barefoot on the bench in front of the church. I looked over there a few times to find her staring at me. I looked away in disgust. I would have loved to confront her, but this was not the time nor the place. Like with Remy, I would have to postpone "the conversation" until another time.

It was so hot outside. I was fanning myself with my hat when from the left, I saw her coming, so fast that I didn't have time to respond. "BOO, HOO, HOO…BOO, HOO, HOO…," she said, pretending to cry. A few of the mourners were staring at her. She was making a complete ass of herself. I wanted to run, but I didn't want to embarrass Remy, so I sat and prepared myself for the shit storm that was headed my way.

She pretended to blow her nose in a handkerchief. "BOO, HOO, HOO…so tragic… She was so young."

Where's the volume button on this chick?
"Lower your voice." I said, extremely frustrated with her presence. "What do you want, Raven, and how in the hell do you keep finding me?"

"You're my baby sister...it's my job to know where you are."

"Well, I need you to leave."

"And why do you want that? I'm here to console you...show you that I care."

"By popping up in my life when you feel like it? I'm starting to think that you got one of those tracking devices on me."

"Yes, I do...you know, like the kind that they stick on dogs...," she said, trying to get on my nerves, not realizing that she already was.

I saw Remy staring in my direction. I wanted to get rid of her before she made a scene, but it was already too late. "Look Raven, it was nice to see you, but you can stop doing what sisters do. Ivy told me that y'all spent the money."

She had a surprised look on her face. "I didn't spend anything and she didn't give me anything."

"Well, that's what she told me after I went to the bank and there was nothing left but a hundred dollars."

There were daggers in her eyes. "That dirty bitch."

I was confused. "Ummmmm, I thought that the three of you spent it all."

Her eyes widened and she said, "Regan...she has Regan."

"Yeah, they both live together." After I said that, she slithered through the crowd like a snake and then she was quickly out of sight.

Remy walked up to me and asked me, "What was that about?"

I smiled and said, "I think the left-hand just found out that the right-hand stole its money."

That night, Remy barely spoke. We both had a long day, so we both went to bed early. During the night, I turned over and reached for him, but he wasn't there. I got up and went looking for him. When I arrived in the kitchen, I found him sitting in the dark. I was about to turn on the light, but decided not to – clearly, there was a reason why he chose to sit in the darkness. I pulled out a chair across from him. "Are you okay?"

He opened the pill bottle and emptied the pills all over the table. I could hear them scatter all over the place. Then he slammed the empty bottle onto the table. "I'm not going to die that way."

I didn't say anything. I just listened.

"My sister and I never got along. On the surface, it may have looked like we hated each other, but really deep down, I think we cared about each other..." he sighed and continued. "I wasn't there for her. I knew that she was sick and I wasn't there. And I have to admit, that my anger kept me from being the brother that she needed me to be. It's hard to love someone who doesn't give love or show love, but I was still her brother...I should have swallowed my pride and reached out to her."

Finally, I spoke. "You can't blame yourself for what happened to her."

"I don't...believe me. I know that nothing I could have done would have stopped her especially if she didn't want to be stopped. I know that. But I saw her laying there in that box and I thought to myself, 'That could easily be me' and I don't want that. I'm saying all this to say...That I love you and you deserve better than this. I made a promise to you and I'm going to keep it." He swooped the pills into his hands, walked over to the sink, poured them down the drain, and turned on the water. After a few seconds, he turned it off and sat back down across from me. "What's wrong?" he asked.

"Remy, I'm glad that you're giving up the pills…I am, but there's some other stuff that we need to discuss."

He looked away.

"You hurt me…"

He interrupted. "I know…I don't even have any excuse for it. I've been hurt all of my life…I had no right to do that to you…no right…and you may not believe this, but I am sorry and I'll never do it again…and I know that it'll be hard to believe me, but I just hope that you give me another chance…"

"And…?" I said.

He sighed. "There's shit in our lives that we wish never happened…but it does and you want to forget it but it becomes a part of who you are…because it won't let you go."

"What won't let you go?"

"All of it…the pain…the memories…the fear…the secrets…my mother…all of it."

I rubbed my forehead trying to get the image out of my head. "Remy…Remy…we are not talking about an ex-girlfriend who dumped you or a motherfucker that stole your bike when you were a kid…that was…is…your mother. Mamas don't do that stuff to their kids. At least, my Mama didn't…You should have called the police…"

348

"First, when you think this mess is normal then it's normal...and I don't think it's against the law to see your mother naked...to wash her..."

When he said it out loud, for the first time, I think he realized how sick all of it was.

"Remy, inappropriate touching is abuse..."

"But I was the one touching her," he said.

"But she introduced that to you, encouraged it, and allowed it...that's abuse...isn't it?" I asked.

We both knew what that term meant and saying it made us both uncomfortable.

"I know...," he sighed. "But that's...but that's..."

I took a deep breath and interrupted him. "But that's messed-up."

"I know...I know..."

I had to address the "elephant in the room" because no matter what, the "elephant" wasn't going away. "Remy, did you have sex with your mother?"

He looked at me. "No, it never went that far, but..."

I interrupted him again. "But what, Remy? I watched you wash your mother's ass...your mother's ass...who does that?"

He didn't respond.

"Remy, look at me...I need you to imagine what that must have been like...must have felt like to me. Can you imagine coming home one day to find your son washing my ass? Can you?"

He shook his head.

"That was some messed-up shit…you should have told me. Do you think that I wouldn't understand? ME? If anyone could understand… it's me."

"Do you understand, Grace…look at your face. That is not the face of a person who understands."

He was right. This was too crazy - even for me.

"And how do you think I should have told you? Ummmmm Grace, your life is messed-up, but guess what? I'm a man who bathes his mother…"

I shook my head in agreement because there was no good way of telling someone that.

He continued. "It's what we were taught…it's what we did."

"You and Nicole?" I asked.

"Me and Nicole," he answered. "Why do you think she got high?"

To get the shit out of her head. I thought to myself.

"Did you…with Nicole?" I asked.

"No, that never happened…and the stuff with my mother…I can't really explain it…but she's my mother…I love her and in her own way, she loves us…"

My head was spinning. "Remy, I need you to stop a minute and think. Now, I may have only recently figured out what love is, but this is not love. I know that a child will love a person…" I paused for a second to think about what I was saying. "….a child, an adult, will love someone who causes them pain…I'm a victim of it…you're a victim of it and there are hundreds, even thousands more, who are victims of it and while love can cause you pain, you have to know that it's not supposed to cause THIS kind of pain. Look at me, I have three sisters who hate me for no other reason than the fact that I was born. None…I've never done anything to any of them, but love them. You know what I got for loving them? I got hurt, a lot. Look at you…you are defending a woman who has clearly convinced herself that if she doesn't have sex with her kids then what she's doing is normal – a loving bond between a mother and her child, but having a child take a towel and wash her…wash her between her legs…especially, when she's capable of doing the shit herself…come on now…that's some sick shit…I'm sorry…"

He looked so confused – like a man who'd been locked up for a long time and have now been set free. "But…but…I needed the pills…"

"But it was because of her that you needed the pills. Think about it."

He paused for a second and said, "But, Grace, she's my mother…"

I shook my head. I couldn't take it anymore. "Remy, she used you…why? I don't know. I've been through my share of bad stuff…been through it…but at some point, we have to realize that it's bad…say it, own it, and then fix it."

He took a deep breath and said, "It's fucked up."

"Yes, it is, but you lived through it…Nicole didn't."

We stopped for a moment to process that – to accept the fact that their mother was behind Nicole's death.

I looked at him. I could tell that he wanted it to be over – this conversation – all of it. "But it's over now. All of it…my family…your family…it's all over now."

He stood to walk away. "Is it, Grace? Is it ever really over?"

I thought about his question for a minute. "Remy, all we have…you and I…is right now…that's all that we got…we have to take care of each other…one day at a time."

"One day at a time?" he asked.

"Yep, one day at a time…" I stood and took his hand. "Now, let's go to bed."

When we walked into the bedroom, I began to climb into the bed. I watched Remy slowly get undressed. My mind drifted back to a place of pain. I closed my eyes and thought to myself, *You are here now…let the past go.*

When he climbed into bed, he glanced at me and said, "Goodnight."

I looked at him as he tucked himself under the blankets. He turned his back to me. I took a deep breath and then slowly slid next to him. I nuzzled my face into the crease of his back and inhaled. *No candy.* I thought to myself. I wrapped my arms around him and fell fast asleep.

The next morning, I woke up with the worst headache in the world. It felt like my heartbeat had traveled north to my forehead. I tried rubbing my temples, but that only made it worse. I closed my eyes because attempting to open them made me want to scream, but I needed to do something because I couldn't begin my day wishing that someone would open my skull, take my brain out into the backyard and shoot the hell out of it.

I glanced over to find Remy resting peacefully. I carefully climbed out of bed being careful not to wake him. I went into the bathroom to find something, but the cabinet's contents only consisted of lubricant, Jock itch cream, and a box of expired colloidal oatmeal that I used to stave off my eczema. I became frustrated, because none of these things were going to work. I squinted my eyes and followed the walls down the hall into the kitchen. I looked into the cabinets, but there was nothing for pain and my purse came up empty as well.

As I walked passed the kitchen table, I saw something white sitting in the middle of it. I walked over to find one pill left behind from the night before. I looked at it. Then I walked over and picked it up. I was about to throw it out, but instead, I looked at it; long and hard. I knew that this pill would relieve my pain as it did for Remy, but it was his prescription medicine. I saw what it did to him. As I tried to focus, I could hear and feel the conga drums playing loudly in my head. Then I thought about running to the local drugstore to pick-up some over-the-counter remedy, but I wasn't feeling well enough to leave the house, so again, I stared at it. *How bad could it be?* Remy was addicted because he'd taken a lot of them over an extended period of time. This was only one pill. *No, I can't.* I thought to myself, but as I shook my head "No" I was quickly reminded of the vice-grip that was squeezing the crap out of my head. I stood to walk it over to its watery grave, but when I did, the headache "bitch-slapped" me in the front, back and side of my head. I collapsed back into the chair and without thinking about it a second longer, I tossed it into the back of my mouth and swallowed.

At first, I didn't feel anything. Then I began to feel really relaxed – like I was floating on "Cloud Nine." I began to giggle – not because anything was particularly funny, but clearly something was because I couldn't stop. The headache had packed-up and left. I was feeling really good. Then I became tired, so I decided to rest my head on the kitchen table. Suddenly, I heard someone call out my name. "Peaches." Slowly, I opened my eyes and answered, "Yes." They called me again, "Peaches."

"Yes," I said, again, but there was no one. I closed my eyes and was about to rest again when someone tapped me on the shoulder. I looked up. This time, I recognized the voice. "Daddy," I said looking across the table.

"Peaches," he said, smiling

Confused, I said, "Daddy, I thought that you were dead."

He smiled and said, "I am."

Rubbing my eyes, I said, "Then…how…why are you here?"

He smiled and said, "I'm not."

Shaking my head, I said, "Huh? But I see you…right there…"

He smiled.

I began to pat myself. "Am I…am I dead?"

"No, Baby-Girl…you're not dead," he said.

"Daddy, I'm really tired…I'm going to lay my head down…and take a nap."

He smiled, again. "You do that, Baby Girl."

"Night, Daddy," I said, resting my face against the cold-hard table.

"Night, Baby-Girl," he said.

When I woke up, I was swimming in my own drool. I lifted my head and there was a paper towel stuck to my face. "Daddy? Daddy?" I said, looking around the room.

He said, "Sorry, Sweetie…I'm not your daddy."

I pulled the paper towel from the side of my face. "What the hell happened?"

Remy was putting some bacon into a skillet. The skillet was so hot that when the bacon hit it, hot grease flew everywhere. He ducked to dodge the flying grease. "I came in here and you were slobbering all over the table...I put the paper down to keep you from drowning."

Confused, I said, "Where's my daddy?"

"I think that he's still in Heaven," Remy said, cracking an egg and putting it into a bowl.

I rubbed my head again, "Son of a Bitch."

He continued, "You must have really been tired."

I looked at him and said, "No, I had a headache and..." Suddenly, I remembered what happened. I couldn't tell him that I took one of his pills. He would never let me live that down. "Yeah, you're right...that's it...I was tired."

He smiled. "If you want to go and lay down for a while, you can...I can bring you breakfast."

"Ummmmm, thanks," I said, standing. I walked into the bedroom, climbed under the blankets, and immediately fell back to sleep.

The next morning, I woke up with my head face down into a plate full of cold bacon and eggs. Then suddenly, the loud drumbeat of the headache that I thought that I'd gotten rid of the morning before was unpacking and settling in for the day. "Son of a Bitch," I mumbled, before I tossed some bacon and eggs into my mouth, chewed slowly, and then I went back to sleep.

Chapter 40

It was easier said than done...The only thing that you should quit cold-turkey is eating cold turkey. He thought that he could get up, declare that he was going to quit and that's it. Even I wasn't stupid enough to believe that. For an addict, drugs are like air - they need it. While many just quit, they all agree that it is not easy to do.

The next few weeks were interesting. It was 98 degrees outside and he was turning on the heat. Then, it was too hot and he was stripping in the middle of the floor. He was having terrible mood swings. He was happy one minute and sad the next. He couldn't eat. He couldn't sleep, but he did manage to get on my nerves and stay on them. While I was proud of him for deciding to quit, I was starting to wonder if we were both going through withdrawal.

One morning, he jumped out of bed, excited about life and prepared to take on the world. "Baby, I'm going to look for a job today." I pretended to be optimistic. "Oh really, baby, that's fantastic...huh-huh...yep, fan-tas-tic." He ran around looking for the want-ads, poured himself a cup of orange juice and he was really going at it, but I knew that it wouldn't last long.

I was getting ready to go to work. He was sitting at the table, staring at a classified ad that was looking for customer service reps. I grabbed my purse and keys and was headed out of the door when I heard, "Nicole would have been the perfect customer service representative."

I dropped my head, glanced at my watch, and decided that I was going to be a little late today.

I turned around, walked back to the table, and sat down.

He continued, "Yep, she was a 'people-person.'"

It took everything in me to contain my laughter because Nicole was a lot of things, a 'people-person' wasn't one of them.

He began to reminisce. "I remember one time, she took all of my underwear and cut the crotches out of them. I walked around for a month with my "stuff" hanging out of the hole and rubbing against my legs. The weird thing is, when our mother did the laundry and she found the holes, she didn't replace them right away because she thought that I was doing it on purpose just to get on her nerves. Her way of punishing me was by making me walk around in them." He paused and continued, "Why would any man want their 'junk' hanging out of their underwear? Man that crap hurt...until I made the holes bigger." He smiled.

It took me a minute to get the joke until I realized what he was talking about. I smiled.

"Yeah, I miss that bitch." A tear rolled down his cheek. "You know what, baby, I'm going to lay down for a minute...I will look for a job tomorrow, okay?"

I nodded my head. "Yeah, baby...tomorrow."

I could tell that it was starting to get to him. His emotions fluctuated from sadness, to anger, to jealousy. He was dealing with too much and he wasn't willing to admit that he needed help to get through all of the stuff that he was going through. It wasn't more evident than one night, when we were just hanging out. I could tell that something was wrong. The tension in the room was thick enough to cut with a knife, but I was really trying to make things lite by making him laugh. I quickly found out that when someone is suffering, it'll reveal itself no matter how hard they try to hide it or how hard you try to help them to forget it.

"So...there we were walking out of the building...she trips and goes flying halfway across the parking lot...she breaks her heel...her wig flies off...and she lands...ass all up in the air...then this guy walks over..."

It was like he'd just awakened from a daze. "What guy?" he asked.

361

"Oh, I don't know. Some guy…but anyway…" I said, trying to get to the funny part.

"Was he cute?"

"Who?" I asked.

"The guy?" he asked.

"Huh? I wasn't really paying him any attention. Now, can I get back to my story?" I asked.

"No, you can tell me about the guy that you can't seem to remember if he was sexy or not, but you remember that he was there."

"Wait…what…sexy?" I was completely confused.

"Did you just say that he was sexy?" he asked, with a wide-eye look on his face.

"Dude, you are trippin'…I can see that you are on some 'special' shit, so I'm going to leave you here to deal with it." I stood to walk away when he grabbed my arm and pulled me towards him.

"You better not cheat on me." Then he raised his hand.

I looked at his hand and said, "You promised."

He looked at me, he looked up at his hand, and then he let me go.

Chapter 41

*T*he next morning, I woke up "tired." Not tired because I worked all day. Not tired because I'd run a marathon or anything. No, I was tired of all of the bullshit in my life. I had been taking the bullshit for so long that "bullshit" had become my normal. I didn't want it anymore. I was tired of making excuses for it. I went from one bad thing to another, "assimilating" as I went along. I learned to get along – to not cause waves, but what has that gotten me? I didn't run away from all of the madness to end-up making love to it every night.

As I contemplated this, the anger inside of me grew more. Today, I was taking a stand. While this would not fix the other battles in my life, I was going to win this one. I looked over at him; sleeping peacefully and knew exactly what I needed to do. I got up, walked into the bathroom and stared at the woman in the mirror. I was no longer the child who had to keep her mouth shut or else. I was a grown-ass woman and today, he needed to learn that. I looked down and saw a jar of Vaseline sitting on the bathroom sink. I took a glob of it and smeared it all over my face to protect my face from scratches and bruises. Somebody was getting their ass whupped today. Either I was getting my ass whupped or he was getting his ass whupped but SOMEBODY was getting their ass whupped TODAY.

I quietly walked down the hall. I looked into the drawer and found the biggest knife that was in there. I slowly crept back into the bedroom and stood over him. He was laying there sleeping, peacefully. As I stood there, I wondered if he was dreaming about me. Slowly, I climbed on top of him and using my legs, I pinned his arms down. He began to stir. Slowly, he opened his eyes to find me staring at him. Groggily, he said, "Wha…what are you doing?" I patted the blade in the palm of my hand – careful not to cut myself. I said, "Remy, I've spent most of my life in fear, but I'm not doing that shit no more."

Afraid, he said, "I'm sorry…can we talk about this?"

I looked at him. "Ain't we talking?"

Trying to find the right words, he said, "I mean…I mean…"

"You mean what, Remy? What?"

He struggled to free himself. "I mean…" he stammered.

"You told me that you would never hit me again and then I look around and your hand was in the air again."

"But I didn't hit you…," he said.

"And I'm supposed to wait until you do?" I asked.

"No, I'm not saying that," he said.

"Well, let's call this an intervention…"

He finally realized that he wasn't going anywhere and stopped moving. "An intervention?"

"Yep, an intervention…," I said, looking at the knife.

I placed the blade against his throat so that he understood the "seriousness" of this moment. The knife was so sharp that it accidentally nicked his skin. I pulled the knife back. I touched the spot where I cut him and showed him the blood. His eyes widened. I continued. "Look…we have both been through a lot of shit, but we are not going to become like the people who have hurt us. We are not going to be afraid of each other. That is not love. That is not respect. That is fear and I won't do it. I don't want to live my life worrying about you hitting me again and you don't want to have to worry about getting stabbed. I leaned in and asked, "Do we understand each other?"

"Yes, we understand…I understand."

"Good," I said. "Now, go back to sleep."

The whole day, we barely said two words to each other. You could tell that he was taking that "wake-up call" seriously. I'm sure that he wondered if I was still carrying that knife around. I'd already put it down, and knew exactly where it was just in case we needed to have another "conversation."

That night, I was awakened to the sound of whimpering. Groggily, I reached out for him, but he wasn't lying next to me. "Remy?" I said, wiping the crust from my eyes. "Remy?" The whimpering became louder. I sat up, threw the covers back, swung my legs, and accidentally kicked something.

"Ouch," he said, grabbing the back of his head. I climbed down and sat next to him. "Oh, I'm so sorry, Remy."

"It's okay," he said, rubbing the back of his head. "I deserved it."

For a moment, we sat and stared outside at the full moon that was staring back at us.

"What are we doing, Grace?" he asked.

"We are sitting on a cold ass floor in the dark..." I looked around the room to make sure that none of our furry roommates were home.

"No, Peaches...what am I doing?"

"Remy...it's the middle of the night and..." I stopped and looked at him. His eyes were swollen. Clearly, he'd been crying for a while. "I don't know, Remy."

"Look at me, Grace. I'm a fuckin' mess. How did I end up here?"

I thought about his mother, his sister, the drugs, the "tree incident" and said, "Well..."

"Peaches, I need help," he said. "I need help. I've been trying to fix this shit on my own, but I can't."

I smiled because those were the words that I'd been waiting to hear for such a long time.

"It would be so easy if none of this ever happened...I wish that I could go back and erase it all...fix my mother...fix my family...bring Nicole back...fix everything," he said.

I thought about that for a moment. *While I couldn't bring Nicole back, maybe it was time that I confronted his mother. I couldn't fix her, but I could tell her how I feel about what I saw that night.*

"Remy, come on…get in the bed. It's going to be okay…try to get some rest."

He stood and began to climb up onto the bed. "Where are you going?" he asked.

"I need to go and talk to a friend about a problem."

Standing in their front yard, I took a deep breath and walked up to the door. Again, the door was left open. *They are really going to regret leaving their door open.* I thought to myself. As I walked down the hall, I heard a loud sound coming from one of the bedrooms. I peeked my head inside to find Remy's father snoring and resting peacefully. As I continued down the hall, I saw a sliver of light coming from under the bathroom door. As I turned the knob, she said in a sexy high-pitched voice, "Remy, is that you?"

This motherfucker. I thought to myself. When I walked in, I saw her surrounded by a tub full of white bubbles. She looked up. "Oh it's you, Peaches...where's Remy?" she asked.

He's not coming back, you bitch. I thought to myself. "Oh Remy...he's at home sleeping."

She took the washcloth and poured some water over her skin. "Well, how can I help you, Ms. Peaches?"

How urban? I thought to myself. "Well, I was thinking about that night..."

She interrupted. "Oh, that night...Peaches, my dear, you shouldn't try to understand the relationship that a son has with his mother. You see...I am the first woman in his life. He fell in love with me before he fell in love with anyone else. My vagina is the first one that he saw...my breasts are the first ones that he sucked...I am his first lady..."

The fuck?!!!! This bitch is nuts. I could not believe that this woman had somehow taken her role as his mother and flipped it into something sick. I couldn't even speak because my brain had completely shut itself down. All I could do was look at her.

She continued. "Yes, he's living with you, but who do you think he's dreaming about? He dreams about me."

No, he has nightmares about you...you crazy BITCH!

"Yes, I loved his sister, but there is something about Remy...he is special...he makes me feel..."

Oh my, Gawd...Oh my, Gawd...STOP IT!!!!!!

She tried washing her back. "Peaches, could you do me a favor?" She extended the hand that was holding the washcloth.

I looked at her. I looked at the washcloth. I thought about Remy and Nicole. I thought about my sisters, and said, "Sure, I'll do you a favor."

"Awwwwww...you're such a 'Peach'...now, wash it good, okay?"

Oh, I'm going to wash it alright. I took the towel and kneeled down beside the tub. I took the bar of soap from her, and said, "Mrs....you know what? I don't know your name...your children never told me your name."

"It's Cruella..."

Of course, it is. I thought to myself. "Well, Mrs. Cruella...," I said, applying the towel to her back.

"Just Cruella...and lower, please."

I looked at her and smiled. "You know...," I began, but decided that she wasn't even worth the energy that was necessary to explain to her why what she did to her kids was wrong. In that moment, I just wanted her to be gone from his life; from our lives. I looked at the washcloth and bar of soap. She turned to me and asked, "Why did you stop?" She took some of the water into her palms and poured it over her skin.

Something in me snapped. I looked at her. *I only wanted to talk to her. My intentions were to stop by, tell her how much of a horrible person she is and leave, but this bitch...THIS BITCH RIGHT HERE? She deserves to die.* I took the bar of soap and shoved it into her mouth, passed her teeth, and into the back of her throat. She began flailing her arms – scratching and clawing at me. In my mind, I kept telling myself that this was wrong, but it just felt so right. She kept struggling. I took the washcloth, dipped it in water and then placed it over her face and I held it there. She kept struggling. Water was splashing everywhere as she kicked – trying to get out of the tub, but I held her there with all of my strength, with every breath, every pore of my being, I held her there. A wave of emotions swept over me. Tears rolled down my face. I started to cry so hard. She continued to struggle and then, suddenly, there was nothing. I removed the washcloth. I looked down at her as she looked up at me. I watched as my tears dropped into the bath water. I stood and dried myself with the towel. As I walked down the hall, I noticed that the loud noise that was coming from their bedroom had stopped.

Nervously, I approached the door. When I looked inside, I saw their father sitting on the side of the bed. I saw a spark of light in the darkness and then the flicker from a flame. He placed the match on the end of something and then put it up to his mouth. He inhaled and looked at me, covered in bath water. He exhaled and said, "Make sure that you lock the door behind you."

Chapter 42

*T*here was always a shadow looming over us. As long as my sisters were around, I knew that I would never be at peace, but I didn't let that stop us from living. Eventually, we did move. We found a small starter home in a quiet suburban neighborhood. It was a "cookie-cutter" that sat in a cul-de-sac surrounded by a lot of trees. It was a step up from what we came from, but because it sat next to water, we couldn't avoid all of the "creature" comforts that came with it. At night, you could hear the "squatters" run across the floor. We caught a lot of them, but there was one that was too cute to kill. I named him, "Blinky" after the fish that I had as a child. It used to piss Remy off that I would feed him, but after a while, he became my pet. As long as he stayed out of Remy's way, he didn't complain.

We thought that no one could find us in our new home. Soon we found that we thought wrong. Technology can be a friend or a foe. Every time you "click" on something, you leave behind digital pieces of cheese making it easy for all of the "rats" of the world to find you.

As a kid, one thing that I could count on, along with eating the exact same cereal from age eight to age thirteen, was my sisters, lurking and looking for ways to torture me. Not like Remy's addiction, being mean wasn't something that you quit cold-turkey. Unless there were other victims in-between, I knew that they will always search-out their "go-to"…their favorite one. I often wondered what they were doing with all of that pent-up-anger. The quote about "keeping your enemies close" definitely applied to my life. At least when I saw them, I knew what they were up to or at least I thought I did.

One day, I was in the grocery store in my old 'hood.' I was in the feminine hygiene products aisle when I overheard two women talking about a woman who stole one of their men. She called that woman every name in the book – some I hadn't even heard of. She was hurt by her husband's betrayal, but more upset that the "floosy" had sex with her man in their bed. I was there to get tampons, not to be all-up in somebody else's business, but I have to admit that I leaned-in closer to listen when she said,

"Called me by her name when we were making love…can you believe that shit?"

"Gurl, nooooooo," the other lady said.

"Yes," she said.

They went on and on until one of the women said, "If I ever see that bitch again, I'm going to kill her."

Boy, I really felt sorry for that woman.

They saw me listening. One woman said, "Girl, let's go…folks all up in your business."

The other woman looked at me and said, "Hey girl…"

I smiled. "Ummmmmm….hey." I said, embarrassed that I got caught being nosey. "Do I know you?"

"Naw, girl…but do you know someone name Regan?"

I was afraid to say "yes" because I wasn't sure if she'd done something stupid or owed somebody some money. I hesitated and said, "Yeah, I know her. What did she do?"

She paused and leaned towards me to get a better look. "Man, y'all look just alike…"

Why did she have to say that?

"What's your name?" she asked.

"My name is Grace, but people call me…" I paused. It was weird. As I said that my name was Grace, I didn't really feel anything, but as I was about to say "Peaches" the painful memories

375

associated with it popped up in my head. "My name is Grace."

"Oh okay…," she had a weird look on her face like she knew that I was lying about something.

I took a deep breath and said, "They also call me Pea…Pea…Peaches."

She smiled. "Interesting, she told me about Raven and Ivy…"

I'm not surprised. I thought to myself. "I'm the youngest."

"Oh okay…but no… she didn't do anything. We used to work together. I'm just so sorry about what happened to her…how is she anyway?"

Confused, I said, "Ummmmmmm, I don't know…what's wrong with her?"

"Awwwwwww man, I'm sorry…she got real sick…had to leave the job…I think she's still in the hospital."

I didn't know what to feel or to say.

"Well, we're going to get out of here, but if you see her, tell her that Sheila said, 'Hi."

"Yeah, sure…" I said.

Later that night, Remy and I were having dinner in bed. We would have eaten in the kitchen, but we hadn't completely unpacked everything. We poured ourselves a glass of lemonade and toasted our success over some catfish, coleslaw, and corn on the cob. Remy had the remote control to his new flat-screen TV and was scanning the channels when he decided that he wanted to watch the evening news. We were discussing current events when a story came on about a domestic violence situation involving two women who were fighting over a man. I'd just took a sip of lemonade when Remy looked at me and said, "What's wrong?"

I picked some of the coleslaw from my teeth and said, "Why do you think that something's wrong?"

He grabbed the remote. "Shhhhhh…."

"We will now go to a story of domestic abuse from an unlikely victim.

"The woman was charged after police found that she attempted to stab her lover after trying to strangle his wife…News 8 caught-up with the victim."

"She's crazy. First she slapped me, then she threw a skillet at me, after she tried to stab me, she tried to run me over with the car."

"And why do you think she did that?" The anchor person asked.

"I don't know…I slept with her a couple of times…" He paused to think about his statement after he realized that this was on 'live' TV.

"What I meant to say was that I never cheated on my wife. I LOVE my wife…love her…I don't know why she was in my bed with her clothes off.

377

I swear," he said, raising his hand like he was giving some type of oath.

The anchor person frowned.

"I'm telling you...she's crazy. We moved six times trying to get away from her, but somehow she keeps finding me and having sex with me...she even threatened me. Yep, that's what she did. She told me that if I didn't have sex with her, she was going to kill my whole family, so I had to do what I had to do."

The story was so funny that you could hear the cameraman cracking up in the background. I couldn't hear the rest of the story because of the cackling coming from the other side of the bed. I turned the TV off.

"Hey, why did you do that?" Remy protested.

"Remy, I ran into a woman today who used to work with Regan..."

He wiped his faced with a napkin. "What did she do now?"

"She didn't do anything...supposedly, she's sick."

"Supposedly?"

"Well, the woman said that she's in the hospital..."

"And you don't believe it?"

"Remy, I don't know what to believe and I'm not sure if I even care."

He took a deep breath. "Wow…that's cold. You know what happened to Nicole…you don't want to end-up regretting never talking to her…even if it's to let her know how much she hurt you…or even how much you hate her for hurting you…you don't want anything to happen without doing something that would finally bring you peace."

I took another bite of the catfish. "I'm at peace now…believe me."

"Look at me…can you really say that?"

"Sometimes, Remy, things are better left unsaid."

"True, but that silence could cause you more harm than good….Reconsider it…you gave me a second chance…"

What I wanted to give her wasn't a "second chance," but he had a point. It was time that I went to see her.

Chapter 43

It was true. Regan was sick. You would think that after finding out, I would be happy. You would think that knowing that she was somewhere suffering would bring me great joy. It didn't. Actually, I didn't feel anything. I couldn't even find it in my heart to feel pity for her. I didn't realize until I found out that she was sick that I've put so much distance between us that I no longer had any feelings for her. There was nothing that connected me to her, but the awful memories and the blood that ran through our veins.

I called every hospital. I made at least thirty calls before I found it – the one that Regan was in. They wouldn't give me much information over the phone, but they did tell me that she was there in the Intensive Care Unit. I hesitated for weeks to go and see her even though I knew that Remy was right.

For several days, I went to the store to pick-up flowers. I brought them home after saying that I would go see her, only to sit and watch them die. At first, I didn't want to buy her any, but after much convincing by Remy, I decided to get them. Now, I just needed to take them to her.

I was staring at a bouquet one day when I asked myself, "Do you want to give them to her now or do you want to wait to place them on her grave?" At least, if I waited to put them on her grave, I wouldn't have to see her face, but would that give me peace - knowing that she was six feet under and unable to ever hurt me again? Would that be enough?

Finally, I decided that I had to do it. While I tried to justify it by saying that it would be something that my parents would want me to do, I knew that I needed to do it for myself in order to move on with my life. So the next morning, I got dressed, stopped by the store, purchased a fresh bouquet, and jumped in my car. All the way there, I tried not to think about anything, but the closer I got to the hospital the more I remembered. All I could do was think about that man lying on top of me. I could remember his big hands grabbing at me, his breath on my face, and the smell of candy in the room. All I could remember was her allowing him to do that to me. All I could do was remember how I wished that she could have stopped it from happening to me. All I could do was remember. *Remember.* I had to pull over and catch my breath. I started to feel everything that I wasn't allowed to feel back then

– fear, anger, everything. I cried so hard until there was nothing until the front of my shirt was soaking wet. When I was done, I took a deep breath, fixed my face, and pulled back into traffic. I was ready to say, "Goodbye."

On the elevator to her floor, I watched the numbers as they lit-up until I arrived at my destination. As soon as the doors opened, I stepped off and was met by the smell of disinfectant. I walked around until I arrived at the room numbered 781. When I walked in, I was immediately met with anger and hatred.

"Why are you here?" Ivy asked.

"She's here to watch her die," Raven followed.

"I just came here to…to…" I said, not really sure why I was there.

"To what?" Raven spat.

"Look…it took everything in me to get here…"

"Well, use everything you got to get the hell out of here," Raven said.

I took a deep breath and said, "Let me just leave the flowers."

"You can take those flowers and stick them up your…" Raven retorted.

Regan interrupted her. "Let us have a minute."

Raven said, "For what?"

Regan touched her hand and said, "I need to talk to her."

Ivy walked out of the room. When Raven walked passed, she intentionally bumped into me. I rubbed my shoulder and then walked over to the bed. I couldn't even look at her.

When I approached the bed, I turned to stare at the television.

"It's been a long time," she said.

I didn't respond.

"Grace...Peaches...look at me."

I took a deep breath and turned towards her.

"I don't have a lot of time left."

"Yeah...I heard." I turned away again. "So what's wrong with you?"

She laughed, "They said that I have something called, 'HPV."

I frowned. "What is that?"

She sighed, "It's Human Papi...Papi...I can't even pronounce it, but it's some type of virus." She laughed again. "I'm going to die from some shit that I can't even pronounce."

"How did you get it?" I asked, already knowing the answer.

"Got it from one of those men...who knows which one..." she shook her head and continued, "I should have listened to Daddy."

I nodded my head and said. "Yep, you should have..." I caught myself. "Damn...that's messed up."

She laughed. "Yeah…some treatable and preventable shit too…it's messed-up to find out that you're going to die over some shit you never heard of until you got it."

"Yep," I said.

She said, "It's weird hearing you curse. You're so grown-up now."

I sighed. "Yep…."

She smiled. "The prices that we pay for the dumbshit that we do to ourselves and to others."

"Yep," I said, again.

"Peaches…I've done a lot of bad shit to you…"

Now, I looked at her. "Yes, you have…"

"I don't even know why I did all of that stuff to you." She sighed, "Kids do a lot of stupid stuff and they do it for so long that it becomes normal whether it makes sense or not." She paused. "We were all wrong for what we did to each other."

I finally spoke. "I didn't do anything to you, but love you."

A tear rolled down the side of her face. "I know and only a messed-up person would take that love and trust and use it against you." She reached out and touched my hand. "I spent more time being your enemy than your sister…and I wasn't born to be your enemy. I was born to be your sister…your big sister…and I let you down."

"Yep, but life has a way of balancing things out…doesn't it?" I asked.

"Yes, I guess it does," she said.

I continued. "Yep…who would have thought that you would just jump in the car of a man that you've only known for an hour?"

She looked at me. "What? What are you talking about?" she asked, now trying to sit up.

I laughed. "Yeah, one of the other two…tried to sell me to a trick…I don't know which one…but whoever did it, I have to thank them."

Regan looked confused. "What are you talking about?" she asked again.

"One night, one of your fucked-up sisters tried to pimp me out…I was so mad that I told him about you…don't know why I did, but maybe it had something to do with you doing the same shit to me…so I took him to you…I was hoping that you'd changed…I guess jail can only fix so much…Predictable Regan jumped her ass in the car of a strange man…" I paused and shook my head. "Did you let him lick the candy from between your legs?"

Her eyes widened. "You set me up????!!!!!"

I sighed. "Naw, I took a man to my sister's job and she did the rest…he didn't rape you and that's the sad part because you would have deserved it if he did. It would have been great for you to find out what it feels like to have someone

386

rip your body apart… rip your soul apart….the unfortunate part is that you gave your shit away, but seeing you in this bed sorta makes up for it."

"You BITCH!!!!!" she yelled.

I laughed, leaned in, and whispered in her ear, "It's going to hurt a lot at first, but after a while, you won't feel a thing." I looked at her and smiled.

Raven and Ivy entered the room.

I reached into my purse and pulled out the $10 bill. "Here…this is for you."

"You bitch…you bitch…I'm going to kill you!!!!" Regan said.

"Not if you die first," I said, before leaving the room.

A few months later, she'd made her transition. I didn't go to the funeral because I wasn't invited. Instead, I decided to deal with her passing the way that I was taught to deal with the rape. I went on with my life - like nothing happened.

Chapter 44

*T*hey were always together. They were so identical that many times it was really hard to tell them apart. They used this to their advantage often times playing tricks on people. When they weren't playing tricks on me, they played them on our parents. I remember one time they played a trick on my mother that, even at a young age, I knew was terrible – funny, but still terrible.

My mother was deafly afraid of spiders. Big, little, dead, or alive, she hated them and we all knew it. When you heard her scream, you knew to come running with a shoe in your hand to kill the intruder.

One day, my sisters thought that it would be funny to make our mom face one of her greatest fears. They caught and trapped a huge black garden spider. They brought it into the house and while my mother was using the bathroom, they opened the jar, cracked the door, and led him into the room. Her response wasn't immediate. It was delayed by five minutes. It took so long that I thought that it'd died from the funk in the room.

Suddenly, there was a high-pitched squeal, the door flew open and all you saw was tits and ass bouncing down the hallway – followed by a trail of what looked like urine. She screamed and screamed. "Kill it! KILL IT!!!!"

The three of them were in no condition to save her because they were too busy rolling all over the floor in laughter.

I stood in the hallway holding my baby doll. My Mama seemed so scared. She was in the living room, jumping from the sofa to the chair in an attempt to run from a spider that was all the way in the bathroom. I didn't want her to cry anymore, so I walked in the bathroom, and there it was perched in the corner of the room. I walked out of the room and re-entered carrying one of my Daddy's shoes. It was one of those pointy-toed shoes, so one hit and it was no longer scaring people. I walked out of the bathroom and down the hall. "He dead, mommy…" Then I went back down the hall and back into my room. When my Daddy got home he interrogated them for hours, but no one would confess to the dirty deed, so Daddy decided to whup them all – and then it was "case closed."

Now, there was one. Her partner in crime was gone. Regan set the bar and Raven did everything to reach it. They had their ups and downs but there was a wholeness about them that wasn't there now. Raven was now incomplete – a puzzle that was now missing a piece. A part of her was missing that could never be replaced.

She didn't take her passing well. Her grief became her life. She wasn't herself anymore. She even stopped stalking me and I'm not complaining about that, but when you spend your life expecting a certain behavior from someone, when the change is so drastic, you have to know that something is seriously wrong.

She fell into a deep depression. Regan was everything to her. Twins hold a special bond. They were the "beginning" to each other's end. It's hard for me to imagine that one of them was gone. I can only imagine how hard it was for her. If Regan and Raven was one born as two, how could the other half exist now that one of them were gone?

It had been so long since I'd heard from the remaining two of the evil trio that I almost forgot that they existed. It was so peaceful that I thought that I'd died and gone to Heaven – a place where I knew they wouldn't be. It was so hard to believe that things could be this good – to live a life not spent looking over my shoulder.

The weird and crazy thing is, when she stopped stalking me, I became paranoid. Spending my life always looking over my shoulder, caused me so much anxiety that I began to follow her – because I needed to know where she was. I felt that it was the only way to protect myself from whatever she had in store for me.

After watching her for several weeks, I realized why she'd stopped messing with me. She was seeing someone. Seeing her with anyone other than my family was weird – especially, if it didn't involve a kidnapping. No, there was someone, out there, who actually, wanted to be with her. At first, my stalking her was a matter of survival, but now, I did it out of curiosity. I followed them everywhere. They both seemed so happy and then suddenly, it all stopped. One night, I saw him alone. This was odd since they'd spent almost every minute of their lives together since I started following them. He walked into a bar. Curious, I followed him inside. I found him sitting in the back of the bar. I watched him for a while, but then he got up and went into the bathroom. When he came back, he found me sitting in a chair across from him. He looked confused. "Who are you?"

I didn't want to waste his time by talking about things that didn't matter. "Why are you seeing my sister?"

He sat down and asked, "Who is your sister?"

"Raven," I confirmed.

"For a minute, I thought that you were her…y'all really look alike….Why do you want to know?"

"Because anybody who deals with her has to be crazy or in serious need of protection."

He sighed. "Why do you say that?"

"Because I know her," I said.

He frowned. "You act like something is wrong with her."

"It is…believe me," I said, folding my arms.

"Well, it doesn't matter anymore because the bitch dumped me."

"Did you say 'bitch'? Do tell…" I said, leaning in to hear all of the juicy details.

"There's nothing to tell…things were good. At least I thought that they were, I gave her everything that she wanted, and then without notice, I was fired."

"That sounds more like Regan…" I began.

"Regan?" he asked.

"Raven's twin sister," I said.

"She has a twin?" he asked. The waitress walked up to the table and then handed him a drink. "Is she available?"

"In hell...but I'm sure that her dance card is already full," I said.

"The bitch tapped-out all of my credit cards and gave me the 'It's me not you' speech." He took a sip from the glass. "Don't she know that I wrote that shit?"

"Yeah, she likes messing over people," I said.

"Anyway...why do you care and again, why are you here?" he asked.

"I wanted to meet the man who was spending time with Raven. For a while, I thought something was going on with her...you know...I mean...she has a lot going on, but..."

"Naw...your sister is all woman...she could do some stuff to a man that would make him want to go home and slap the shit out of his wife."

"You're married?" I asked.

"Naw, I'm Greg...the nag at home is married."

I shook my head. "And my sister?"

"Your sister was the love of my life," he said.

"Why not leave your wife?" I asked.

He leaned in and said, "Why you all up in my business?"

"Because Raven is my business," I said.

"That bitch…" he said and shook his head. "And I still love her."

"Your first mistake…" I took a deep breath and said, "Let me tell you about some of the things that she's done to me." As I spoke he ordered more drinks. By the time that I was done, twelve empty glasses sat in front of him.

"Damn…that's messed-up…that bitch needs to be dealt with…," he said.

"Yes, she does…it would be a shame to see her do this to someone else," I said.

His right eye was twitching. "Yes, it would…"

I smiled. "Yep…it would be a shame." I stood to walk out. I reached into my pocket, grabbed some cash and said, "The drinks are on me."

I didn't sleep the whole night. All I could do was think about her. The next morning, I got up and looked into the mirror. *You look just like her, he said. I do, don't I.* I thought to myself. I laughed. I applied my makeup, put on a beautiful navy blue dress, and a pair of heels and decided to put it to the test. I drove to all of the locations that I followed them to before pulling up in front of a beautiful single-family home on Chicago's West-side. Greg was leaving out of the house when suddenly, a woman wearing a robe yelled behind him, "Sweetie, you forgot your lunch." He smiled, walked back to retrieve the bag from her, and then placed a kiss on her forehead. She smiled before saying, "Have a good day...I love you." He didn't respond – just jumped into his car and pulled off. When the car was completely out of sight, I exited my car. I looked around before approaching the door. *Ding Dong!* "Coming!!!" she yelled from the other side of the door.

I fixed my clothing. The door opened. She frowned. "You...you...you bitch...didn't I tell you to leave my husband alone?"

This surprised me. I wasn't expecting this response to my visit. She continued, "My husband loves me. He doesn't love you."

Thinking on my feet, I said. "I just stopped by to tell him that I'm never going to leave him and...and...and...I think I'm pregnant."

She slammed the door in my face. I stumbled back to the car in those heels. Once inside, I looked in the rearview mirror and said, "Now, who is fucking who, Ms. Raven?"'

I went about my life trying to replace my horrible past with beautiful memories. It was so good that I should have known that it wouldn't last.

We were going through some boxes when my cellphone rang. I didn't recognize the number. I was afraid to answer – wasn't sure if it was a bill collector or some other type of annoyance, but when they called back, I decided to answer it. "Hello?" I stopped to hear what they were saying. Then, I said, "Oh…do you know how it happened? Ummmm…and you couldn't call anyone else? Oh…she had my number in her purse…of course, she did…well, I guess I will be there…sure…thanks," I said before hanging up.

Remy looked at me. "What was that about?"

I sighed and said, "It was about Raven…"

"What's wrong?" he asked.

I thought about the question for a moment and then said, "Nothing…nothing's wrong."

I walked in to find that I was the only person there. I chose to sit in the back even though every other chair in the room was empty. A woman walked up and asked, "Are you a friend of the family or are you family?" I took a deep breath and said, "I'm family."

"Well, we're going to wrap things up…if you would like to come up…"

I hesitated and said, "Give me a second…I'll be up there."

I took a deep breath, trying to remember the last time that I saw her. It was weird because every image or memory of her contained a frown on her face. I stopped trying to find a "fond" memory of her because one did not exist.

I stood, fixed my clothes and walked up to the front of the room. The look on her face was frightening. I grabbed my chest. "What happened to her?" I asked the woman standing next to me.

"Well…," she began. "I was told that she was dating a married man."

"Really?" I asked, already knowing the answer.

"Yep…and the wife found out," she said.

"Wow, that's terrible," I said.

"Yep, it is," she said.

"What happened to her face?" I asked.

"That is what happens when you mess with the wrong person," she said.

"I didn't know that she had a boyfriend," I said, lying.

"'Had', is the perfect word," she confirmed.

"Do you know what happened?" I asked.

"Well, I was told...she was seeing him. Things got hot and heavy fast, but something went wrong and she called it quits, but he wasn't having it. He asked her to come over so that they could talk things over...patch things up...but she wanted it over. Some say that she was just playing with his head, took him for his 'paper and plastic,' but he loved her...and anyway...she was done. Well, I guess he felt that it wasn't over until HE said that it was over...one night, he tied her to a bed...raped her repeatedly...starved her and tortured her for seven days." She stopped and shook her head. "When they brought her in, she had everything, but the kitchen sink shoved-up inside of her. That man was a sadist....a sick bastard...shoved a lamp inside of her...can you believe that? But that didn't kill her. Nooooo...you know what he did next?"

I couldn't catch my breath long enough to answer her.

She continued. "He played Russian Roulette with her every day...stuck a bullet in the gun...spun the barrel...stuck it against her head and then pulled the trigger...he did this every day for seven days...and finally, on the last day, he put a bullet in the chamber, spun the barrel, and then…well, as you can see…she didn't win…"

"Look at her face." I said.

"Yeah, that is the look of a woman who was tortured until the very end…terrible…we couldn't remove the "fear" from her face…we tried to "fix" it, but without breaking the bones…well, it would have taken too much. If you want, we could close the casket."

I looked at Raven. "No, leave it open…what happened to the person who did this to her?"

"They found him lying in her arms…a bullet to the head."

I didn't take my eyes off of her. I've never seen that side of her before. Fear was not an emotion that she was capable of and here she was, dead, with it stuck on her face, forever.

Finally, my nightmare was over. It was weird. When Raven died, I felt like I'd lost a part of myself. Once the stalking stopped, I actually felt alone. In a strange way, we were probably the closest of the four. I spent most of my life running, hiding, cursing, begging, and pleading with her that now, I felt weird – lost. I still looked over my shoulder though. I realized a long time ago that it will always be a part of me – them, the memories, the fear, but now, I can sleep a little bit easier.

Chapter 45

*T*he stalking didn't stop. I thought that Raven's death would surely put an end to the madness, but it didn't. At least now, I knew who was behind it all. I could see her doing it, I just couldn't understand why? The leaders were dead. What would be her motivation?

I needed to catch her in the act, so we purchased a surveillance system. One morning, I woke-up, poured a cup of coffee, fed my friend, and sat down to watch the video of the night before. I was watching it and for several hours, it seemed like an uneventful night, but then a shadow swept across the front lawn. I wiped my eyes because I thought that I was seeing things and rewound the tape to see it again and again; the figure swept across the lawn. I watched as they gawked into all of the windows while being careful not to touch anything to set-off the alarms. The shadow started kicking the few remaining flowers that were left. Then you could see them pulling down their pants and doing something on the front porch. It was weird, funny, and even sad watching her. I just couldn't wrap my head around it. *Why would she do this?*

I went outside and stared at the pile of shit sitting in the middle of my front porch. I looked at my yard and looked at all of the damage that was done to it. I scooped the poop into a brown paper bag, and decided that it was time that Ivy and I had a little talk.

I showered, dressed, left a note on the counter for Remy, grabbed the bag, grabbed my friend, and picked up some flowers and things out of my yard to give to her – since she loves my yard so much. All the way over there, I thought about what I would say to her, but I couldn't think of anything. When I pulled up, she was getting out of her car. She saw me and stood in her driveway like she wanted to fight me. I shook my head. I was on a mission and to get it accomplished would require me to revert back to the old "Peaches"…just for a little while.

I grabbed the items off of the car seat and jumped out of my car. "Hey Ivy," I said, forcing a smile on my face.

She frowned. "What do you want?"

"It's only you and I…why can't we try to get along?"

"Why?" she asked.

That was a good question. I thought to myself. Thinking fast. "Life is too short. Like you once said, 'It's time to let it go.'"

She forced a smile on her face. "You're right." She motioned for me to follow her. "You wanna come in?"

I smiled. "I…would…love…to." I looked around before following her inside.

Once inside, she offered me a seat. She filled the sink with water and dish detergent. She began to fill the sink with dirty dishes. "It's been a long time," she said, splashing soapy water everywhere. "I can't say that I didn't think about you."

"Well, I thought about you too…I was just thinking about you this morning and thought to myself, 'I wonder what Ivy's been up to?'"

She began to rinse the dishes.

"What happened to the dishwasher?" I said, looking around the room.

"Well, after the money was gone…," she paused and then said, "Well, you know…"

"Yes, I do know…," I said, thinking about how much I hate her right now.

She looked at me. "Would you like something to drink?" she asked.

"Naw, I don't plan to stay long." I heard a rustling sound. The bag began to move.

"So how have you been?" she asked, as she turned on the faucet – filling a glass with water.

"I've been okay...," I said. "How about you?"

"Well...," she said, drinking from the glass. I watched as water dripped down the front of her shirt onto the floor. "I'm tired, Peaches."

"Tired of what, Ivy?" I asked.

"Just tired...," she said.

"You're tired...got it," I said.

She chewed on her bottom lip before speaking, "I am so tired of the lies...so tired of carrying this weight on my shoulders....this 'cross' is too heavy to bear."

"What are you talking about, Ivy?" I asked.

"I was always in your shadows...the oldest and the baby. Nobody ever really cared about the middle kid. You never heard anyone introduce a middle child with any type of importance or excitement as they did when they spoke of the oldest and the baby. It was always 'here's Regan and Raven, they're the oldest, there's Ivy, and then there's Peaches the baby girl.' I was nothing, but Ivy...the one who wasn't lucky enough to be born first or last." She took a deep breath and then continued. "And I tried, Peaches, but nothing that I did was good enough...nothing. The only time that mom and dad saw me was when something went wrong and we were all being swept up to be punished together whether I did anything or not. The only time Regan and Raven noticed me was when they wanted to hurt me or use me, and the only time that you saw me was when I wasn't hurting you."

I was confused. "That's not true, Ivy. I always thought that you were the good one...at least compared to the other two."

She softened for a second. "Really?"

"Really...We had our problems but you weren't as bad as the other ones...and..."

"And what?" she asked.

"And nothing," I said. I had to stop. The lies were starting to get to me. Plus, the 'bag' was getting louder.

She took a deep breath and said, "But nothing matters now..."

"Ivy, remember how I used to tell you to tell me when you were changing the subject?"

She scowled and said, "And they did that type of shit to us...pitted us against each other...why would they do that? Why would they leave you everything? What is so fucking special about you?" Then she paused. We were just looking at each other when she went into a drawer and removed some papers. "Here..."

I took the papers and then looked at them. I looked up at her, numb and confused.

"You didn't see that coming, did you?"

The bag began to rustle louder.

"You didn't think that I could have done that? Poor little stupid, Ivy...not even capable of..."

Suddenly, things were becoming clear. "You did that to me…I can't believe it, Ivy. Why?"

She sighed. "At first, I didn't want to, but…" She began to laugh. "You know what? I can't even lie…that shit was funny as hell."

I looked at the pieces of paper. They were images of me naked and in the shower. I was disgusted. "You know what? I used to feel sorry for you, but you are no better than they are. You deserve everything that they did to you." I threw the pictures into her face.

She began to stare at something behind me. I turned to see who or what was there, but there was nothing. Now, she wasn't talking to me. It was more like she was having a conversation with herself. "You know…I almost hesitated. I stood outside of the house and watched them…for ten minutes…before the strength that I needed to destroy the root of all of this shit came to me…and then I thought that it was over, but killing them changed nothing." Then suddenly she looked at me and smiled.

My heart was beating so hard that I thought that it was going to jump out of my chest and strangle her for me. I was praying that I heard "wrong" but the look on her face indicated that I heard "right."

She continued. "When I knocked on the door, I walked in and we sat down and talked like old times. Their memories of our childhood was beautiful. The whole time that they were talking, I wondered who the hell they were talking about. Who the hell was this big happy ass family that they speak of? I was confused. Then, they started to talk about what happened to you. When I told them that the same thing happened to me, you know what they had the nerve to say?"

Her admission left me speechless. "You were raped too? I asked you about this, Ivy, and you didn't say anything." The 'bag' was getting so loud that I had to pick it up and sit it into my lap. "And what exactly would you have done? You couldn't do shit to stop what happened to you. After they found out, what exactly did they do? Not a damn thing. When I told them, they glazed over that shit like I'd just told them that there was a boil on my ass…nothing…absolutely no reaction, but let it have been you with the boil on her ass and they would have move mountains to get it removed. THEN…then, if that wasn't enough, she had the nerve to call me Raven. RAVEN…that crazy bitch."

Who are you calling crazy, bitch? CRAZY BITCH. I thought to myself.

She continued. "I simply excused myself, went into the kitchen, and came back and reminded them who I was…bet she knows which one I am now...the middle one, damnit...THE MIDDLE ONE and her NAME IS IVY!"

She has lost her damn mind. "How could you do that? Kill Mama and Daddy?" I asked, trying not to jump up and put my hands around her throat.

"It wasn't as easy as I thought it would be...but I thought about all of the unearned ass-whuppings and punishments...how they never really loved me...here they never thought that I could do anything right...I wonder if they feel that way now?"

My hands were shaking. I swallowed hard, took a deep breath and then handed her the bag. "Whew...I feel so much better now that I've gotten that off of my chest," she said, sipping from the glass and dripping more water onto the floor. Looking at the bag, she asked, "What is this?"

"Well, after everything that you just told me, I feel kinda stupid...I should have brought you something else..." I began to ball my hands into fists and continued, "But this would have to do." She sniffed the bag. "This smells like shit...is this shit?"

I smiled. "Look in the bag, Ivy..." I said.

She looked closely at the bag. "What is this? She asked, before it jumped out and revealed itself. It squealed as it jumped out smearing feces all over her face and shirt. She screamed and as she tried to run, she slipped and fell on the soapy water surrounding her feet. She tried to get up but fell again. The rat ran around the room – running back and forth across her feet. She screamed and tried to stand again, but this time when she fell, she hit her head against the kitchen counter. She grabbed the back of her head. There was blood all over her hand. "Grace, help me." She kept looking around for the rat.

"Remember my birthday party?" I asked, walking over to the refrigerator.

"What? What the hell are you talking about?" The rat ran across her legs. "Oh my GAWD...I am so sorry, Peaches...please...I'm begging you...HELP ME!!!!!"

I stuck my head inside of the refrigerator. "What do you have in here to snack on?"

"Peaches...I can't move." Suddenly, she began to heave and then she threw up all over herself and the floor.

I grabbed an apple, sat down at the table, and watched her struggle. Next, the rat stopped running and began to eat the vomit from her lap. She screamed, "Awwwwwwwww...Oh my Gawd... PLEASE...HELP ME!!!!"

I watched and finished the apple. When I was done, I walked over and sat next to her. I stuck the core down her shirt and said, "Like you said, Ivy, 'Sometimes, some shit…some shit happens for a reason.'" I stroked Blinky's head, as he ate from her lap, before standing to walk out of the door.

"Peaches!!!!!!!" She screamed. "PEACHES!!!!"

And then there was one.

Chapter 46

The seasons came and went…A year had passed before we stopped sleeping with the lights on. We had been through so much together that we spent the next year, waiting for the next messed-up thing to happen. While we waited, we tried our best to get back to some form of normalcy, but after about six months I started feeling terrible. I wasn't able to keep any food down and was having a difficult time sleeping. After I'd missed my period for three months straight, I decided to go to the doctor. All the way there, all I could think about was the possibility that I might be pregnant. The thought that I could be or would be someone's Mama scared the hell out of me. When I was younger, I told myself that I would never have any kids, because I was a mess. What could I possibly give a baby? What type of mother would I be? I never really had any experience taking care of anyone but myself. How could I be someone's Mama? As these questions crossed my mind, I realized that I was getting ahead of myself. Maybe, I wasn't pregnant. Maybe it was something else.

When the doctor was done examining me, she said, "Well, it looks like you're going to be a Mama."

"Damn," I said. "How did that happen?"

The doctor smiled and said, "Well…when a man puts his penis…"

I interrupted her. "I know how it happened." I rubbed my forehead in disbelief.

"What's wrong?" she asked.

"Wow…me…a mother."

She smiled. "Yes, it happens."

I sighed. "Yes…I guess it does."

She rubbed my shoulders. "It'll be okay."

I smiled and said, "I hope so."

When I returned home, I saw Remy waiting to find out what the doctors said. I smiled at him and said, "You're going to be a father." He stood and smiled back, then all of a sudden his body went limp and he hit the floor. When he came to, I was smiling. "Are you okay?"

"Yes, I'm fine…so I'm going to be a Daddy?"

"Yeah, and you might want to fix that 'fainting thing' before we go to the delivery room." We both laughed.

For the next three months, he catered to my every whim. He held my hair when I had to throw up, he picked up all of my 'cravings', and he rubbed every part of my body to make sure that I was comfortable. He was incredible and I couldn't ask for a better father for the little person growing inside of me.

But something was wrong. I was getting big really fast. Either they had my weeks of gestation miscalculated or I was having a really big baby. I was concerned, so I made an early appointment to make sure that everything was okay. All the way there I felt the baby pulling and tugging on my insides. I was in a lot of pain.

They prepped me for an ultrasound. The doctor poured some cold jelly onto my stomach and began rolling the 'ball' across my belly. After a few sweeps back and forth, the doctor said, "I see what the problem is."

"Problem, problem, what problem?" we both asked.

She smiled and said, "Yeah…the problem is that there's two of them in there."

I looked at Remy who was again faced down on the floor.

The doctor shook her head. "I'll help him."

I smiled and looked at the ceiling, while she tried peeling him off of the floor.

Chapter 47

"*O*uch!" I shouted. "Oh my, Gawd…these babies are killing me. I don't know if I can make it another day let alone another month." I rubbed my stomach in the spot where one of them kicked me. "I don't think this is normal." I couldn't take it. I couldn't sleep, I'd gotten so big that I couldn't remember what my feet looked like. My ass was so big that Remy had to help me wipe it. I was miserable. Every day, I cursed Remy for getting me pregnant, cursed God for making men, and cursed sex for feeling so damn good, because I enjoyed every moment that it took to make this moment in my life happen.

Remy rubbed and kissed my stomach. "They're going to be boys…football players…or maybe even soccer players…"

"I don't care what they do when they grow up…what I need them to do right now is hurry up and get out."

He smiled. "Are you evicting our babies?"

"Yes…" I buckled over in pain. "Awwwwwww damnit!!!"

He rubbed my stomach. "Okay boys…this is your daddy talking…y'all need to settle down."

The babies kicked me harder. I screamed. "Awwwwwwww!!! I can't take this much longer."

Remy sat up. "And y'all gotta do this for nine months? I am so glad that I'm a man."

I shifted my body, trying to get comfortable. "Whatever...just please make it stop...it hurts."

"Baby, I can't make it stop. I can only try to make it better."

"Awwwwwwww...then make it better!!!!!"

And this went on for the next six weeks. It felt like they were trying to cut me open from the inside. I was in so much pain. I didn't know what to do and every visit to the doctor yielded the same results – nothing was wrong.

Just when I thought that I was going to have to reach up inside of myself and pull them out, God must have heard my cries. On my way to the bathroom, I felt a warm liquid running down my leg. I looked down, hoping to find a clear or brown fluid, but it was dark red. I screamed for Remy and he rushed me to the hospital.

Chapter 48

Something was wrong...All the way there, blood was pouring out of me. We were so scared. I prayed all the way there. I didn't want anything to happen to my babies. The doors to the Emergency Room flew open and I was being pushed through. I clutched Remy's arm as they swarmed around me. It seemed like they were all trying to talk at the same time.

"What do we have?" the doctor asked as she rushed to the stretcher.

"We have a 28 year old woman, pregnant, in labor, BP 90 over 60."

"What's her name?"

"Grace," Remy said.

"Grace, my name is Dr. Williams, where are you having pain?"

"It hurts all over,"

"Doctor...is she going to be okay?" Remy asked.

"Aaaawwwwwwwww!!!!!!!!!!!"

"Are you having any contractions?"

"Yes...don't you hear me screaming? Aaaawwwww...please save my babies..."

"Babies? She's having twins?"

"Yes," Remy said.

"Take her into room three…," the doctor directed.

"Doctor, look…," the nurse said.

"Okay…she's bleeding."

The doctor applied a stethoscope to my abdomen. "The babies are in distress."

"How many weeks is she?"

"BP dropping 68 over 40…"

"What's does that mean?" Remy asked.

"It means that we have to get her blood pressure back up. Did she fall or hurt herself?"

"She's 36 weeks." Remy said. "No, she's been having a lot of pain throughout her pregnancy, but nothing, according to the doctor, to worry about."

BEEP! BEEP! BEEP!

"What's happening?" I asked.

"There's nothing to worry about…I need you to relax…think about your babies."

"Fetal heartrate is 60," the nurse said.

"Is that bad?" I asked.

The doctor looked at me. "We're going to have to give you a C-section…your babies are in distress."

"Please save my babies…"

"Doctor, please save my babies," Remy begged.

"Aaaaawwwwwwww!!!!!!!!!!!!! It hurts."

"We're going to start an Epidural. It'll help with the pain. Sir, we're going to have to ask you to wait outside."

"No, I'm not leaving her," Remy said.

"Sir, please…"

"I'm not leaving her," Remy said.

"Okay…then stand back out of the way."

BEEP! BEEP! BEEP!

The doctor rubbed my forehead and said, "Your placenta is detaching itself…you are bleeding into your uterus…we have to perform a C-Section to save your babies."

"Okay…okay…," I said.

"I know that you're scared, but it's going to be okay."

"Doctor, she's losing a lot of blood," said the nurse.

"We don't have a lot of time…if we don't stop the bleeding they both may die."

"DIE! DIE! What do you mean die?" Remy asked running back towards me.

"He has to go…Sir, if you don't leave, we're going to have to call security. I know that you're scared, but you have to let us save your family."

"Aaaaaaaaaaaaaaaaaaaaaaaaaa!!! God, please!!!"

BEEP! BEEP! BEEP!

"Start a central line…let's prep for surgery."

"Here doctor?" one of the nurses said.

421

"We don't have time to move her. If we wait any longer…"

"Grace…how are you feeling?" the doctor asked.

"Huh…I'm tired," I said.

"But do you feel any pain?" the nurse asked.

The medicine was kicking in. I shook my head, "No."

"Set up…hand me a scalpel."

"Doctor, her BP is dropping."

BEEP! BEEP! BEEP!

My eyes began to close.

"Okay, Grace…I need you to stay awake. Okay, stay awake."

"Okay…," I said.

"Starting the incision." The doctor began to cut across my stomach. "Okay…I need you to pull this back while I go in."

"Okay doctor…"

"We're going to clamp off the bleeding… clamp."

"Clamp."

"How are you doing, Grace?" one of the nurses asked.

I mumbled.

BEEP! BEEP! BEEP!

"Doctor, her blood pressure is down to 50 systolic…"

"Pull back…I see another one…clamp…"

"Clamp…"

"My baby…my baby…," I mumbled.

"Hang on, Grace…"

"There's the uterus…scalpel…"

"Scalpel…"

"She's lost a lot of blood…"

"Send for some units…"

"We're losing her…"

"We need to start oxygen…"

"I'm going to 'bag' her…"

BEEP! BEEP! BEEP!

"Extracting the babies…suck out their nose and mouth…we're cutting the umbilicals…"

"Grace…are you there…are you with me…?" the nurse asked.

"Where's the damn blood?" the doctor asked.

"It's here, doctor…it's here…"

"My babies…" I mumbled. I smiled and then closed my eyes.

BEEP! BEEP!

"Grace…Grace, wake up! She's exsanguinating. She must be losing blood from somewhere else."

"She's coding," the nurse said.

BEEP!!!!!!!!!!!!!!!!!

"Start her on Dopamine…"

"She's in V-fib."

"Starting manual ventilation."

"It's not working…"

BEEP!!!!!!!!!!!!!!!!

"She's asystolic…"

"Charging at 200…"
"CLEAR…"
"300…"
"CLEAR…"
"Nothing…"
BEEEEEEEEEEP!!!!!!!!!!!!!!!!!!
"Keep trying…"
"CLEAR…"
BEEEEEEEEEEEEEEEEEEEEEP!!!!!!!!!!!!!!!!!!
"Doctor…she's gone."
The doctor sighed, "Call it…"
"11:01pm…"

The nurse slowly wheeled the twins over to Remy.
"They are so beautiful," she said.
Remy didn't speak.
The nurse continued. "I'm so sorry for your loss."
Remy looked up. With eyes that were filled with tears, he said, "What?"
"Their mother…your wife…I'm so sorry."

Remy glanced into the hospital cribs. "Yes...their mother...she's gone."

"But she died, so they...these little angels could live."

"Yes...live...," he mumbled.

"That's such a terrible way to start your life...without the person who gave it to you."

Remy didn't speak. He stared at the beautiful baby girls.

"Have you thought about names, yet?"

"Huh?" he asked. "Names?"

"Yes, do you know what you're going to name them?"

He stared at them. "We never talked about names."

"Well...if you don't mind me saying? It would be beautiful if you named them after their mother."

"Yes...their mother...her name was Grace...," he said.

"That's so pretty...and the other baby...what are you going to name her?" she asked.

He continued. "And...they called her...they called her..."

The nurse interrupted. "Awwwwwww look."

"Peaches...," he said, as they both looked down into the cribs. One baby was fast asleep, resting peacefully, while the other one looked up and smiled.

And then there were none...

If you feel like you are a victim of physical or sexual abuse or a victim of any type of bullying, please contact someone. You do not have to suffer. There are people and agencies who will help.

Illinois Domestic Violence Help Line at 877-863-6338; your local domestic violence program; or the National Domestic Violence Hotline at 800-799-7233 or TTY 800-787-3224. If you do these things to your partner you should seek help by contacting a Partner Abuse Intervention Program.

National Domestic Violence helpline: 1-800-799-SAFE

Call the 24-hour Child Abuse Hotline at 800-25-ABUSE (800-252-2873 or TTY 1-800-358-5117) if you suspect that a child has been harmed or is at risk of being harmed by abuse or neglect. If you believe a child is in immediate danger of harm, call 911 first. Your confidential call will not only make sure the child is safe, but also help provide the child's family the services they need to provide a safe, loving and nurturing home.

For bullying, Cyberbullying, or Sibling Bullying, Please call 877 N0BULLY (877 602 8559). When the Help Chat Line is not available and you are in crisis please contact the National Suicide Prevention Lifeline at 1-800-273-TALK (8255) or the GLBT National Youth Talk-line at 1-800-246-PRIDE (1-800-246-7743).

And for more info about HPV (Human papillomavirus), please visit https://hpv.com/

A preview of my next novel,

Six Degrees of Separation
Coming in the Spring of 2017

"Six Degrees of Separation (also referred to as the "Human Web") refers to the idea that, if a person is one step away from each person they know and two steps away from each person who is known by one of the people they know, then everyone is no more than six "steps" away from each person on Earth." -- Frigyes Karinthy

So now we must ask ourselves, "Where the hell did he come from?"

Prologue

"Excuse me sir, do you have any change?" she asked, with the most beautiful blue eyes I've ever seen.

I looked into my pocket and retrieved some small bills and handed them to her. It was cold out. Her teeth 'clicked' together as she thanked me. I had to admit that I felt sorry for her.

"Look, let me buy you a hot meal," I said.

"Oh, thank you, that would be nice," she responded.

We walked down to the corner diner. From the moment we entered, all eyes were on us. I ordered us some coffee to get us started. While we waited, the woman went on and on about the road that led her to this place — this moment in her life.

"He was a football player," she said, as if I gave a shit. "Yeah, he even went pro," she continued.

I looked around the room for the waitress who was taking so long to bring us our coffee that I was beginning to think that her ass took a trip to Columbia to hand pick the beans herself. The woman sitting across from me was still rambling. "I really loved his ass too…for real…no kidding. Everybody thought that I was only with him for his money, but I ain't no gold-digger. No matter what they say," she spat through the gap in her front teeth.

The people in the diner watched and whispered as she took me down memory lane. She noticed it. I couldn't tell if she was embarrassed or not because her face was hidden under several layers of dirt. When the waitress finally arrived with the coffee, the woman excused herself, went to the bathroom, and when she returned it looked like she tried to clean herself up. She had pulled her matted hair back and she tried to wash her face. It was evident that she scrubbed really hard because now her pale skin was even redder than before.

As I ordered, I could tell that the waitress was staring at me. I didn't acknowledge her because I wasn't interested. When she realized that I wasn't going to give her the attention that she was seeking, she took the menus, placed them under her arm, rolled her eyes at the woman sitting across from me, huffed and then walked away.

Still talking, the woman said, "That motherfucker even had the nerve to be on the down-low. Man, I heard she cut the shit out of his ass."

Now, she had my attention. "She who?" I asked.

"The bitch he dumped to marry my fine ass." She smiled. "Then he dumped me to get back with her. That's why I'm glad that he's dead...with his triflin' ass," she said, like a person who was trying to make Ebonics a first language.

Curious, I asked, "So, she killed him?"

"Naw," she began. The waitress walked over with our plates. She paused and threw some fries into her mouth. "Like I was saying...naw, that motherfucker got him some 'jail-house justice.' They raped his ass to death. He was a loser in life. Now, he's a loser in Hell." She went on like this for another hour. I watched her thinking about what she may have looked like when she was younger. She was probably really pretty 'back-in-the-day.' Now, she was just an empty shell — one of life's walking dead.

When she finished, I paid the tab and then we left the diner. I was about to walk away when she said, "I really appreciate what you did for me. Nobody has been that nice to me in a long time. Let me do something nice for you." She looked down at my crotch.

Frowning, I said, "There's nothing that you could do for me. Just take care of yourself."

"Please let me do something…it's the least I could do," she pleaded. She began to lick her lips seductively.

What a waste. I thought to myself. "Look, I'm good."

"Well, I promise that I'm going to do something really nice for myself. I might even use the money you gave me to go to the clinic and get myself cleaned up. Wouldn't that be nice? Change my life…become respectable," she said. I looked at her. "Take care of yourself." I turned and walked away.

Later that evening, I was walking back in the direction where I left the woman. I walked passed an alley where I could hear someone both crying and laughing. I walked towards the sound. In the dark, it was hard to tell who it was. As I got closer, there she sat with a rope wrapped around her arm and a needle sticking out of her vein.

"Hey, I told you I was going to do something nice for myself," she said, recognizing me.

I looked at her; disappointed and angry. It was disgusting looking at her lying in the alley like trash that someone had thrown out. I leaned over her and then removed the needle from her arm. Lying on the ground next to her was a spoon, a lighter, and a couple of rocks that looked like heroine. I placed a 'rock' on the spoon and began to heat it. She laughed to herself. When the rock melted and became a liquid, I filled the syringe with it. As she mumbled and laughed to herself, I asked her for her name.

"My name is Sandy," she said, enjoying her buzz. I hit the syringe with my finger, found her vein, and then plunged the needle deep inside of it. Initially, she smiled and closed her eyes. Suddenly, she looked at me as if becoming lucid just long enough to realize what was happening to her. I smiled at her. Before ramming the needle deeper into her arm, I said, "My name is Izrael. It was nice to meet you."

- ✓ *NEVER WHAT IT SEEMS*
- ✓ *AUTUMN LEAVES*
- ✓ *SOMEBODY ELSE'S BABY*
- ✓ *NEVER WHAT IT SEEMS II – A MOTHER'S LOVE*
- ✓ *FALLEN ANGEL*
- ✓ *KISS MY ASS – THIS IS NOT YOUR TYPICAL SELF-HELP BOOK*